NOW IS EVERYTHING

NOW IS EVERYTHING

Amy Giles

HARPER TEEN
An Imprint of HarperCollinsPublishers

HarperTeen is an imprint of HarperCollins Publishers.

Now Is Everything

Library of Congress Control Number: 2017932865
ISBN 978-0-06-249573-0

Typography by Katie Fitch
17 18 19 20 21   PC/LSCH   10 9 8 7 6 5 4 3 2 1

First Edition

For Pat, Maggie, and Julia

now

Emergency first responders scramble up and down the hill around me like ants, trying to see what can be salvaged. We're on different frequencies. Theirs is manic and frenzied, searching for life, while I watch without seeing. What I escaped below eclipses everything. Blank eyes. A blood-soaked Cornell sweatshirt. Necks bent unnaturally. Angry fists of heat pounding at my back as I crawled away from the wreckage.

But the sky is a perfect crisp blue, like someone forgot to tell it to wipe that smug smile off its face.

No one survives a plane crash. I shouldn't be here.

Feet crunch across the ice-crusted leaves. "She's in shock."

A man in a navy windbreaker with yellow reflective "NTSB" letters on the sleeve crouches down in front of me. I stare down at his cheap black leather shoes, not at all like the rows of expensive Italian shoes that line my father's closet.

"Hadley?"

My eyes travel up to a craggy face with kind, crinkly blue eyes that reach for mine carefully. He smiles gently when I meet his gaze. "They're going to take you to the hospital now, okay?"

Fingering the claddagh pendant hanging at the base of my throat, I glance down at my left arm resting against my stomach.

"It hurts," a small voice says, sounding nothing like mine.

"They're going to take good care of you." He glances at the two EMTs handling a gurney. It was a long climb up the rocky incline. Bramble and rocks tore at my clothes, at my flesh, trying to drag me back down into the fiery pits of hell.

A firefighter races past me down the gulley to the billowing smoke. I should tell him there's no need to hurry. They're dead.

"Your grandmother has been notified."

My eyes bounce up. He takes it as a ray of hope. It makes those kind crinkles around his eyes deepen.

His hope fills me with guilt. I'm bound to disappoint this complete stranger.

BRADY: *The date is January 6. Time . . . 8:03 a.m. Do I have your permission to record your statement?*

CW: *Sure.*

BRADY: *Please state your name and age.*

CW: *Claudia Wiley, seventeen. I'll be eighteen in May.*

BRADY: *Miss Wiley, I'm Gerald Brady, senior air safety inspector from the National Transportation Safety Board. As you are aware, the McCauleys were involved in a plane crash. Hadley was the only survivor. Since we have yet to determine a probable cause for the accident, we're interviewing witnesses as well as family and friends who knew the McCauleys to get a broader picture, if you will.*

Your name came up as someone who spent time with Hadley. I understand you played lacrosse on the same team?

CW: *Well, yeah. We both played on the travel team in the fall and the school team in the spring. But that's kind of it.*

Honestly, I really don't know why my name came up. Hadley and I weren't friends . . . we didn't really like each other all that much.

BRADY: *Why's that?*

CW: *They're kind of a hard family to like. Were, I mean.*

BRADY: *Well, tell me a little about that. What was it that made them hard to like?*

CW: *Everything. Like how they never let you forget how rich they were. The McCauleys were ALL about the money.*

You're looking at me like I'm a bitch, but I'm not. It's just true. Ask anyone.

BRADY: *Maybe you could provide an example?*

CW: *There's, like, so many, where do I even start?*

So okay, here's one: when the band was selling oranges and grapefruits to raise money for our trip to the Rose Parade, Hadley didn't sell any. Not even one crate. Just showed up at band one day with a big fat check from her father. I don't know how many zeroes were on that check, but Mr. Rosen's eyes bugged out. If he were in a cartoon, they would have bounced out of their sockets on springs with a loud BOING and hit the floor.

That's how the McCauleys rolled.

BRADY: *Hmm. So who was Hadley close to at school?*

CW: *Really just Meaghan and Noah. Meaghan Maki and Noah Berger, that's who you should be talking to. Not me.*

And Charlie. Charlie Simmons. If anyone knows anything, it's going to be Charlie.

BRADY: *The date is January 6. Time, 8:37 a.m. Do I have your permission to record your statement?*

MM: *Yes.*

BRADY: *Please state your name and age.*

MM: *Meaghan Maki, seventeen.*

BRADY: *Miss Maki, could you please tell me a little about your relationship with Hadley?*

MM: *I don't know what you want to hear. I mean, Hadley's my best f—frrr—*

. . .

BRADY: *Miss Maki, do you think you can continue?*

MM: *Yes. Sorry. This is harder than I thought.*

BRADY: *How long have you known Miss McCauley?*

MM: *Forever. We met in second grade. We're both "Ms"— McCauley, Maki—so we sat together. Ms. White said it helped her learn our names that way. We just hit it off—me and Hadley, I mean. Not me and Ms. White. Because we did not hit it off. That was a bad year. All I can say is thank God for Hadley.*

Sorry, I know that doesn't help you.

BRADY: *It's all helpful. Why don't you tell me a little about her family?*

MM: *Well, I know things weren't great at home, but Hadley didn't like to talk much about her family. Except for Lila. Hadley always had a funny Lila story.*

BRADY: *She was close to her sister?*

MM: *Super close . . .*

BRADY: *Take your time.*

5

MM: *Sorry . . . I'm having a hard time with all of this. Processing it all.*

BRADY: *Are you okay to continue? We can reschedule.*

MM: *No . . . I'll try.*

BRADY: *Tell me about her father. What was Hadley's relationship like with him?*

MM: *[groan] The Drill Sergeant? He was horrible. Did you know he used to make her get up at four thirty in the morning to run with him? And she did it, even though she hated it. And lift weights with him. I think he was one of those dads who wished he had sons, not daughters, you know? He was like . . . obsessed with her.*

BRADY: *Obsessed? How?*

MM: *He was a control freak. He was living Hadley's life for her, pressuring her to go to Cornell because he went there . . . play lacrosse because he played lacrosse . . . take flying lessons because he had his pilot's license. Oh, and he had this strict no-dating rule.*

BRADY: *Mm-hmm . . . But Hadley was seeing a boy named Charlie Simmons, correct? Did her father know about him?*

MM: *Well, eventually. She got into a lot of trouble when her dad found out.*

BRADY: *What kind of trouble?*

MM: *The usual. Grounded. Um . . . when do you think they'll let me see Hadley?*

BRADY: *The time is 9:07 a.m. Do I have your permission to record your statement?*

. . .

BRADY: *Mr. Simmons, the purpose of the Safety Board investigation is to determine a probable cause of the crash in order to improve transportation safety. At this time, we have not been able to determine if the accident was due to mechanical failure or medical emergency or something else. We would appreciate your cooperation in our investigation.*

. . .

BRADY: *If we find you have information that would help us, the Safety Board is authorized to issue a subpoena to obtain your testimony.*

CS: *Fine. Get a subpoena. Because I'm not talking to you, or the reporters, or God himself until someone lets me see Hadley. So unless you can get the hospital to waive this "family only" bullshit, everyone can just fuck off.*

then

The sky is black and unwelcoming outside my bedroom window. It tells my body to go back to sleep, but even the heavens have no jurisdiction in this house.

Downstairs, the metal spoon clangs against the glass container that holds Dad's precious gourmet beans, followed by the obnoxious grating of the coffee grinder that's like a buzz saw against my eardrums. *Whirr, whirr.* That's my alarm clock, five days a week.

Gravity presses down on my sleepy body, sinking me deeper into my mattress. But a couple more z's aren't worth the grief of falling back asleep. I slip out from under the warm duvet and change out of my pajamas, tugging on my black running tights with the reflective stripes down the legs, then a sports bra and a top. I'm tying my sneakers when he bangs on the door loudly.

"I'm coming," I whisper. Leaning over, I grab the doorknob and open it.

Dad slurps his coffee noisily. It always amazes me that he can run with all that coffee sloshing around in his gut.

"We're late." He doesn't even try to modulate his voice for a sleeping house.

I hurry, if only to get him away from Lila's door. When I was her age, I could sleep fourteen hours straight, no problem, if anyone ever let me. Which they didn't. Being the firstborn has no advantages at all, despite what Lila thinks.

At ten, Lila thinks my life is exciting. I go to award banquets with my lacrosse team. I take flying lessons at McKinley Airport. She still doesn't see how much of my life isn't actually my own.

"Come on, let's go," Dad says, looking at his watch. If we run for an hour, he has time to take a quick shower and still make the 6:17 train. This ungodly 4:30 wake-up fits *his* schedule. I come home, take a shower, eat, then help Lila pick out her outfit for the day. Left to Mom, Lila would walk out the door looking like a miserable American Girl doll. Left on her own, she'd walk out the door looking like she's off to host the MTV Video Music Awards. She's really into music and dancing, so I begged her to let me be her stylist.

"Every self-respecting diva has one," I said.

It's fun playing dress-up with her. I had been an only child for seven years when she was born. The day she came home from the hospital, Mom put her in the carrier on the floor. I sat in front of her watching her for hours, making sure she didn't stop breathing. That actually terrified me, the thought of her lungs quitting because it was too hard; this whole living, breathing thing was completely overrated. By not tearing my eyes off her, I was willing her into existence. And then they let me hold her in my arms. Light and fair like my mother, with big blue eyes—unlike me and Dad with our brown hair and brown eyes—she looked just like my very own baby doll.

"You're a big sister now," Mom said, smiling down at me as I held Lila, as if the big pink "I'm a Big Sister" t-shirt they bought me at the hospital gift shop wasn't enough of a clue. "You have to protect her and take really good care of her."

It's probably the one and only thing my mother's ever said that I've taken dead serious.

We stretch in the driveway, and Dad takes the lead down the blackened streets. Motion lights go off at every McMansion we pass, lighting the path behind us. Our block is one of those newer developments built on a patch of land that was once a potato farm, which means we have to worry about imidacloprid, DDT, and other pesticides in our groundwater responsible for cancer pockets across Long Island. The Poland Spring delivery truck is a regular fixture around here.

Our particular house model came with the requisite five bedrooms, four and a half bathrooms, gourmet kitchen, granite countertops, and twelve-foot coffered ceilings. Instead of the theater room all the other models have, Dad made the builders turn our basement into a home gym. He works out like he's training for the Olympics. Which means I do too.

A few dogs bark as we run by their homes. The neighbors must love that. No one should be up at this hour. Not us, not the dogs. I pant to the rhythm of my feet hitting the pavement. It's like meditating, I guess. Focusing on my breathing helps me forget the ache in my hip that shoots through me with every step. The October air holds just enough chill that I can see my breath. It'll get really cold soon, but weather never interferes with our runs.

"Early decision deadline is coming up." He huffs, white clouds punctuating his words.

I nod. He looks at me for an answer, but I pretend to focus on my run.

"November first."

"Yep." I pant.

"Cornell's lacrosse team did really well last year. Brown did a little better, but . . ." He trails off.

"I know." *You told me.* Monitoring my exact words is an important survival skill, like building a fire out of twigs or foraging for cattails and conifers in the wilderness.

"We should fly up one of these weekends. Take another look around. Talk to the coach this time."

I nod.

He pants. "Pick up the pace; you're lagging."

I'm not sure how I'm lagging since we're neck and neck, but I pick it up, just enough that he has to struggle now to keep up with me.

Suddenly he stops running and doubles over, clutching his chest. He coughs and gasps for air.

"Dad, are you okay?" Fear and panic and something unspeakably luminous in the periphery root me to the ground. He doesn't answer. Finally, he straightens up and spits a loogie across the street.

"Something flew down my throat," he gasps, his eyes watering. "I'm okay."

He runs and I follow.

Meaghan and Noah wait for me by my locker before third-period Spanish.

"Hey, Muscles." Meaghan reaches over and squeezes my bicep hello. Noah leans back against the lockers, arms folded, his lips twisted to the side. His eyes narrow as he assesses me.

"You're walking like my nana before she got her new hip," he decides.

I'm limping slightly, but nowhere near the way Noah's grandmother used to shuffle and rock. Though even after two ibuprofens, my body feels as creaky and ancient as hers. I twirl my combination, making sure to hit the numbers just right. My lock is as rigid and inflexible as everything else in my life.

"My hip's acting up." I dig into my locker for my Spanish book.

"Again?" Noah sighs and takes his phone out, tapping on it. With a satisfied nod, he turns it around to show me a fitness website. "You need to show your father this."

"Drill sergeant." Meaghan coughs into her fist.

Noah smiles in agreement at Meaghan then continues. "Ten warning signs you're *over*training. First one on the list is prolonged muscle soreness." Noah stares purposefully at my aching hip.

Behind Noah, Charlie Simmons walks up the hallway toward

us, his Spanish textbook tucked under his arm. Our eyes lock. It's probably just my imagination, but he seems to course correct a few degrees in my direction. I'm not certain because I take this opportunity to spin around and look in my locker mirror, pretending to fuss with my hair until I see his reflection walk away behind me. His tall, beautiful reflection.

When it's safe to turn back around, Noah is still reading through the list with a smirk. "Number five is interesting. How's your menses going?"

"None of your business." I slam my locker shut.

Noah jabs a finger in the air as if I just made his case. "Irritability. Number seven." He pockets his phone.

Mrs. Marino sticks her head out of her classroom door and glowers at the stragglers in the hallway. "Why are you dawdling? Get to class."

With a quick wave to Noah, I race Meaghan upstairs to Spanish. Even with an aching hip, I smoke her. I'm conditioned to run through pain. It's when I'm still that the ache settles in, a combination of my muscles stiffening and the inability to ignore what demands to be felt. We settle into our regular seats just as the bell rings.

Opening her homework folder, Meaghan turns to me. "Come with me to the mall after school? I want to get something new for Mike DiNardi's party." By the twinkle in her green eyes, she's crushing on someone new.

I pull my homework out to have it ready. "Really? Who's the lucky guy?"

She rolls her eyes. "Mike DiNardi!"

"Oh, the host! Okay then." I laugh.

"So you'll come?"

"Can't. I have a flying lesson."

She looks away, irritated. "Shocking."

Shuffling my papers, my eyes flutter down, trying to pretend that didn't sting as much as it did.

She sighs and bites her lip. "Sorry. I was just kidding. I—"

I tilt my head at her and smile. She nods solemnly and lets it go.

"You *are* coming to the party though, right?" she asks, with her dead-serious, don't-try-me look. Meaghan always bugs me to stand up for myself more.

"Grow a pair!" she'll say with two clenched fists.

"I would if I could, but my Y chromosome is still on back order!" is my go-to comeback. I've gotten lots of advice from her over the years about how to handle my dad. Her father happens to be a real softie.

I nod. "I'm going to try."

"Not try. *Do!* I need you there! You're my—"

"Wingman?" I ask, and we both laugh.

"Sure, let's go with that."

Señora Moore sweeps into class flushed and breathless, wearing a long peasant skirt and a peasant shirt, off the shoulders today. She looks ready to fiesta.

"Hola!"

"Hola, Señora Moore." A cacophony of apathy greets her, except for the large cluster of Highsteppers. They continue talking as if

14

they are the sun and we orbit them. Today is Madelyn's turn to have her hair French braided. Some days I watch them and think of Jane Goodall's chimps grooming each other.

Pat Michaels, his legs spread in front of him in a wide, slouchy V, raises his hand. "Can I go to the bathroom?"

"*En español, Patricio.*" Señora raises her finger.

Across the classroom, Charlie Simmons hunches over his desk, doodling, as always. She walks over and taps his desk.

"*Presta atención, Carlito.*" She points two fingers at herself, and he straightens up in his seat.

I stare at his honey-brown hair that shimmers even under the fluorescents and the slim inverted pyramid of his back underneath his fitted short-sleeve gray shirt. He has the long, toned body of a swimmer. He used to be on the swim team but quit. Charlie Simmons quits everything. He was also in the Robotics club and on the debate team. Smart, but a quitter.

He turns around at just that moment, catching me staring at him for the second time today. I bend over my notebook and start scribbling random notes, feeling the blush creep up my neck. But not before he smiles at me.

I wish I lived in a world where there was hope for me and Charlie Simmons.

BRADY: *The date is January 10. Time . . . 10:17 a.m. Do I have your permission to record your statement?*

KM: *Of course.*

BRADY: *Please state your name and your relationship with Hadley McCauley.*

KM: *Kathleen Moore. I was Hadley's Spanish teacher her junior and senior year.*

BRADY: *What can you tell me about Hadley?*

KM: *Hadley was a bright, conscientious student. She has always been a delight. A pleasure to teach.*

Isn't that what we always say about the quiet ones?

Some teachers prefer the quiet students. We have to contend with so many fresh mouths, year after year, that a quiet student is a blessing. But Hadley was quiet in a way that worried me. Her quiet felt . . . silenced.

BRADY: *Silenced? How?*

KM: *[sighs] With Hadley . . . I could never really tell what was going on beneath the surface. She was quiet, but really only around adults. In class, I wouldn't hear a peep from her until I called on her. Only if I called on her.*

So early last year I mentioned it in her first-quarter progress report. Now, you have to bear this in mind, when we do the progress reports, we don't have a blank field to write personal notes. We have a selection of comments we can check off. In Hadley's case, the one that came closest to what I felt was suitable was "More Participation Needed."

Well, when that poor girl came to school the following Monday, she was near tears. She asked to speak to me privately. She begged me to take that comment off her permanent record. I said, "Hadley, honey, you have a perfect grade in my class. I just want you to raise your hand more, that's all." And she asked me, "How many times?" I thought she was joking. But I saw the look on her face. She wanted to know how many times it would take to make sure this never happened again.

I swear to you, from that day on, that girl raised her hand three times in every class, every day. She was counting. Someone put the fear of God in her, and I promise you, it wasn't me.

then

It's easy to find Mike DiNardi's house thanks to all the cars parked haphazardly on both sides of the road. We're forced to park a few blocks away on Jackson Street. Along the way, we spot Claudia's white Acura by the deep gouges on the side mirror and door panel, the wheels half up on the curb. The girl can't drive to save her life, let alone parallel park.

"These boots were *not* made for walking. They're for standing and looking cute." Meaghan stops and leans against Noah to rest her feet squished into her new stiletto boots.

Noah laughs. "And for adding a few inches so you're not stuck under everyone's armpits all night." He links his arm through hers and mine, and we walk down the sidewalk at a leisurely pace. All down the block, impatient homeowners have decorated their yards for Halloween, which is still three weeks away. RIP tombstones turn front lawns into cemeteries while inflatable pumpkins staked to the ground bob in the wind, desperate to escape.

Noah turns to me. "I feel a tiny bit guilty that you're always our designated driver."

I smile back up at him. At six feet five, Noah looks down on everyone. "Couldn't drink if I wanted to. I have a game tomorrow. Go nuts. Unless you don't want to be too hungover for Matt."

He looks away. "He's not coming."

Meaghan jerks her eyes over to me, exasperated, then pivots back to Noah. "What's his deal *this* time?" She snarls. Matt hasn't been down to visit once since he left for college. Noah shrugs it off.

A breeze scatters a few fallen leaves around our feet. Meaghan stops again to lean against an old maple tree, its wide trunk taking up half the sidewalk. Noah deftly changes the subject.

"Yeah, but you know who else is really hot? Charlie Simmons."

A great yawning chasm opens up in the sidewalk, ready to swallow me whole.

"What?" I stare up at him in horror.

Noah slaps a hand to his cheek, wide-eyed with feigned embarrassment. "Well, *this* is awkward. Not you too?"

My heart stumbles to regain its footing. "You're *messing* with me?"

"A little." He wraps a long arm around my shoulder.

Still leaning against the tree, Meaghan pulls an impaled leaf off her heel. "The first step is admitting you have a problem."

"I don't have a problem," I say, but my nuclear-meltdown cheeks betray me.

Meaghan and Noah exchange knowing looks, the kind that push me outside our comfortable threesome, making me feel like

I'm a topic of conversation when I'm not around. "You *so* do!" Meaghan laughs. "You stare at his back every day in Spanish. Then when he looks at you, it's like you try to make yourself invisible."

Lifting my head a notch, I snap, "So what? I look. I'm human." I storm ahead, up the brick stairs to Mike's house.

Noah runs up behind me, meeting me at the top of the stoop. "I may need to see proof of that one day to believe it." He tilts his head down to look at me from under his thick eyelashes. Then he waves his hand in the air like the whole conversation reeks. "Anyway, I heard he likes Claudia."

My stomach free-falls. "Not *her*," I moan.

Noah laughs and claps his hands. "It's like shooting fish in a barrel."

Meaghan catches up. "Had, Charlie's perfect for you. He's hot, he's obviously into you, and he's the hookup king of our class." She ticks off Charlie's perfect trifecta on her fingers. "One and done."

She winks at me to let me know she's only half kidding.

Noah stops me with a hand on my shoulder before I open the door. "Seriously, though, Claudia has a huge hard-on for him. So if you're going to make a move, you better do it tonight."

I stare back at him with worried eyes.

"Great. She's traumatized. Happy now?" Meaghan opens the door for us.

"Me?" Noah protests with a hand to his chest. "That one's all on you, Ms. 'One and Done.'"

Mike DiNardi's parties always draw a huge crowd; people are jammed shoulder to shoulder near the entrance. Couch cushions and laps have already been claimed for the night. I follow Meaghan and Noah to the kitchen, dodging the group of guys passing the funnel around. Meaghan fills a Solo cup with soda and hands it to me, a prop so I don't look too dorky, then we find a spot in the dining room. The house is swampy with body heat. All around me, straps of skimpy dresses slip off drunken shoulders. I push my sleeves up to my elbows.

The party is divided into a bunch of mini clusters, the corner of each room hosting a cafeteria table from school. Noah is the Godfather, fist bumping and hugging his way through the party. Meaghan and I hang by his side as people swarm over to kiss his ring or whatever, chatting with the two of us just to be polite. After a while, Noah gets antsy and scans the party with his periscope vision, his head bopping to the music.

"Time to cut the cord, ladies." He darts off into the party, but I never lose sight of him; at his height, his head breaks the surface wherever he goes.

Meaghan is at my side for only a blink longer. "There's Mike. I'll be back."

This is why I hate parties. The bigger the crowd, the more alone I feel. Sipping my soda, I hug my waist with one arm, searching for a friendly, welcoming look. Eyes intentionally skirt around me, through me. Everyone's so into their conversations, no one budges to wave me over into their circle. Over in the den, Kim's peals of laughter draw my attention. She's bent over with her butt high up in the air like a cat in heat while Winona giggles and snaps a picture on her phone. She'll have over three hundred likes on

Instagram by tomorrow. Kim's ass pictures always do.

A path clears to the living room, and I catch Claudia's eye. She turns to Faith and says something. The way they both laugh at the same time tells me I am the joke. It's the final blow. I'm used to Claudia's crap, but Meaghan and Noah know better than to ditch me like a social pariah. They're just going to have to find another ride home; I didn't sign up for public shunning.

"Need a refill yet?" A mop of honeyed hair dips over my shoulder and peers into my cup.

I start and glance over my shoulder.

I'm not surprised to see Charlie Simmons here; he's good friends with Mike. Actually, Charlie is friends with everyone, a nomad who fits in comfortably wherever he goes. What's surprising is that Charlie is talking to *me*.

"Um. Actually, it's soda," I try to yell back, but my tongue swells ten sizes too big for my mouth, wicking every ounce of saliva, like those pellets Lila and I threw in the tub to watch them grow a thousand times their size into spongy sea creatures.

"Are you driving?" he shouts, and mimes with his hands a steering wheel in case I can't hear him over the noise from the speakers.

I nod. "Yeah. Always the designated driver," I shout back. He points to his ear, shakes his head, then gestures with his hand to follow him before turning away.

I stare at his retreating back, paralyzed for just a few seconds. Then I follow him.

Charlie leads the way, burrowing a hole through the kitchen crowd for us to worm through. He turns to look over his shoulder to make sure I'm there. When he sees I am, he smiles. He points to the back door, then reaches behind him and grabs my wrist to lead the rest of the way.

Pushing the metal screen door out, he holds it open as we walk down three cement steps to the patio. Glowing cigarette tips circle in the night like fireflies. Goosebumps prickle up my arms thanks to the autumn night breeze. I rub them away, wishing I hadn't left my jacket in the car.

Charlie notices. "Cold?"

"No," I say, afraid the truth will drive us back inside.

He unzips his hoodie and hands it to me.

"Liar." He smirks. His dark eyes catch the floodlights and sparkle.

I push his sweatshirt back. "But I don't want *you* to be cold."

He reaches over and wraps it around my shoulders, his fingers brushing against my neck. Another shiver zings through me.

"I hardly ever get cold. Has to be below freezing." He's wearing a blue short-sleeve shirt underneath, the same style as the gray one he wore the other day. It's fitted without being tight in a *really* good way.

"I remember seeing you skateboard through town in shorts last February," I blurt out, then cringe inwardly. God, I just admitted I've been stalking him for almost a year!

"Told you. I don't get cold."

I smile and bite my lip, pretending to be interested in the soaring height of the pine trees that line Mike's property, but really I'm scouring my brain for something to say. Meaghan never has this problem. Meaghan probably came out of the womb flirting with her mom's obstetrician.

"So," he says, trying to catch my eye. I look up at him nervously, hoping he's better at keeping this going. Because I don't want it to stop. "I figured it was time to take it to the next level," he says with mock seriousness, followed by a flirtatious smile.

"The next . . . *level*?"

"You know, all that hot and heavy staring. Thought it was time to have a real conversation."

My cheeks burn, remembering how he caught me staring *twice* yesterday. "Oh. I . . ."

His eyes dart along my face. "Doesn't take much to make you blush, does it? It's cute." Standing under the backyard floodlight, where apparently my blushing is center stage, I'm completely exposed. Being ignored inside is sounding more appealing. A hot, sick sensation swirls around in my stomach.

Noah was right. It's like shooting fish in a barrel. "Do you get off on making fun of girls or something?" My eyes sting with humiliation.

"What?" His face flattens, and then he winces. "Crap, no! I thought I was flirting. Was I that bad?"

I stare at him blankly then burst out laughing. "If that's flirting, then yes. You suck at it!"

He flicks his thumb and finger in the air. "Command Z!" I get it. Erase, do over. We both crack up, which relieves at least some of the tension building up inside of me.

"I probably should have stuck with something safe like, 'you have really pretty hair.'" He reaches over and gently touches a strand falling down my shoulder.

I'm horrified at how nervous I am around him. My tongue is vibrating in my mouth like a tuning fork. I feel alive—excruciatingly, painfully alive.

We find a bench under the tree and sit down. The temperature is dropping. I don't want it to chase us back inside, so I push my arms through the sleeves of his hoodie. Something primal makes me whiff a sleeve when he's not looking, to catalog his boy scent, mixed with something else. Stale cigarette smoke. From the party, I assume at first. Then I push my hands in the pockets.

"These yours?" I hand him a pack of cigarettes.

He glances down at the pack in my hand. "Yeah," he admits grudgingly, taking them from me.

"You smoke?" I ask, dismayed.

"Does it help if I say I'm trying to quit?"

I grimace. "I really hate everything about it. The way it smells. What it does to your body. I mean, they're your lungs." I point to his chest. "I just never understood how anyone could have such a lack of regard for his own life."

He nods. "I know. It was stupid to even start."

"Why did you?" I ask. "You used to be on the *swim* team," I say, like we're in the same club. The *athletes'* club.

He bristles. "Look, I said I was trying to quit."

I back off. And I told him *he* sucked at flirting. "Okay, I get it. Sorry for the lecture."

Folded over, his elbows on his knees, he stares at his sneakers and then looks back up, studying me. He opens the pack and takes one cigarette out, holding it up between us.

"In case of emergency." He pops it behind his ear and twists over his shoulder. "Hey, Willie. Catch."

Charlie tosses his pack over to Willie then turns back to me.

"I'll try harder." His eyes are serious, full of promise.

"Thank you," I say, recognizing that gesture as a huge, giant, big deal.

He reaches over and grabs my hand. I stare at it, the warmth of his palm spreading through my body.

I'm seventeen and I've never had a boyfriend, which, according to Meaghan, is a bigger crisis than the national debt and a measles/Ebola/Zika outbreak combined. It's not like no one's ever asked me out. A few weeks ago, Dylan Finnegan asked me to the movies, tapping his fist nervously against my locker, his jug-handle ears flaming red. But even someone as sweet as Dylan isn't worth the heap of trouble I'd get into by saying yes. My father made that abundantly clear last year when he threw my mother's wineglass against the kitchen cabinet at just the mention of a boy *possibly* asking me out.

But Charlie Simmons, who wears his confidence like a second skin, he's been my secret crush for years. I just never expected anything to come of it.

This one little dream I held for myself, that I hid away and stoked privately, is unexpectedly becoming a reality, which makes my toes curl in the best and worst ways possible. I know my world will snuff it out the first chance it gets.

"So, Hadley. Have any amusing anecdotes you want to share?" His eyes crinkle.

"Any amusi—?"

"Nah, scrap that. Tell me something about yourself. What makes you tick?" he presses.

With his hand in mine and his eyes searching for bits and pieces of me that hide below the surface, I find it very hard to form a coherent sentence. The warmth radiating off his body together with his warm eyes undermine my ability to think straight. My weighted 4.34 GPA is useless in the real world.

"Um . . . I play lacrosse?"

"Tell me something I *don't* know." He laughs. "You're kind of a legend on the lacrosse field. Muscles McCauley." He lifts his arms and flexes, showing off his biceps like a superhero.

"What? Nooo!" I gasp. "Only Meaghan calls me that!"

"Sorry to break it to you, Muscles. Everyone calls you that." He reads my face and tries to make light of it. "Relax! It's hot!" He chuckles.

"Hot?" I cry. "It is anything *but* hot! It makes me sound like the Terminator!"

He laughs hard at that, which eases my humiliation a little.

Charlie leans closer. "I promise you, you are not built like the Terminator." Just when I'm about to let it go, he wraps his long fingers loosely around my bicep. "Though you do have enviable guns. I may need to keep you around to open those tricky pickle jars." I cover my face with my free hand.

"But seriously," he says between laughs. "Is lacrosse *it* for you?" he asks, trying to probe a little deeper.

"No."

"You're fierce though. I've seen you play. You're like a machine out there. Unstoppable." He lifts his arm and mimes a toss.

"Yeah," I say vaguely.

He squints, scrutinizing me. "Are you bad at accepting compliments? Or are you still mad about the pickle-jar joke? Because I was just kidding. Kind of." He searches for eye contact and smiles, as if I'm in on the joke, as if we already have our own secrets.

Then I sigh and admit, "I only play because of my father. He was really big into lacrosse when he was in college. He gets to live vicariously through me."

"Really?" He leans back in surprise. In the shadows here under the tree, with only a dim stream of light from the party reaching us, his eyes are dark as the night sky. But I know in the right lighting, they're amber. I know because I've watched him for so long now.

"It really looks like you put your heart into it though," he says. I stare at his eyes long enough that I fear a part of me gets trapped and crystallized there forever.

"I'm a very good liar, I guess."

"Hmm." Charlie takes his cigarette from behind his ear and rolls it between his fingers. Just when I think he's about to light up in front of me and ruin everything, he puts it back and takes my hand again.

"Okay . . . well, so what does Muscles McCauley like to do off the lacrosse field?"

"I take flying lessons," I offer.

He stomps his foot on the ground. "Daaamn! *Flying* lessons? That's so badass! How was that not the first thing you told me?"

I laugh then look down at our clasped hands. "I'm not all that into it, to be honest. My father kind of makes me do it."

"That too, huh?" Charlie scratches his cheek, giving my embarrassing admission some breathing room.

"*Cupcake Wars*!" I blurt out.

"*Cupcake Wars*?" he repeats, then laughs.

"Yes! I watch it with my sister all the time!" I filter out the part about how we watch it because cupcakes, and any kind of junk food, are the forbidden fruit of the McCauley household.

"Okay." Charlie nods his head and chuckles. "What else?"

"Disaster movies," I admit.

"Seriously? Me too!"

"I love them. The cheesier the better. Volcanoes, tornadoes, earthquakes, major historic landmarks crumbling to the ground. Even better if it's in 3D."

Charlie nods his head in agreement. Then he points his finger between us. "You and me? We are going to a disaster movie together, Muscles. Okay, keep going. You're on a roll."

I bite my lip. "I like ceramics." I don't know where that one comes from. I took a class in summer camp years ago, when I was about Lila's age. I loved it. Loved the feel of the cold, wet clay under my hand taking shape. Our ceramics teacher gave us a demonstration on his pottery wheel. We weren't allowed to use it yet. "Someday," he said, looking at me. My hands itched to take a turn. I couldn't wait to take ceramics when I got to high school, but there was never any room in my schedule for it.

I tell Charlie all of this and he listens intently, and then Meaghan and Mike DiNardi come outside and join us, ruining my perfect oasis alone with Charlie.

"Move over," Mike orders. Charlie squeezes in closer to me on the bench and wraps an arm around my shoulders. Mike sits next to him and pulls Meaghan onto his lap.

"Yay! We're going to double date!" Meaghan shakes her fists in the air in victory.

"Where's Noah?" I ask.

"Matt surprised him. They took off," she says right before Mike reaches up and cups the back of Meaghan's head, pulling her lips to his. The two of them make out loudly, right here next to us.

I eye my noisily slurping friend with a mixture of amusement and shock. "She's shy that way," I say to Charlie.

"Why don't we give them some privacy." Charlie takes my hand and pulls me up. "Your hands are freezing." He takes both of them between his and rubs them between his much larger, much warmer hands. "Come on, let's go in and warm you up."

Inside, the party has thinned out.

Charlie leans down to my ear. "Let me just get a refill," he says before walking over to the keg. From the kitchen, I watch Claudia in the living room dancing on the coffee table with loud "look at me" *woo-hoos!*, her short skirt hitching up with her wild kicks. Every so often I get a flash of her underwear. I think that's the point. She's going to be useless on the field tomorrow *again*.

Which reminds me. I glance at the kitchen clock. It's after eleven.

"Keg's almost kicked," Charlie shouts over the music as he wraps an arm around my shoulders.

"Charlie?" That happy light in his eyes dims when he sees my grim expression. "I'm sorry. I have to leave. I have a game tomorrow morning in Riverhead." Stupid, *stupid* game.

"Oh. That . . . sucks." He looks as disappointed as I feel, which shouldn't make me happy. But it does.

He checks outside the kitchen window at Mike and Meaghan, who are still trying to swallow each other whole out on the bench. "I don't think Meaghan's going to want to leave yet. Mike can drive her home. Come on." He takes my hand again. "I'll walk you to your car."

He cuts through the crowd, towing me behind. As we get closer to the door, Claudia leaps off the coffee table.

"Charlie!" she screeches. "Where are you going?" She throws herself at him, looping her arms around his neck. Her makeup, always heavily caked on before a party, is beading on the surface from the sweat she worked up dancing. Frizzy blond bangs cling to her damp forehead.

He lets go of my hand and reaches behind him to untangle the knot of her arms.

"Hey, Claudia." He gently pushes her a few steps back. "I'm heading out."

She blinks and squints, struggling to focus. "Charlie, don't go," she pleads, her eyes and hands devouring him. "I've been wanting to talk to you all night. Where *were* you?"

"Out back." Charlie squirms away from her.

The music isn't as loud in this part of the house, which is how I know I don't imagine what happens next.

"Charlie." She leans forward, planting her hands on his chest to steady herself. Her eyes are wide and earnest, her voice a loud whisper. "Do you want a blow job? I give really good blow jobs."

I turn to look for her friends. Why aren't they running interference? Why aren't they looking out for her? Instead, Faith and the rest of Claudia's so-called friends stand only a few feet away, all laughing at her.

Charlie peels her hands off him again. "No, Claudia. Stop. Go home or something."

She pulls back, wounded then angry. "What's *wrong* with you?" she says, then sees me. *Really* sees me. Layers of understanding slowly rise to the surface. She shoots me a withering look through half-mast lids.

"Whatever." She turns and stumbles away. Charlie grabs my hand and tows me out the front door. On the sidewalk, he runs his hand through his hair.

He shakes his head, his eyes focused on the pavement. "Sorry."

"You didn't do anything," I say, though I'm still shocked. "What *was* that?" I thumb back over my shoulder.

"That girl's in serious need of an intervention," he says. "Which way is your car?"

I point to the left. "On Jackson." We walk together, hand in hand, down the tight sidewalk, stepping carefully over the ancient tree roots that push through the cement squares every few feet.

"So . . . are you going back to the party?" I ask.

He squeezes my hand apologetically. "Yeah . . . Shouldn't go for much longer, though. Once Mike runs out of beer, everyone will tear out."

It scares me to think that he's going back to the party after *that*. What if he only said no to Claudia because I was standing right there? What normal, red-blooded, healthy seventeen-year-old guy *wouldn't* say yes?

As if he's reading my thoughts, he says, "I'll steer clear of Claudia."

I shudder; how much of my internal dialogue did he manage to figure out?

He laughs, and we stop outside my car. "I swear, you practically had a thought balloon over your head. I could see it. It was all in uppercase and in bold with four, no, *five* exclamation points." He mimes a big balloon over my head.

Meaghan's still making out with Mike, and Claudia's probably back on the coffee table, and I have to leave this perfect night just as it was getting interesting to get some rest before the game. I have never resented my life more than I do in this minute.

I glance away. "I have no right to expect you to do . . . or *not* do . . . anything." I don't mean it, not one bit. I just say it to herd my own wildly out-of-control expectations.

I unzip his hoodie and hand it back reluctantly. Instead of taking it, he puts his hands on my shoulders and holds me in his gaze.

"Except, you kind of do," he says. He leans over and kisses

me. I clench my arms against my sides to stop them from lassoing around his neck. I don't want this kiss to end. Ever.

He pulls back and smiles. "I've been wanting to do that for a long time."

BRADY: *The date is January 10. The time, 1:05 p.m. Do I have your permission to record your statement?*

NB: *Yes.*

BRADY: *Please state your name and your age.*

NB: *Noah Berger. I'm seventeen.*

BRADY: *Noah, what is your relationship with Hadley?*

NB: *We're friends. Good friends.*

BRADY: *Tell me about Hadley.*

NB: *Well, Hadley is hands down one of the kindest, most compassionate people in the world. Period.*

BRADY: *Okay, continue.*

NB: *Look, Hadley is a really private person. I don't feel comfortable talking about her like this. Is she in trouble or something?*

BRADY: *No, nothing like that. We're just trying to learn a little more about her.*

NB: *Yeah, but why?*

BRADY: *The investigation is ongoing. We're still looking for answers about the crash. I promise you won't be betraying Hadley. You'll only be helping her. I just want to ask a few questions about Hadley's home life. We're getting the impression that Hadley's father was very controlling. Do you agree?*

NB: *Oh God, yes.*

BRADY: *So, tell me a little about that.*

NB: *Well . . . okay . . . so last year, he wouldn't let her be a Peer Helper. Hadley and I were both picked, which is a big deal. There are only about ninety Helpers out of more than fourteen hundred students in our school. Basically everyone gets a survey to fill out anonymously,* to find out which students you'd be most comfortable talking to about your problems. Hadley's name came up . . . a lot.

But Hadley had an SAT-prep class the same day as the Helper retreat. Her dad wasn't happy with her SAT scores . . . he made her take that test five freaking times last year. I would've killed for her LOWEST score! But he thought she could do better.

Mr. Murray—he's our dean who runs the Peer Helper program—said it was absolutely mandatory to attend the training weekend if you wanted to be a Helper. Mr. Murray even called Mr. McCauley to try to convince him to change his mind. I mean, she could've missed one class, you know? But when Mr. McCauley said no, it was a hard no. That's just the way it went down at her house.

BRADY: *Was Hadley disappointed?*

NB: *Well, yeah. But this kind of thing happened all the time. She just got used to being disappointed. Which is really sad. I probably made a bigger deal about it than she did.*

Listen, all of this stuff I'm telling you isn't anything she'd ever broadcast to the whole world, okay? We're tight. She confides in me and in Meaghan. And now Charlie. That's it. Everyone needs someone to lean on. Isn't that like a song or something?

now

I'm aware of nothing and everything.

Rubber wheels squeak across the linoleum floor as I'm rushed through the emergency room. From the corner of my eye, I see the hallway is bumper to bumper with occupied gurneys. Overhead, fluorescent light fixtures flare in a blur. Faces float over me, their expressions flat and professional. We pass a woman whose repetitive cries bleat like a car alarm.

But there's a hollow emptiness in my chest.

Someone says, "Find her a room. The news crew is already trying to get in."

"They're all taken. Must be a full moon today," another voice answers, and they laugh. They *laugh,* even though people are dead or dying all around them.

A whiff of coffee as we pass the nurses' station jolts me. A hand presses me down. "Lie back, Hadley. Don't try and get up."

More hands reach for me and move me onto a bed. I'm not in

a room, but I do have a privacy curtain that swishes open and shut on metal rings. Behind the curtain, two nurses discuss me as if I'm not right behind the thin veil of fabric.

"News Twelve already got wind of it. They're trying to get in to talk to someone."

"Has she said anything?"

"No, poor thing. She's still in shock."

A doctor sweeps in with a nurse to examine me. The dark circles under his eyes tell me his shift has been long. His bushy eyebrows bunch together, annoyed, but his bloodshot eyes take in everything.

Probing at my arm, he juts his chin toward the corner of a room.

"What's that still doing here?" he asks gruffly.

The nurse and I both glance over at the red cart with one open drawer. "Oh . . . from the cardiac patient. They took him to ICU—"

"Lock it up. If anyone—"

"Heeeelp meeeeeeee! Please, someone help meeeee!"

Chaos breaks out just beyond my curtain.

"Now what?" the doctor mumbles to himself. He juts his chin at the nurse this time. "See what's happening out there."

She steps out then rushes back in a moment later, pushing the curtain aside with an abrupt swish.

"Dr. Garfield, they need you . . . *now.*" She holds the curtain open for him, and he follows her. She swishes the curtain closed again as if this were a matinee, only I'm not sure if I'm in the audience or the performance.

Something crashes. A stampede of feet run to help. It takes an army of shouting hospital personnel to get whatever is going on out there under control.

The noise, the chaos, all belong to another world, another dimension. Not mine. I'm not really here. I died with them. I must have. I *should* have.

I shouldn't be here.

My feet touch the ground, walking over to the cabinet in the corner. I pull the slightly ajar drawer open all the way. Inside a plastic, shrink-wrapped tray is a neat row of glittering medical instruments.

With my teeth, I tear the package open and pluck the scalpel out.

I know they just want to help put me back together again, but it's not just my arm that's broken. I'm a million shattered pieces. Tiny shards that will cut anyone who tries to clean up my mess.

The first slit is easy enough, left to right, along my wrist. The blade is sharp; the flesh is soft. Blood pools up in a rush, looking more solid than liquid until it streaks red down my arm.

The next cut is harder. My left arm hurts so much, but the pain reminds me why I have to do this, why I have to finish what's already in motion. Because the pain in my arm is nothing compared to the pain of everything I've lost.

then

Between my damp, sweaty uniform and the cold rain that set in toward the end of the game on Saturday, my body is racked with chills. The heater was broken on the bus, so the ride back to the Duck Pond Park parking lot was brutal. Even Charlie's kiss last night—which has been on a constant loop in my head—isn't enough to warm me up. Inside my car, I crank up the heat and race home, if only to take a hot shower. Dread clamps its familiar fist around me as I pull into the driveway.

I kick off my sneakers and walk through the foyer to the kitchen. Mom is at the island chopping vegetables, an open cookbook at her left, a glass of wine at her right. She glances up from her work, and her nose wrinkles in distaste.

"Hadley, use the mudroom entrance." She points to the mudroom door off the garage. "Especially if you're going to come home like *that*." She gestures up and down at me with the knife in her hand.

"I'm just sweaty." I lean over the island to pluck a grape from the fruit bowl. She shakes her head, the dank, slightly smelly body of her own daughter ruining the carefully curated illusion of perfection in her home.

My father bursts out of his study, a gust of wind before the storm, his footsteps the rolling thunder, approaching closer, closer. He stands in front of me, hands on hips, ready to grill me like he does after every game he doesn't personally attend. I really should have hightailed it to the shower first.

"Did you win?"

"Yeah."

"How many goals did you score?" His dark falcon eyes interrogate me.

"One."

His lips curl with distaste, like I'm sour milk. Unimpressed, he dismisses me for the stack of mail on the kitchen island. He flips through quickly, then stops at one letter.

"What's this?" He holds an envelope out at arm's length. It's from the high school, addressed to me. Not to "The Parents of Hadley McCauley." To Hadley McCauley. I shrug and hold my hand out. He ignores my hand and tears the envelope open.

"'Dear Hadley,'" he reads out loud. "'You're invited to attend the Peer Helpers' Awareness Weekend . . .'" He mouths a couple more lines under his breath then looks up. His eyebrows unite in a bridge of indifference over his nose. "Not this shit again."

I can't stop the grin from spreading across my face. "Oh yeah. Noah told me about this. When is it?" I stick my hand out again, but he holds it out of my reach.

"I thought we told them no last year," he says, irritated.

My hand drops by my side. "I did. They're doing a training session for people who were interested in being a Peer Helper but didn't get in."

"So . . . it's not for the club?" he asks again, confused.

I shake my head and swallow hard. "It's just to learn the skills to be a Helper, you know . . ." I shrug.

He looks at me like I just sprouted two heads. "So what's the point?"

I lift a shoulder helplessly. "I'd really like to go," I plead. I try not to let him ruin this for me again, but a steady trickle of disappointment burns in my stomach anyway. He shakes his head and continues reading.

"It's another one of those overnight training sessions. November eleventh." He looks up at the calendar pinned to the kitchen bulletin board. "You have a tournament on the twelfth."

"Oh." I scramble to rebound, to come up with a solution that will work for everyone. "Coach Kimmel won't mind if I miss one."

His face darkens, storm clouds building before the onslaught.

"You're kidding me, right?" He turns to Mom, as if she's as much to blame for my temporary lapse of sanity. The air sparks with tension.

Mom lifts her glass of wine and takes a sip. Her blue eyes telegraph a message to me over the rim. *Tell him you're kidding.*

"Fall tournaments are just for practice, Dad," I explain. My hand reaches for the letter, pleading.

"You are the team *captain*," he says quietly. "*Every* game is important. Every . . . one." He holds up a pointer finger, a furious exclamation point.

I shoot my mother a beseeching look. *Once, just once, be on my side.* Her gaze skitters away, focusing instead on the fascinating pile of green and orange vegetables in front of her. I'm on my own, as usual.

"I wouldn't ask if it didn't mean a lot to me, Dad." He leans forward, bracing his knuckles on the granite countertop. He stares me down, pinning me with his eyes until my fleeting moment of courage incinerates under his stare. "Sorry."

"Miles," Mom speaks up finally. "She made a mistake. Let it go." She raises her glass again, her hand shaking.

He turns his back to me, shoulders squared, fists clenched like sledgehammers by his side, the letter still clasped in one hand. He balls it up and tosses it in the garbage on top of the used coffee grounds. Turning to me one last time he snaps, "Get your priorities straight," before storming out of the room.

Mom exhales, as if she'd been holding her breath the entire time.

"Why do you always have to make things more difficult than they already are?" she asks tremulously.

He broke her years ago. Now he's trying to break me too. They both poison me, little by little, mutating me at a molecular level. I'm terrified someday he'll snip my already fragile backbone in half, just like he did to my mother. I'm just grateful that they leave Lila alone. I make sure of that.

I turn and walk away. Upstairs, in the bathroom, I turn the shower on, hot. As hot as I can stand without my skin blistering off me.

My bedroom is straight out of a showroom, a showroom my mother saw in a magazine and hired painters and designers to duplicate. I was fourteen when she got the itch to redecorate my room, old enough to choose the colors I liked. I wanted green. Calm, soothing green. And blue. Tranquil, like the sea. Instead, she had my walls painted fuchsia and Pepto-Bismol pink. An enormous crystal chandelier scaled more for a ballroom than a bedroom dangles heavily from the high ceiling. Sometimes I wake up in the middle of the night with a scream in my throat, convinced it's crashing down on me. This is Mom's taste. It's pretty. There are plenty of girls who would love it. Just not me.

Lila and I lounge across my bed flipping through a copy of *Rolling Stone*, laughing at the glossy pictures of singers with ruby lips and plunging necklines. My hair is still damp from my shower.

"Look at *her*!" Lila points, curled up with my faux tiger-fur throw. She rubs the soft fabric against her cheeks while she reads. "Her boobies are so big!"

"So's her booty."

She pulls the magazine closer to her face. "Do you think they're real?"

"Her boobies or her booty?" I ask, trying to stifle a laugh.

Her hand circles the page. *"Everything!"*

I take a closer look. "I think her ears are real." Lila bursts into giggles, revealing a gaping hole where a molar should be. "Hey, how much did the tooth fairy give you for *that* thing? She should pay you by the pound."

She feigns the bored maturity of a grown-up. "There's no such thing as the tooth fairy, Hadley."

"Really?" I snap my fingers. "Too bad. I'm kind of hard up for cash. I was hoping you could bankroll me with all those teeth falling out of your head." She pretends to blow her nose in my throw. "Go ahead! I can't stand that thing!"

Her eyes grow wide and serious. "Hey, you need to help me practice my act."

The school talent show is coming up. When I was her age, I performed Bach's *Allemande* on my flute. Lila? "Beg for It" by Iggy Azalea. It doesn't even faze her that the song is already old as dirt. "I'm into retro hip-hop," Lila said, even though Iggy hasn't been out of circulation long enough to earn the distinction of being retro.

"Lila, the lyrics—"

"I'm going to use the karaoke version! Just to dance to!"

"Lila! 'Beg for It'?"

"The teachers won't know what it means!"

"Any . . . other . . . song! And don't do that thing with your butt!"

She jumps off the bed and turns her back to me.

"You mean like this?" She sticks her butt out and gyrates around.

"Lila!" My hands fly to my face in shock.

"God, Hadley! You're such an old lady!"

I put a hand to my ear, pretending I'm hard of hearing. "Eh?"

My phone rings and interrupts our giggles. I don't recognize the number.

"Hellooo?" I warble like a little old lady for Lila's benefit, watching for her reaction.

"Hadley?" the voice asks, confused.

"Yeah, ha! It's me. Sorry. Who's this?"

"Charlie."

"OH!" The heat climbs up my neck to my cheeks. Lila's head pulls back in shock like a turtle retreating into its shell. "Sorry! I was just goofing around with my little sister."

She takes offense at that. "LITTLE?" she repeats with her hands on her hips.

"Is it a bad time?" he asks.

"Yes. No. Um . . . Hold on one sec!" I press my hands together and mouth, *Give me a minute . . . please?*

Lila sashays out the door. "It's a boy, isn't it?" she shouts, then runs out as I throw a furry pillow at her.

"I'm back," I say, trying to compose myself.

"How old's your sister?" Joy warms his voice, heating me from the inside out.

"Ten going on twenty-one. She was just practicing her booty dancing for my viewing pleasure. I can't unsee it."

"Oh no."

"Oh yes."

He laughs softly. "You sound really happy when you talk about her."

"Really? I guess so."

"It's cute."

I rest a cool palm to one flaming cheek. "Like my blushing and constant staring?" I shoot back, half jokingly.

Charlie clears his throat. "For the record, last night I was referring to *my* constant staring. Now I know why you were offended." He laughs uncomfortably. "And yes, you blush ridiculously easily. I bet you're blushing right now."

I nod even though he can't see me. "I am."

An awkward moment of silence echoes for a millennium. "How'd you get my number?" I blurt out, panicked for something to fill the dead air.

His tone changes. "I'm sorry," he says. "Should I not have called?"

"No . . . I mean, yes. I'm glad you did. I'm just curious."

"Meaghan. Before Mike took her home."

"Oh." I grin. Now I know why I haven't heard from Meaghan all day. She was probably sitting on her hands waiting for me to tell her Charlie called. "How was the rest of the party?"

What I *really* want to know is if Claudia propositioned him again. I pick up the fake-fur throw and rub it against my cheeks like Lila did. It's so soft and soothing, like rubbing your face in a cloud. I get why she loves it now, even though it's ugly.

"Claudia cried then threw up then cried some more."

"Yeah, I'm not surprised. She was useless today. Coach benched her for most of the game."

"Yeah." Pause. "Did you know that lightning strikes six times around the world every second?"

"Uh . . . no?"

"And bees beat their wings two hundred and seventy times every second?"

I frown, trying to follow his random train of thought. "Charlie, what are you looking at?"

"BuzzFeed. I started thinking how every second I'm not spending with you is a wasted opportunity. Holy crap! Listen to this: in just the amount of time it took me to explain that, five babies were born. We're squandering precious seconds. Let's get off the phone and go out, see a movie or something."

"Now?" I drop the throw, as stunned as if my chandelier actually did come crashing down on my head. "I mean, now is fine," I say, without thinking it through.

"Well then, yes, now. Look at all the amazing things that happen every second. Time's a-wasting, Hadley. I'll come get you—"

"No," I say firmly. "I'll meet you. Where?"

"Okay." He pauses again, trying to read my mood, my words. "How about the AMC? In an hour? We'll just see whatever movie is playing when we get there. Maybe we'll get lucky and there will be a cheesy disaster movie on."

"Okay. See you in an hour."

I hang up and grin.

Just go and see what's playing? Who does *anything* without a ten-step plan in advance?

Charlie Simmons, that's who.

I try on and discard several tops before settling on a pair of jeans and a navy-blue sweater. My laptop rings; Noah's FaceTiming me. I hit accept, and his face appears.

"Hey." He smiles at me, but it wavers at the corners. He eyes me suspiciously. "You're literally beaming. What's going on?"

"So Charlie Simmons just called. I'm heading out the door right now to meet him at the movies!" I squeal.

Noah's eyes narrow. "Wearing *that*?"

My shoulders slump. "I changed *four* times!"

He waves me away. "You're fine. Fill me in on all the dirty deets in the morning."

Noah reaches over to disconnect. "Wait!" I stop him. "How was last night? With Matt?"

He makes a slightly nauseated face. "Meh. I'll tell you later. Go have fun." He sweeps his hand like he's brushing me away. I blow him a kiss and close the laptop.

Before I run downstairs, I pop into Lila's room. Music is blasting. She's standing on her bed staring at herself in the mirror, thrusting her hips to the beat. Her shirt is tied up high, showing off as much of her belly as possible.

"Hey, kiddo. Change of plans. I'm heading out."

"Was that a boy?" Her tongue flaps around behind the crater of her missing tooth.

"No, it wasn't a boy, wise guy." I lie to her for her own good. "Stay out of Dad's way, okay?"

She rolls her eyes and works on her booty thrusts. I die a million deaths just picturing what would happen if my father walked in and saw *this*.

"And stop doing that!" I point at her and slam the door then I run downstairs. I don't have a plan or an excuse. Where am I going? How am I getting out of the house?

Wearing only a pair of nylon workout shorts, my father stands at the kitchen counter glistening with sweat, drinking a glass of water. His skin is an unnatural shade of nutmeg for October; I try not to gag picturing him getting a spray tan. He puts the glass down and pinches his waist to check his body fat. Even I can see he doesn't have an extra ounce on his lean frame that he obsesses over almost as much as he obsesses over mine.

Dad is kind of manorexic. He was the fat kid growing up, picked on for his Michelin spare tires and man boobs, especially by his father, who died before I ever met him. There are no pictures of my father as a kid in the house. He hates seeing his "before" shots. The summer before college, he got serious, lost the weight, and went off to school a new man. Joined a fraternity, and *voilà*, transformed himself into a frat-boy asshole, a legacy that continues well into his middle age. And since he associates his unhappy childhood with his own lack of discipline and weakness, he makes it his mission to make sure none of us ever turn into "fat-asses" by monitoring every crumb of food that goes into our mouths.

There is one picture Dad is particularly proud of, framed in the den on top of a floating wall shelf, of him and his frat brothers standing behind their Alpha Kappa Douchebag basement bar in their Ray-Bans, Hawaiian shirts, and plastic lei garlands (it was a

Get Lei'd party. Get it? *Hilarious!*). Over their heads hung a crude handwritten sign: No Fat Chicks Allowed.

"You haven't been down to the gym in a while. Monday morning instead of cardio, we lift."

"Okay." I nod agreeably, slipping my arms through my jacket sleeves. His expression changes instantly.

"Where the hell do you think *you're* going?"

"Library." I come up with it quickly, because library has "lie" in it.

"What for?"

"History project. I need to present my notes on Monday. I was so busy worrying about the game, I totally forgot." The lie comes easily. *He's* been the one obsessing about today's game. Using that against him is somehow satisfying.

He lifts his glass of purified water and glares at me over the rim. "When will you be back?"

"Couple of hours. Depends on how good or bad it's going."

He opens a kitchen drawer to pull out the calipers. I bolt before he can say no or decide it's time to check my body fat again.

Outside, the air is fresh and welcoming. The more distance I put between my father and me, the easier I breathe.

then

Charlie waits outside the movie theater. A breeze ruffles through his shaggy hair as I walk down the sidewalk to meet him. He sees me and smiles, and that constant little "Charlie" flutter in my belly thrashes wildly in response.

"Hey." He bends down and kisses me softly on the lips, as if he's making certain last night wasn't just a fluke. My head tilts up to meet him halfway. I clamp my elbows by my side again; the impulse to knot them around his neck is just too powerful. I guess I have to forgive Claudia for last night. Charlie is pretty irresistible.

When he pulls back, his eyes are happy.

Glancing down at my boring outfit, he says, "You look pretty."

"Liar," I tease him, picking up his joke from last night. But his eyes are serious.

"Nope. I never lie," he says. And I believe him.

He wraps his arm around my shoulders, and we walk inside.

We look up at the movie listings.

"Hey, look at that. *Monkey Apocalypse* starts in five minutes. Perfect timing," he says, and I can't tell if he's joking or not.

"Seriously?"

"Oh, because you're such a movie snob, queen of disaster movies!" He squeezes my shoulder and laughs. "It got a four percent on Rotten Tomatoes. We should go, just to make fun of it. I think the special effects are supposed to be halfway decent." His grin is infectious. His happiness passes through to me like osmosis.

"Okay," I agree, because, really, all I care about is spending time with Charlie. I take my wallet out of my purse.

"Stop." His face pinches. "We're on a date. I'm paying."

"You don't *have* to," I say. His entire body stiffens.

"I said I got it." He takes his wallet out of his back pocket. He puts a twenty and a five down on the counter. "I got paid yesterday," he adds, a little less prickly.

He picks up our tickets from the counter, and we walk across the lobby, cutting through an oppressive cloud of buttery popcorn scent.

"So . . . where do you work?" I try to smooth over whatever *that* was.

"Well, I have *three* jobs." He laughs, but it sounds embarrassed. "I have a paper route in the morning. I drive all around town at four thirty in the morning and throw papers on front stoops. It's very Norman Rockwell."

"I'm surprised we haven't run into each other. That's what time I get up to run with my father."

An usher dressed like a down-on-his-luck bellhop stands by the velvet ropes. Charlie hands the tickets to him and smiles over his shoulder at me like I'm teasing, then his eyes widen in surprise. "You're kidding me, right?"

I shake my head. "Nope. I always thought we were the only lunatics up at that hour. It might make it easier to get up knowing you're out there too."

"Looks like our timing is off. My route keeps shrinking. People are starting to figure out that they can get all the news they need on Facebook."

"*Mom* news." I laugh.

"Exactly. Then a couple of days after school, I stock shelves at Greenway. And on Sundays, I bus tables at the diner my mom works at."

"Oh," I say, unable to find a response that won't come out all wrong. "How do you find time to study?"

"I don't," he answers easily.

I bite the inside of my lip. "Is that why you quit the swim team?" *And the Robotics club. And the debate team.*

He opens the door for me with one arm and places the other on my lower back to usher me into the dark theater. "Bingo."

That's when I realize Charlie isn't a quitter. Charlie's a survivor.

The movie is awful. On the plus side, we are the only people in the theater, so we laugh and make fun of it loudly.

Charlie wraps his arm around my shoulders, drawing me closer; the armrests stop us from getting too close. A couple of times during the movie, Charlie glances around to make sure no one has entered the empty theater, and then pulls my face to his for a few long kisses that leave me breathless. We're kissing when the credits roll. If I were quizzed right now, I don't think I'd be able to tell anyone what the movie was even about.

The lights slowly go from dark to dim. It's our cue that we have to leave, that our date is over.

I bite my lip and smile, more than a little embarrassed by this new public-display-of-affection side of me. "Well, that was fun. I should probably—"

He shoves his hands in his pockets and points with his shoulder behind him. The words pour out of him in a rush. "I live right around the corner. Do you want to come over?"

I'm not ready to say good-bye. "Okay," I say, without even weighing the options, the many obstacles and potential hazards I'm completely ignoring.

We walk hand in hand through town. A few short blocks from the movie theater, Charlie stops outside Sal's Pizza, right across from the library where I'm *supposed* to be. The overpowering smell of oregano and marinara is as appetizing as a loaded diaper. I'm about to tell him I'm not hungry, but he pulls out his keys, opening a metal door to the side of the restaurant entrance. Up the warped, creaky stairs is another door. He takes a second key and pushes in.

I don't want to see Charlie's apartment through my family's distorted lens, but I can't help it. Everything looks like a yard sale find. The ratty brown couch with an orange-and-yellow afghan tucked over it. To the right of the couch is a small round table for eating. The kitchen is right off the living room, surrounded by three closed doors. The apartment reeks of Italian food and mothballs.

"Where's your mom?" I ask, glancing around.

"At work." He tosses his keys and wallet in a chipped ceramic bowl on the table. "She won't be back till late."

"Oh." We're alone. "Can I use the bathroom?" I stall until I sort out how I feel about this.

He shows me through the kitchen, past an ancient oven too tiny to fit a Thanksgiving turkey.

"Here you go." He opens the last door and flicks the light on.

I bump the door closed with my shoulder when the old wood sticks on the frame. Once inside, I sweep the shower curtain aside with a finger. A tub that, while not dirty, is permanently stained algae green and muddy orange from years of drips. The white tile bathroom floor, old and chipped, sparkles.

Charlie sits on the couch watching a football game when I get back. The kind of boxy television set you find out on the curb on garbage day. I cringe inwardly that I notice this, that I *think* this. His arm reaches out for me, and I join him on the couch. He puts his hand to my cheek and pulls me toward him, kissing me, harder, more urgently than at the theater. He starts to lean forward, pushing me down on the couch.

I come to my senses and push him way back. "Whoa. Slow down."

He winces. "Sorry."

We stare ahead in awkward silence, our eyes glued to the game. It could be C-SPAN for all I notice; my thoughts are a tangled mess. I glance down at my lap, wringing my fingers, the tight atmosphere of his apartment pressing down on me.

"Command Z?" he teases. When I don't smile back, he sighs. "I really am sorry. I don't want to blow this. I kinda . . . I've just liked you for a while." He plucks at a tear in the cushion between us where the afghan inched up to expose the worn couch underneath. "I tried to talk to you so many times, but you have this amazing talent of looking away just as I'm about to open my mouth. I had some great opening lines too." He laughs awkwardly. "Like, 'Hey, how'd you do on the Spanish test?'"

He tips his head back and scans the ceiling, his Adam's apple bobbing with a nervous swallow, exposing a vulnerable, less confident side of him than the boy I fantasized about all this time. Relief starts to undo the knots in my stomach.

"I've liked you for a while too," I say, feeling the heat rush to my cheeks just by admitting that out loud for the first time.

He cautiously reaches his arm around my shoulders, testing the waters. I lean back and let his arm curl around me, nestling in, as if we've been doing this for years. But we haven't. Last night was the first time we actually ever *really* talked. And here I am, making out with him, first in public, and now back in his apartment.

Charlie, the hookup king. Is that all this is?

How many Monday morning conversations did I listen in on in the girls' bathroom, where the weekend gossip would be rehashed and Charlie's name would come up? "I heard _____ hooked up with Charlie." Maybe that's all I am, someone whose name will fill in the blank next to Charlie's on Monday morning in the bathroom.

"Charlie?" I ask hesitantly. "So . . . what are we doing?"

He gestures to the TV with the remote. "Want me to put something else on?"

"No . . . I mean *this*." My hands flutter by my sides, trying to define this space, this moment. His mouth twists, still not tracking. "Are we just hanging out?"

He gets a dopey, earnest look on his face, but his lips twitch with a barely suppressed smile.

"Muscles McCauley." He takes my hand. "Will you be my steady girl?" A tiny snort scrapes at the back of his throat, which makes me crack up.

"You're an idiot. You know that, right?" I push him away with a laugh.

He wrestles me back into the crook of his arm, and we watch the game.

After a few minutes, he squeezes my shoulder. "You didn't answer my question," he says, more serious this time.

I bite my lip and glance up at him. "Yeah, sure."

"Yeah?" he repeats, like he can't quite believe it either.

A small flame ignites inside my belly, one I thought was extinguished a long time ago. A tiny torch of hope.

now

I lean my forehead up against the hospital window to watch the snowflakes fall from low clouds, the cold glass bracing against my skin. The barren trees are coated in a layer of fresh snow, their branches raised toward the heavens in prayer. Or maybe surrender.

The grounds go on forever. I can't even see the road from my room. I think that's the point. My window doesn't open either. I know it's all to keep me safe. But they can't keep me here forever.

Janet comes in, her white orthopedic shoes squeaking across the linoleum. Her chubby face is cheery.

"Oh, good, you're up," she says, bringing me breakfast. "How are you feeling today?"

Loopy, I want to say. But I don't. Mostly because the meds I'm on make me not want to do or feel anything. Without anger, guilt, grief, even happiness, I have nothing. I want to go to sleep and never have to wake up again.

She walks over and lifts my right hand, examining the dressing, then gently lifts my left.

It should have been over by now. But no, I had to pass out at the sight of all that blood and fall into the curtain and out to the hallway. Dr. Garfield got to me just in time to stitch me back together again.

"After you eat, I'll change those for you, okay?"

Sitting on the radiator, I stare out the window. She waits to see more of a reaction from me.

"I think we need to look into adjusting your meds."

I shrug and gaze out the window.

"Do you need help eating?" she asks.

I glance down at my broken arm. They took the sling off yesterday and gave me a cast, with a window cut out where they sewed me back up. The cast should have names and funny pictures scribbled in Sharpie across it, but it doesn't look like I'll be seeing my friends anytime soon.

Charlie drew funny pictures, I think, and my stomach clenches with a fist of regret.

I shake my head.

"Come on, Hadley. You need to eat something."

"What's the point?" I ask through dry, gummy lips. I try to lick them, but even my tongue is lethargic.

"The point," she says with dire seriousness, "is to *live*."

Her eyes are wide and blue, like a baby doll's. Like Lila's.

"My sister . . ." But I don't say anything more.

I turn my right wrist over to look at the bandage.

then

"Hold still!" Charlie says, trying not to laugh, but he can never completely erase the smile from his eyes. He squints them now in concentration, the blue pen working across my bicep. "There!" He lifts the pen away. I pull my arm forward, struggling to see his artwork.

"What *is* it?" I ask. Meaghan leans around Charlie to look.

Everyone in Spanish class knew we were dating that first Monday back after Mike's party. Charlie met me at my locker between second and third period and walked me to class for the first time, taking the desk next to mine. Meaghan's jaw dropped when she walked in and saw him sitting in her seat; I patted the desk to my left for her to flank my other side.

"That's April's seat," she said tightly. Then she put on a brave smile and took a seat to Charlie's right.

Now she says, "Nice," nodding her head in approval at Charlie's artwork.

"Flex your bicep," Charlie says.

So I do, which makes them both laugh really hard.

"It's a rabbit!" Meaghan squeals. "His ears wiggle when you flex! Charlie, that's hysterical!" She high-fives him.

"I can't see!"

Meaghan pulls a compact out of her purse and leans across Charlie's desk to show me. I stare at the reflection, flexing and laughing. I look up at Charlie.

"Muscles like those should flaunt some ink." He wiggles his eyebrows at me.

Whereas Meaghan (and apparently the entire student body) calls me Muscles jokingly, Charlie says it in a way that makes my knees weak. At my locker this morning before the first bell, he whispered in my ear, "Morning, Muscles," as his hand traveled down my arm, down my back, inching down . . . and then our principal, Mr. Johnson, stepped in.

He hooked two fingers in the air. "You two, come with me."

Shutting his door behind us, we took our in-trouble seats, something as completely foreign to me as the in-school detention room, which, rumor has it, is somewhere in the west wing. He took a piece of paper out of his drawer and highlighted it in yellow with a dramatic flourish then passed it across the desk to us.

PUBLIC DISPLAY OF AFFECTION

Melville High School is an educational
institution. It is inappropriate to display
any form of affection (e.g., hugging or kissing, whether friendly or romantic) while in

attendance at school. PDA may be written up
as a Behavior Report if excessive or reoc-
curring.

Charlie and I read it together. I must have looked as terrified as I felt because Charlie's hand found mine under the desk and squeezed.

"Are we clear?" Mr. Johnson asked.

"Crystal," Charlie answered for both of us.

"Okay, then. Get to class," he dismissed us. We both stood up. "I don't want to have to call your parents about this." I sensed that warning was for my benefit. Icy dread trickled down my spine. When we were far enough from Mr. Johnson's office, I turned to Charlie.

"Seriously, he cannot call my parents. We have to chill a little."

"No, I know." Charlie nodded, but his face was confused. He glanced over. "Have you told your parents we're going out?"

I bit my lip. "Not yet. But I will when the time is right." That was a lie. I know there'll never be a right time. I just don't know how to explain it to Charlie.

Señora Moore sweeps in.

"Hola!" She wiggles her fingers at the class.

"Hola, Señora Moore," we say.

My shirt sleeve is still pushed up to my shoulder, my lacrosse hoodie on the back of my chair. Señora Moore glances my way, a quizzical smile on her face. She steps over to look at Charlie's artwork.

"Ah!" she gushes. *"Muy buen trabajo, Carlito!"* She turns to the classroom and enunciates very loudly, *"Un conejo."* She puts her fingers over her head like rabbit ears.

The students turn in their seats and laugh at my Bic pen bunny tattoo, which sets off my hair-trigger internal thermostat. Charlie reaches over to squeeze my hand as my cheeks flare. His hand, so solid and sure, both buoys and anchors me.

Even though it's only been three weeks since Mike's party, it feels like Charlie and I have been together for much longer. I've canceled flying lessons two weeks in a row, telling Phil, my flight instructor, that I had a big paper coming up I needed to work on. I've also been spending a lot of time at the "library" whenever I can squeeze it in around lacrosse practice and Charlie's work schedule. It shaves a few hours off my studying. But for the first time in my life, I'm putting something on my schedule for myself, something that puts a smile on my face when I wake up, even at the ungodly hour of four thirty.

"Hey, Muscles." Meaghan pulls me aside in the hallway on our way to lunch. "Just so you know, the whole school is abuzz about you and Charlie."

It hits a nerve. I frown. "Why does anyone care?"

She shrugs and lifts her hands up. Then she looks away. "It's just weird, Had. No one gets that tight that fast," she says as if she's just relaying a message. But it doesn't sound like that; it sounds like it's coming from her.

I stare her down. "I have been your wingman for way too long for you to have a problem with me and Charlie now," I snap.

"No, you're right." She glances away. Her eyes bounce back up. "I think I'm kind of jealous," she confesses, her nose wrinkling up.

That makes me laugh. "You? You can have any guy in this school!" Then I lean forward. "Unless you already have."

She shoves me playfully, then her eyes dim. "But I've never had what you guys have."

Seeing how gloomy it makes her confirms what I already know in my heart about Charlie: what we have is real. People see it, are talking about it. Even Meaghan. If that's the case, then my fears that we're moving too fast are really just excuses, because the thought of having sex terrifies me.

My mind drifts back to last night, like it's been doing all day.

Our dates have fallen into a predictable pattern. We start off making out on his couch. After a few minutes, we make our way to his bedroom, our lips barely parting during the short walk across the apartment. Collapsing on his springy twin bed, pushed up against the wall of his sliver of a bedroom, his touches are confident. Mine are still hesitant, inching along nervously. I'm afraid to explore *too* much, but his soft groans and deepening kisses encourage me to keep going.

Last night we went further than ever before.

Then came the inevitable moment when my fear of what was about to happen next if we kept going became a thunderous drumbeat that drowned out everything else.

"Charlie, wait." His tightly coiled body slumped against me in defeat.

"Okay," he groaned into my hair. We curled against each other, both of us afraid to move.

Finally, he propped up on his elbow and reached an arm out to twirl a strand of my hair around his finger.

I took a deep breath. "It's not that I don't want to. I mean . . . I do. I just . . ."

He leaned over and kissed me. "I can wait."

"I want to, Charlie. I really do. I just want to be ready." I held his eyes, trying to find courage in those amber pools. The last person I need to be afraid of is Charlie.

"Hellooo?" Meaghan waves a hand back and forth in front of my face, dragging me back to the clamoring school hallway.

My eyes dart around to see if anyone's listening.

"I have to ask you something . . . serious," I whisper. Meaghan leans closer. "I think . . . I'm ready . . . I want to go on some kind of birth control," I finish with false bravado.

Meaghan leans back and squeals with delight. People stop and stare.

I pinch her arm. "Stop that! Don't make me regret telling you!"

Meaghan rubs her bicep. "Ow, all right. What kind?"

I run a hand through my hair. "That's the thing. I'm not sure which one is right . . . for me. I mean . . . a *vaginal ring*? I freak out when I can't find the tampon string!"

Meaghan roars. I once called her in a panic convinced I had lost the tampon somewhere deep inside the cavernous depths of my uterus. After several failed attempts to find the string with Meaghan staying on the line with me, I remembered I had taken the tampon out in the middle of the night and forgot to put a new one in.

"Just go on the Pill," she says with an aloof lift of her shoulder, like this isn't the biggest decision I've ever made.

"I don't know . . . ," I hedge.

Meaghan's lips twist to the side as she weighs other options. "Well, there are condoms. If you're with a player, which you are." I groan. "Well, I'm not saying he *is* anymore," she assures me. "But Charlie has history. In good news, it helps when at least *one* person knows what he's doing your first time. But unless he gets tested, I'd say go with condoms."

I grimace.

She reaches over and puts a steadying hand on my shoulder. "Look, this is *you* we're talking about. Condoms aren't always the safest, you know. Accidents have been known to happen."

Just the *thought* of getting pregnant almost sends me into full-body hives. "Oh, I absolutely, positively have to have *the* safest—"

"I know, I know," Meaghan cuts me off. "Which is why, for you, I'd say go on the Pill. It's 99.9 percent effective. But make Charlie get tested."

"Maybe we should use both. Condoms and the Pill. Just to be certain."

Meaghan giggles. "Had, this isn't like extra credit. You don't get more points for doing more. If he gets tested and you take the Pill, you're covering all your bases. Don't overthink it."

It's the most logical plan.

"Makes sense," I agree.

Meaghan laughs and pats my shoulder. "Yes, Muscles, sex makes sense."

Mike DiNardi walks by with his crew. I sense Meaghan tensing up next to me. Her hand raises up by her waist, ready to wave. Mike glances over at Meaghan and quickly looks away. Farther down the hallway, Billy squeals in a falsetto voice, "Can I cooome?" The guys crack up, too hard, too obviously at Meaghan's expense. Mike shoves Billy into a locker. "Don't be a dick," Mike warns. He glances back at Meaghan with an apologetic wince.

"What the hell was *that*?" I ask her. Her eyes tighten, and her lips pinch.

"Nothing."

"It's not nothing—"

"Look, you've been so wrapped up in Charlie, I haven't been able—"

"Don't." I hold up a hand to stop her. "I've been right here. What's going on?" I jerk my head down the hallway toward Mike and his friends.

"Not here." Her eyes dart around, making sure no one's listening. "Do you think you can come over after school? Just you and me? You can help me wrangle all the trick-or-treaters."

She asks hesitantly as if I might say no, as if I'd ever do something so hurtful. Which makes me fear maybe that's exactly what I've been doing to her this past month. "Definitely. Not a problem."

I don't tell her I have a flight lesson. I'll just have to call Phil and cancel a third time. Then after Meaghan's, I'll stop by

Charlie's. Once you pull at that thread, the lies start to come easily.

"Charlie, wait."

Shot down again, he slumps next to me, draping a heavy arm around my waist. With his head resting on my chest, my fingers run through his hair, down his neck where I feel his pulse racing, then trace the steel curves of his forearm. When my fingers trace his jaw, he leans into my palm.

"So, I've been thinking," I hedge.

"Thinking is good," he says absently, his lids closed.

"I'm going to go on the Pill."

His eyes fly open, and he props his head up on an arm, a flicker of hope darting across his face like a shooting star. "Are you sure? I mean, I have condoms." He gestures to his desk, ready to leap across the short distance and grab one.

I pull him back by his wrist. "I know. And I know they're safe, just not as safe as I need them to be. I just . . . I can't take *any* chances."

He relaxes back against me. "Gotcha."

"But." I raise a warning finger and trace a line down his nose to his lips. They part under my pressure and I pull away, smiling. "If I have to get my girl parts probed, you have to get tested."

His lips close and turn up into a smile. "It's only fair." His hand roams down my side, dipping in at my waist, resting at my hip. He takes a deep, satisfied breath.

"So . . . this is really going to happen? Like, soon?"

"Soonish," I qualify.

His eyes roll up into his head, and he buries his face in my neck, groaning.

"Are you okay?"

"What do *you* think?" he asks, and I laugh, sensing his predicament.

The next day after the last bell, Charlie meets me at my locker.

"You sure you don't want me to come?" He holds my backpack for me while I load it with textbooks.

"No, go to work. I'm nervous enough," I say as Meaghan struts over in her high heels, grinning all the way down the hallway.

"Ready to go?" She makes a V sign with her fingers when she reaches us.

I cringe. "Meaghan," I groan.

Charlie shakes his head and squeezes his eyes shut. "I think I know what she's talking about. I just want to pretend I don't."

Meaghan thumbs over to him. "Never took *him* to be a prude."

Charlie and I both shift uncomfortably.

I really wanted to do this alone. But yesterday at her house, Meaghan filled me in on the fallout after she and Mike broke up last week. I just assumed it was the usual: Meaghan likes boy, Meaghan hooks up with boy, Meaghan tires of boy, Meaghan breaks boy's heart. I didn't realize this time was different.

Sitting on opposite sides of a leftover Entenmann's chocolate fudge cake at her kitchen table, we attacked it with forks, not even bothering with plates.

"He told his friends I was too *needy*," she said, the word

sounding bitter despite the fudge frosting melting in her mouth. "The worst part is he was kind of right," she added. "I mean, he's being a dick, don't get me wrong. But *needy*? That's not me. You know that. I know that."

She stopped to lick her fork, then stared pensively into space. "Seeing you and Charlie together . . . I don't know, I guess I was trying to make Mike be 'the One.' I mean, you date *one* guy and hit the mother lode? I've dated *sooo* many guys, I'm exhausted! And I'm not even eighteen!"

I sliced off another bite of cake with my fork. "You're the one who told me Charlie would be perfect for me." I laughed.

She didn't.

Meaghan shrugged one shoulder and stared at the cake. "I thought you guys would just hook up. I never thought you'd get serious."

I glanced up and tried to read her. Her words bugged me.

"So you were hoping Charlie would dump me the next day?" I asked, the heat in my voice hard to disguise.

"NO!" Her eyes shot up at me and widened in alarm. "No," she said again, quieter this time. "I thought you'd dump *him*."

She leaned back over the box and speared her fork into the last piece of cake. Any other time, I would have fought her for that last bite.

"So . . . why didn't you tell me all of this was going down with Mike?" I asked.

Her nose wrinkled. "I *tried*. I sent you a text, but you never got back to me."

My mouth fell open. I vaguely remember a cryptic text that

came from her while I was at Charlie's. I was going to text her back that night when I got home and forgot all about it.

"Oh, Meaghan. I'm sorry. I meant to—"

She waved her fork around, dismissing it, me. "It's fine. Noah was around."

Her words were intended to hurt me, and they did.

"Well, I'm glad Noah was there for you," I said, staring at the empty tray of cake we had devoured.

She leaned across the table. "You *know* things have gotten shitty with Matt, don't you?" she asked.

"Well, yeah," I answered, not letting on how little I know.

"So Noah told you . . . they agreed to see other people?" Meaghan asked. "Meaning, Matt's already found someone, you know?"

My involuntary gasp gave away that I clearly knew none of this.

She took the side of her fork and scraped a thin layer of crumbs off the tray. "Noah's not talking about it much, but he's devastated."

The silence was heavy; I could feel her judging me.

I exhaled loudly in defeat. "Guess I should put my stretchy pants on and go apologize to Noah over an entire chocolate cake too." We both snorted at that, and it seemed like we were ready to move on.

Meaghan waved her fork in the air like a conductor. "Okay, call Planned Parenthood. Make the appointment so you and your man can start doing the deed."

I laughed in relief, glad that the awkwardness between us was over. The doorbell rang and Meaghan got up with the bowl of candy for the first wave of kids. My palms started to sweat as I dialed.

"Tomorrow? At three thirty?" Wiping my free palm on my jeans, I repeated what the receptionist said as Meaghan came back into the kitchen.

Meaghan nodded. "Works for me," she said, as if we were making the appointment together. After neglecting our friendship these past few weeks, I needed to make things right between us, so I didn't fight her on coming with me.

Now that the appointment is just an hour away, my palms start to sweat again.

Charlie leans over to peck me good-bye.

"We'll have her pumped up on hormones in no time." Meaghan pats him on the back reassuringly as he leaves, looking over his shoulder one last time.

I glance around the hallway to see if anyone *didn't* hear that exchange.

"Meaghan!" I slam my locker shut. "Seriously! Keep it down."

Noah slides next to us, dipping his head between us. "I like secrets. What are we whispering about?"

"Nothing," I say, never releasing Meaghan from my glare. Noah tilts his head forward, scrutinizing me.

"*Something's* going on. Meaghan?" He turns to her.

Meaghan shrugs. "Come on, Had. It's *Noah!*" He bends down, and she reaches up on her tiptoes to cup a hand to his ear. "Hadley's going on the Pill!" she whispers loudly.

Noah blinks in shock. He turns back to me. "You *are* human!"

"On second thought, I'm doing this alone," I shoot over my shoulder, storming off. They run to catch up, flanking me on either side.

"I'm still coming," Meaghan decides. She turns to Noah, who keeps pace with us. "You're coming too?"

"Sure, why not? It'll be fun. Like a field trip. Buddy check!" Noah grabs my hand and lifts it up in the air. He releases it and wraps his scarf around his neck before he pushes through the doors. "Besides, they hand out free condoms like lollipops there."

As we walk to the parking lot, Noah assesses me in his analytical way. "You're not walking like my nana today. Drill Sergeant ease up on the training or something?"

I laugh nervously. "Yeah . . . for a little while at least." It's not a lie if there's a shred of truth in there.

Later that afternoon, I come home through the mudroom, lugging my backpack.

"Hadley?" Mom calls from the kitchen. She has the Chardonnay lilt in her voice.

"Yep." I kick off my shoes and hang up my jacket. Then I run past her and up the stairs.

"Where are you going?" she calls after me.

"Homework." I add, "Lots of it."

I need to catch up on what I've missed by sneaking out to be with Charlie. I have three quizzes tomorrow, and I haven't even started to study. But more important, I have my first month's prescription, and I need to find a good hiding spot for it.

Upstairs, music blasts from Lila's room. My hand is poised, ready to knock on her door when my phone rings. I pull it out and see Charlie's number. I pivot and run back to my room.

"Hey." I close the door behind me.

"How'd it go?"

"Okay, I guess."

He's quiet.

"What?" I ask.

"I feel guilty that I wasn't there with you."

"No, don't. Trust me. That was an experience I preferred not to have anyone witness."

He sighs. "Okay."

"How about you?"

"Good. I'll have the results soon. I should be fine. I've been really careful."

My stomach writhes with jealousy knowing he's been with other girls. Even though it's completely irrational, I hate these other girls for sharing something so intimate with him.

I walk over to my calendar on the bulletin board over my desk. Cornell's early decision deadline is today, circled in red. Almost everything circled or penned in is about deadlines, tests, lacrosse practice, or flight lessons. Week after week, for years, I've given everything of myself to the things that matter the least to me.

Circling a date in the middle of next week, I tell him, "They said I'll be safe in seven days."

There's more silence.

"Charlie?"

I hear him exhale. "I'm here," he says. "My imagination was running amok."

Instead of submitting my early decision application to Cornell, I take the plastic dome out of my backpack and pop the first pill out. With whatever dregs are left in my water bottle, I toss it back.

"There. First one down. Six more to go."

Charlie laughs suggestively. "Let the countdown begin."

Dad calls as we're setting the table for dinner.

"Tell your mother I have to work late," he says, and hangs up. I wait for the dial tone to mumble, "Tell her yourself."

"Was that your father?" Mom asks, putting forks by each place setting.

"Yeah. He's working late."

"Did he say late or . . ." She glances up, letting me finish the sentence.

"Just late," I answer, and walk away.

She knows. We all know. But Mom's got her head buried so far into her wineglass, she pretends to ignore it. Me, personally? I'm thrilled when my father "works late" or, more often lately, doesn't even make it home. I may even go to the "library" tonight.

After dinner, Lila and I help clear the table. Lila turns her head away and gags as she scrapes her barely touched dinner into the trash can and hands the plate over to me. I rinse and load it into the dishwasher. Lila scrapes the next plate clean, her shoulders heaving.

"I don't know why they call it spaghetti squash," she whines, leaning as far away as possible from the discarded dinner. "It doesn't taste anything like spaghetti."

"Agree," I say, taking the plate from her.

"They had *real* spaghetti at lunch yesterday," she confides to me quietly. Her eyes roll back in her head in ecstasy. Dad doesn't let us eat spaghetti; he says refined white flour will turn us all into "fat-asses."

Rinsing the plate, I laugh. "Sad state of affairs when you start fantasizing about cafeteria lunches." Then I jerk my head toward Mom, who's fluffing pillows in the den. "Don't let *them* know, though. She'll start packing you spaghetti squash lunches."

After the last plate is scraped clean, Lila grabs the neck of her shirt and pulls it up over her nose before bringing the bowl of leftover spaghetti squash to the counter.

"Is this a stickup?" I stare back at her.

"I'm gonna hurl," she says, and I believe her.

"Go," I tell her. "I'll finish."

Mom and Dad think Lila's refusal to eat certain foods is just her being defiant and that she'll learn to like them if she just tries harder. It's so obvious she's not faking; even Lila can't force her face to turn that sickly shade of gray.

She murmurs a "thank you" through her shirt and tears off upstairs. Within minutes, the ceiling rattles with Lila's music and dancing.

Mom comes back in the kitchen with the everyday wineglasses and sets them on the table. Because there really is such a thing in this house as "everyday wineglasses" and "formal wineglasses." We even have Christmas wineglasses, with boughs of holly etched around the rims.

"Who's coming?" I wipe my hands on a dishcloth and toss it on the counter. Mom walks over and folds it once, then again, before laying it carefully over the farmhouse sink.

"PTA executive committee meeting here tonight. We're going to talk about the Valentine's Day dance at the high school."

"Mom," I groan. "Trust me, no one is going to want to spend Valentine's Day at the high school." I know I won't.

"But it falls on a Saturday this year!" she whines.

"More reason *not* to spend it at school!"

She pours herself another glass of wine. "Well, I think you're wrong." She props herself up against the counter and shakes her tousled blond hair before taking a sip. "Besides, if you had a boyfriend, you'd feel differently."

I stare back at her in disbelief. "Is this your first day living here or something?" I snap. She takes a long swig and pretends she doesn't understand.

Last year, a month before the homecoming dance, Mom was well into her wine. Sitting at the dinner table, she chirped, "Marie told me that her son Jake is trying to work up the nerve to ask Hadley to the dance. Isn't that adorable?"

I had no interest in Marie's son Jake, but no one actually asked my opinion. And no one ever would.

Dad turned red. He grabbed Mom's wineglass out of her hand.

"I won't have my daughter fucking every jackass that looks her way!" he hollered, and hurled the glass across the room, shattering it against the kitchen cabinet.

She turns to me now and sneers, "You know what? You're mean. Just like your father."

I turn my back and go upstairs to call Charlie. I suddenly need to cram for a test at the library tonight.

Downstairs, the PTA moms are cackling. I have to walk past them to get my coat out of the mudroom.

"Hadley!" Mrs. Giovanni howls a greeting, stopping me in my tracks. Her eyes are already glassy. I look over at the counter; three empty wine bottles in under an hour, four more to go.

I raise my hand and wave to everyone. Mrs. Wiley, Claudia's mom, sends a frigid smile my way. Like mother, like daughter.

"Mom, I'm heading to the library." She's too far gone to care. She wiggles her pretty manicured fingers at me.

Mrs. Wiley's eyes lock on mine. "Are you going to meet Charlie there, Hadley?" she asks, and takes a sip. An arctic blast rushes through the room and enters my bloodstream.

"What?" I ask, careful to erase any look of shock or understanding from my eyes.

"Charlie Simmons. The boy you're seeing," she says with a laugh. It's tinny with sharp edges.

I force a laugh, playing along. "Charlie *Simmons*? We're not dating. We're just friends."

"Charlie?" Mom blinks, trying to force the conversation into focus.

"Really?" Mrs. Wiley says. "Claudia told me you two were dating."

"No." I shake my head again. "We're just good friends. We're in Spanish together."

Mrs. Wiley looks across the table at Mrs. Wheeler. With a flick of her eyebrows, she telegraphs a message: *she's lying*. Mrs. Wheeler looks over at my mother and back at Mrs. Wiley and shrugs.

"Charlie Simmons." Mrs. Giovanni searches the air in front of her to place the name. And then it dawns on her with a gasp. She leans over and clutches Mrs. Wiley's arm. "Jillian! Remember? Field day, when the kids were in third grade? Charlie's mother— what's her name? Nancy?—she showed up *drunk*!"

Mrs. Wiley nods. "Oh, I remember. She was also drunk at Claudia's seventh birthday party. It was *embarrassing*," she says as she refills her wineglass.

"That was around the time her husband left her, right?" Mrs. Giovanni tips her glass to Mrs. Wiley for a refill.

Mrs. Wiley sips. "Well . . . you could see why."

"Isn't she a *waitress* at the diner in town?" Mrs. Wheeler asks as if it's as shameful as being the town prostitute.

Mom looks up at me with that same wounded expression as when Dad calls to say he'll be working late.

"You're not interested in this boy, are you, Hadley?" Her face tells me she doesn't really want to know the truth.

"No, Mom. Of course not." Mrs. Wiley's eyebrows flick again. I'm not too concerned about whether Mom believes me or not. We both know she would never tell my father.

I turn to leave when Mrs. Giovanni calls me back.

"Hadley, what do you think for the Valentine's Day dance: famous couples in history or movie theme?"

I pause and pretend to give a crap. "Definitely movie theme," I decide before escaping through the mudroom door.

I don't know who I hate more: them or me.

now

Janet plays a game of rummy with me in my room while Linda the social worker talks to Grandma outside in the hallway. Their voices drift in and out while I try to keep track of the sevens and spades in my hand.

Grandma's voice warbles in the background. "But *why?*"

I'm glad for the meds today. I couldn't take the guilt of Grandma's tear-streaked face without them. Even as she hugged me and thanked God I was alive, I knew.

"It could be survivor's syndrome . . ."

I discard and pick up a new card from the pile.

"The trauma of leaving her family behind . . . not being able to save them before the fire broke out . . ."

Janet watches me over her cards, her eyebrows drawn in at such a sharp angle I've asked her "What's wrong?" three times today.

The room glows bright but cold, a reflection of the sun off the mountains of snow outside. We got eighteen inches from the storm, Janet told me, explaining why she was late this morning. I used to love playing in the snow with Lila. There's a hill outside my bedroom here that would be great for sledding. Lila would have loved it. But so far no one has made it behind the building. The grounds are pure and pristine, not a footstep in sight.

"We need to keep her a while longer, you understand. To make certain she won't try again."

"What I want to know is how you allowed this to happen in the first place? Where were all of you?"

I want to tell Grandma it wasn't anyone's fault. They were right to leave me to go help someone else. The ER was packed with people who wanted to live. Who deserved to live.

then

Cradling the ball, I rush the goal, panting through my mouth guard. The redhead on defense from the other team has it out for me. She holds her stick up and screams in my face, trying to psych me out so I drop the ball, but it's really no use. On the field, I'm fearless. Coach Kimmel says I'm *too* fearless. I really don't care what happens to me out here. An injury might be a nice break. I pass the ball to Faith seconds before Red rams her big shoulder into me.

The ref blows his whistle and calls foul, but not before Dad screams at him. Coach Kimmel blows her whistle in Dad's ear.

"If you want to be a ref, by all means, volunteer!" Coach Kimmel yells at him. "Otherwise, stop getting in my way!"

Dad grins and walks behind her to give her stiff shoulders a vigorous massage. "Relax, Coach! I'm on *your* team!" She cringes as if the Grim Reaper latched his claws on her.

I've learned to tune my father out. When I was younger, his

voice would unnerve me, make me second-guess my instincts. Which is one of the reasons why Coach Kimmel isn't a fan of Dad's. She doesn't agree with his scrimmage tactics, especially when they go against her warning to play clean and fair.

I take the penalty shot, passing the ball to Olivia, but she misses.

"Get your head out of your ass, Hadley!" Dad hollers through cupped hands, which translates into "blah-blah-blah" as I run back onto the field. Faith scoops up the ball and passes it to me. I cradle it, weaving toward the goal. But then I hear it, the *other* voice.

"Go, Hadley!" Followed by a loud *"Woooo!"*

His voice is unmistakable.

I turn to look over my shoulder. Charlie's standing not ten feet away from my father, clapping. My father shoots him an annoyed sidelong glance. Flustered and panicked, I turn back to the game and run right into Red's stick.

Moments later, I look up at a huddle of four concerned faces: Coach Kimmel. The ref. My dad. And Charlie.

Coach Kimmel pulls my mouth guard out and peels off my protective eyewear. I try to bounce up off the ground and escape.

"Don't try to get up." Coach presses her hand against my shoulder, pushing me back down.

The ref looks in my eyes with a flashlight.

"Pupils are dilating, but she's pale," he says. "How do you feel, Hadley?"

I look up at my father's annoyed face. "Fine." Dad grins in a rare "atta girl" nod of approval. The ref puts an icepack on my head. I hold it in place.

"She should sit the rest of the game out," he says.

"Like hell," my dad argues. "She just said she felt fine."

Coach Kimmel shoots him another dark look.

"Hadley, you should sit it out," Charlie chimes in. "I felt that blow down to my toes." He reaches over and puts his hand on my shoulder and squeezes. Dad stares at Charlie's hand as if he's honking my boob.

"Who the hell are you?" Dad asks, turning red.

Charlie's mouth drops open. He's about to answer, but I can't let him.

"A friend from school, Dad. We have Spanish together." A pounding fist of self-loathing knocks the wind out of me.

Charlie's mouth slams shut. He looks at me, hurt, then angry.

"Yeah. Just a friend." Charlie stands up and walks away from the huddle.

The ground is cold and damp under me. I want to get up and run after Charlie. But my father's eyes have me pinned to the ground.

The ref shakes his head. "I'm calling it. She's sitting out."

"This is *bullshit*!" My dad storms off the field.

Coach Kimmel glances down at me, the watery sun behind her forming a halo around her head, her weathered face sympathetic. She reaches out a hand and pulls me up off the ground.

When I look at the sidelines again, my father is glaring at me, arms folded. Charlie is gone.

Dad lets loose on the ride home. At least his anger wasn't directed entirely at me. It was my fault I got hit; that he made clear. Apparently, my head was in my ass again. But most of the ride was spent cursing out Coach, calling her horrible names that questioned both her intelligence and sexual orientation.

Then he turned to me. "And who was that guy?"

My ears hummed. "Who?"

"Don't act dumb. The guy who came over when you got hit?"

I cleared my throat so I didn't squeak. "Charlie? We're friends."

Dad stopped at a red light and stared at me, too long. "Well, watch out for him. He likes you."

I tried to laugh it off. "No h—"

"Hadley?" My name was a direct order. "Don't try and play me. Just stay away from him. Understood?"

I nodded and looked out the window so my father couldn't see the lie on my face.

Now home and showered, I call Charlie three times, but he doesn't pick up. It's Saturday. His day off. Finally, I get in the car and drive to his apartment, throwing my backpack in the backseat as always.

They don't have an intercom or any way to buzz visitors up. Charlie has to come downstairs to open the door when I ring the bell. His face folds in angry creases.

"Please let me explain," I beg.

"I get it, Hadley," he says annoyed. "I had a feeling something wasn't right."

A cold wind rushes down the sidewalk. I rub my hands over my arms, chilled, but more chilled to the bone by the angry look on his face.

"It's not what you think."

He scowls at me.

"Can I come up? Please?"

He opens the door to let me in. I walk up the stairs ahead of him, my back prickling with his anger. Upstairs, he shuts the door behind him. I sit on the couch, waiting for him to join me. But he doesn't. He stands, arms folded.

"Charlie, I haven't told my parents about you because . . ." I wince. "I'm not allowed to date."

He raises one eyebrow. "*What?* You're seventeen!"

"And counting the days till I'm eighteen."

He lets out a deep breath, looking more confused than angry now.

"Why didn't you just tell me that?"

I shrug and look away. "I don't know." I'm not ready to explain it to Charlie. Lies are easier to unspool. The truth is a tautly wound coil. "It's not the easiest thing to cop to."

"So . . . you've been sneaking out to see me?" I hear a pleased smile in his voice.

I point out the apartment window where the large redbrick building stands across the street. "I've been at the library a lot these days. Kind of funny, though. Since it's always in my view, I really don't feel like I'm lying."

He sits down next to me and wraps his arm around me. I lean

against him, so grateful he's not mad at me anymore. That's when I smell it.

"Charlie!"

"What?"

"You smoked!" I pull back and stare at him in disappointment. He bites the inside of his cheek.

"I know. Sorry. I was pissed off."

"But you were doing great!"

"It's not easy," he argues. "But I am trying. It was just today."

I frown, but I have to let it go. He pulls me back against his chest where I rest, smelling the smoke on his shirt and hating it.

"So your dad . . ." He hedges, and I can tell he's drawing his opinion from firsthand experience at the game today.

"Yeah . . . he, uh, gets overly enthusiastic at these games." I pluck at a piece of lint on his shirt.

He reaches his hand over and touches my head, gently grazing the knot.

"How's your head?"

"It's fine. I can take a hit." I try to laugh it off. I reach up to kiss him, but he pulls away.

"Hadley, is there something you're not telling me?"

I stall, alarmed by the knowing look in his eyes.

"No."

then

It's Wednesday. The date circled on my calendar in blue pen to remind me that, as of today, my body is no longer ovulating. I can have sex now. The calendar doesn't lie.

My date with Charlie tonight takes over my mind so much that I trip in a pothole during my morning run with my father.

"Hadley, what the hell?" He pulls me up roughly. "You could've broken your ankle and then what?" He starts complaining about the highway department. "I'm going to call those assholes down at town hall and tear them a new one. I pay enough taxes—"

I take off running, the slapping of my sneakers on asphalt tuning out his words.

My stomach is in knots all morning. I can't eat breakfast, so I just drive over to school. Charlie finds me at my locker.

Leaning over my shoulder, he whispers in my ear, "We still on for tonight?"

I turn around in his arms and force a smile I don't feel. "Mm-hmm."

He leans in for a quick kiss then takes my hand in his.

"Your hands are freezing." He rubs them between his larger, always warmer hands. "You okay?" He leans closer, resting his forehead on mine.

"For fuck's sake, get a room!" Claudia walks by, sneering at us. Charlie scowls back at her while a wave of blood rushes to my cheeks. It's as if the whole world knows about the date circled on my calendar.

Meaghan meets me at my locker later that morning before Spanish.

"V-Day," she says, making the peace sign with her fingers again.

"Stop it!" I hiss, slamming my locker.

She looks at my angry face and raises her hands up in the air in surrender. "Easy, woman. What's going on? Too many hormones wreaking havoc with your mood?"

I lean my head against my locker. "Meaghan, I'm scared to death."

"Ohhhh. Now I get it." She links her arm through mine. "I just thought you guys were counting down the minutes."

My shoulders slump. "We *are*. I don't know why this is freaking me out so much."

With our arms looped together, we walk slowly to class, our heads leaning toward each other.

"I bet once you guys are together, you won't be nervous. You're overthinking it, like you always do."

I want to believe her. "You're probably right."

"I *am* right."

I nod and draw a shallow breath into my tightly clenched lungs.

I drive around Charlie's block three times, trying to find the courage to park, to march up those stairs. But every time a parking spot opens up—and there have been plenty—I keep driving. My stomach hurts. Maybe I'm getting sick. Maybe I should go home so I don't get him sick too.

But as I drive around and around, the ache passes and I know it's just nerves.

The clock on the dashboard tells me I'm officially late. I pull into the spot in front of Sal's that just miraculously freed up, as if even the universe is fed up with my stalling. When I ring the bell, Charlie's footsteps race down the steps, faster than he's ever answered the door before. It makes me want to run away. He opens the door with a big smile. The tips of his hair are still damp; he took a shower for the occasion. The fresh lingering scent of soap reaches over and clamps its diaphanous fingers around my throat.

"I was about to call you," he says, kissing me hello. "I thought you got cold feet or something." He laughs at the absurdity. So I laugh too, a strangled bark. He takes my hand as we walk up the stairs together.

The apartment flickers in a soft glow of several lit candles. On the little table for two is a plastic two-liter Coke bottle, cut in half, with a half dozen red roses sitting in it.

I breathe through my nose so I don't throw up.

Charlie runs a hand through his hair, oblivious to my sweaty palms, my dry throat, my churning stomach. "You would think there'd be *one* vase in the place, but no." Then he adds, "I wanted to get champagne, but you don't drink."

I nod briskly, thinking how I would have made an exception tonight.

There are plenty of girls who would swoon over Charlie's efforts to set the mood. Probably the same girls who would love my Pepto-Bismol room with the ballroom chandelier. Me? All it does is ratchet up my anxiety, highlighting the pressure of having to follow through on the date circled on my calendar *in ink*.

He takes my coat and hangs it on a chair. Then he pulls me into his arms and lifts my face, kissing me, one hand cupping my head tenderly behind my ear. I raise my arms, looping them around his neck. My hands are heavy blocks of ice, visibly shaking. He pulls back and rests his hands on my shoulders.

"Are you sure you're okay?" He looks all the way through me.

An anxious tremble tears through my core.

"I'm just a little nervous," I admit through chattering teeth.

He wraps his arms around me, rubbing his hands vigorously up and down my arms to warm me, more utilitarian than romantic.

"Does it help to know I'm nervous too?"

"Why would *you* be nervous?" He's done this before; if I'm to believe the school rumor mill, a Hugh Hefner *ridiculous* amount of times.

He leans back and smiles. "Because it's you."

He pulls me over to the couch and sits down, tugging at my

arm to join him. Are we going to do it here? On the couch with the scratchy afghan? At least I'll be lying down; my knees can't hold me up for much longer. I just want to get it over with. It's going to be terrible the first time anyway.

To my surprise, he turns on the TV.

"It doesn't have to be tonight, you know," he says. "Whenever it happens, I want it to be because you want to. Not because you're doing it for me." He grabs the remote. "Want to watch a movie?" *Instead* is implied as he wraps an arm around my shoulders.

"Yes," I exhale in utter relief. Elasticity returns to my lungs; I can breathe again.

Charlie gets up for a moment. When he comes back, the smell of freshly blown-out candles follows him, soothing me.

He wraps his arm back around me. "It was the sawed-off soda bottle, wasn't it?" He kisses the top of my head.

"That was actually my favorite part," I say. The candles, the flowers, were over-the-top romantic. But what we have right here on this couch, in his arms, *this* is real.

Nestling next to him, I tilt my head up, allowing the words to rise to the surface.

"I love you, Charlie."

A look of shock crosses his face, and my body crackles with an electric surge of regret. I shouldn't have said it. I just freaked him out. Am I totally wrong about us? Command Z!

Just as I am about to lose it, he pulls me into a hug, burying his face in my hair. "I love you too. I'm sorry. I should have said that before tonight." He pulls back and looks around the room, at the flowers, the candles, rolling his eyes at the one thing missing from the night. "I really am an idiot." He kisses me, and everything is right again. More than right. About as damn perfect as my life can ever be.

We settle back and watch the movie. My phone vibrates in my back pocket all night. Texts from Meaghan.

Did you do it yet?

How about now?

Now?

What about now?

I know she's trying to be funny, but after the fourth text, I stop checking.

When the movie's over, I glance up at him.

"You're not mad, are you?" I ask with a twinge of guilt.

"Mad? Are you kidding? You were literally shaking like a leaf. There was just no way it was happening tonight."

Footsteps stumble up the stairs. Charlie's head jerks up, alert and listening keenly. Keys jangle as someone approaches closer to the door.

"Charlie, what's wrong?"

"Nothing," he whispers. He's up on his feet in a flash, pulling me off the couch with him. "Do you mind waiting in my room?

Just for a couple of minutes."

"Yeah. Sure."

He tows me through the kitchen by the hand to his bedroom. He doesn't quite push me in, but it's close. "It'll just be a minute. I'm sorry," he says, closing the door in my face.

His footsteps retreat through the kitchen to the living room as the front door opens. I press my ear to his bedroom door to listen.

"Hey, Ma," he greets her casually.

"What's this?" she asks, a teasing lilt to her voice. "Flowers?"

"Yeah."

A chair scratches across the floor.

"Was Hadley here?"

I squeeze my eyes shut with guilt. Unlike me, he's told his mother about us. But then why am I hiding from her?

"Yeah. We were watching TV. What happened?"

After a couple of thuds that sound like shoes kicking off, she grunts in relief.

"Slow night. Gus let me and Regina off early." I hear it then. The too-loud voice, the slurring.

Charlie's silent. I can barely make out what he says next.

"Where'd you guys go after work?"

There's another long pause.

"Charlie, don't judge me, okay? I've been doing good. It was just one night."

Now I know why I'm hiding.

I pull my phone out of my back pocket to check the time, and I see three missed calls, all from home.

My heart pounds in my chest as I listen to the messages. The first is from my mother.

"Hadley . . . we were just wondering what time you were coming home. Call me when you get this."

The second one is from my father.

"Where the hell are you? The library closed a half hour ago."

The third one came in a few minutes ago.

"Hadley. Answer your fucking phone."

Shit. Shit shit shit shit shit shit shit.

Charlie manages his mother in the other room, trying to convince her to go to bed and sleep it off. I have to call my parents, but I don't want Mrs. Simmons to hear me.

Outside Charlie's bedroom window is a fire escape. I ease the window up and sneak out. It's only one flight down. I could try to go down the rusted steps, but the ladder doesn't reach all the way to the ground, and I have no idea how to fix that, or what kind of hellacious racket that would make. So I settle on calling my parents from outside his bedroom window.

My father picks up on half a ring.

"Where . . . are . . . you?" Each word is loaded, intended to strike a blow.

"Hi, Dad, I'm sorry. I had the phone on vibrate in the library—"

"I asked you where you were. The library closed forty-five minutes ago."

I glance down at the dumpster behind Sal's.

"I was hungry and got some pizza. I ran into some girls from school—"

"Pizza?" he asks, annoyed in a different way. Getting busted for eating a "fat-ass" food is better than the truth right now.

"Yeah . . . sorry."

"Get your ass home. Now."

"Okay," I stammer through chattering teeth, from nerves and the chill.

I hang up. Charlie peers out his open window at me with a perplexed look on his face.

"Everything okay?" he asks, looking around the fire escape for clues.

"I have to go home now."

He reaches his arm out and helps me back in. "I'll walk you to your car."

I follow behind him quietly, past his mother's closed bedroom door.

Outside on the street, we stop at my car. I lean against the door and grab his belt loops to reel him closer. He focuses on my hair, pushing it back over my shoulders, my jacket, straightening the collar. Finally he looks me in the eyes.

"Are you in trouble?"

"A little."

I don't tell him how my entire body coils into a tight knot every time I walk through my front door, whether I'm in trouble or not. How every fiber of my body goes limp with relief as I put distance between my home and myself, especially when I'm headed to see him. How I will lie, cheat, and steal to protect our few hours together. Whatever trouble I get into because of him is worth it, because being with Charlie is the only thing that helps me forget what waits for me at home.

"Is everything okay?" I glance up toward his apartment.

His face hardens. "I won't make excuses for her."

"Charlie." I reach up to touch his cheek. "I didn't ask you to."

He glances away, twisting his lips to the side.

"It is what it is. She goes long stretches. Every so often, she has a night like this."

I choose my next words carefully. "I just wanted to make sure *you* were okay."

He leans down and pecks me on the lips. It's quick and meant to send me on my way.

"I'm fine. You better get going before you get in more trouble."

He stands on the sidewalk watching as I drive off.

now

They move me to the children's psych wing. It's like going from solitary confinement to the penitentiary yard.

There are two beds in my new room. Mine is neatly made, blankets tucked tightly under the mattress. The other is a disheveled, knotted rope of blankets that looks like an epic battle was waged and lost between the occupant and the bedding.

"I have to share a room?" I spin around to face Janet.

"'Fraid so," Janet says, taking in my alarmed expression. "Patients are carefully screened before they're admitted. If they act out or try to hurt another patient, they are sent to another facility."

Janet takes me by the shoulder and guides me down the hall to the rec room. I glance in, and Janet nudges me from behind through the door like my mother urging me to go make new friends in preschool.

"Everyone, this is Hadley," she announces. Heads spin to face me. An orderly sits on the radiator, arms folded, watching the TV mounted high up on the wall. When I turn around, Janet is gone.

Half a dozen kids lounge across the two couches, one bright blue, one forest green, watching TV. The girls keep to themselves on the blue couch, legs folded up under them like origami swans, the boys take over the green one with their guy spread. Searching for courage, I finger the empty space at my clavicle, where my claddagh pendant used to rest. They took it from me when I got here; I'm not allowed to have jewelry, zippers, or shoelaces.

I try not to take *too* much in all at once, but two of the girls I can't ignore. The blonde, who's missing at least 40 percent of her short hair in a bizarrely abstract pattern. Her scalp doesn't have the clean lines of being shaved; instead, it looks like it fell out, leaving just a few strands behind, beginning around the top of her head and around her right ear. Chemo, maybe, though this wouldn't be the right wing for her. The other girl has curly auburn hair and clutches her sleeves in tightly clenched fists.

I find a seat away from everyone at a round game table and pull out my deck of cards. It was one of the few personal belongings Grandma brought that I was allowed to keep. I start a game of solitaire. It gives me something to do, so I can ignore all the "new girl" looks from around the room.

Curly gets up and sits across from me.

"I'm bored." She folds her arms in front of her on the table, still clutching her sleeves in her fists. I suspect we both have matching gauze bracelets.

"Join the club." The new pills are the Goldilocks of meds, keeping my mood at a steady plateau, not too high, not too low.

"Are you open to playing something else?" She stares at my cards like they're a box of chocolates.

"Rummy?"

She nods and waves Wacky Hair over to join us.

"I'm Rowan," Curly says. "And this is Melissa." Melissa slides into a seat and blinks back a greeting, her face slack, emotionless. I stare, fascinated by her hard blinks, as if she has new contacts and they're bone dry. She barely has any eyelashes or eyebrows, just a spattering of blond fuzz that makes her look like a baby bird.

She notices me staring. "Trichotillomania," she says, her voice as flat as her expression.

"You kiss your mother with that mouth?" Rowan grins and winks at me, showing off two cavernous dimples in her round cheeks.

Shuffling the deck with one good hand takes a little longer. Dealing ten cards each, I say, "I'm Hadley."

Rowan looks at my cast in the sling. "Does it hurt?"

"Not really." I focus on my cards, trying not to stare at Melissa's hair, at Rowan's hidden wrists. I don't want to know their stories. I don't want to dig in any deeper here than I already am.

Rowan shuffles the cards around in her hands. Her sleeves fall back, revealing big-boned wrists clear of gauze or sewn-up slashes. Instead, her forearms are a brutal crosshatch of ropy white scars and newer scabs. She catches me staring and looks at my bandaged wrists.

"Amateur mistake," she says, organizing the cards in her hands.

"What's that supposed to mean?" I shoot back.

She gestures with her chin to my wrists. "Everyone knows you bleed out faster with vertical cuts. Horizontal cuts are for drama queens."

My blood boils.

"You think I did it because I *want* to be here?"

She smirks, one dimple pressing into her cheek. "Nobody wants to be *here*," she says, looking at her cards. "I'm just telling you how you fucked up."

then

On the way to the cafeteria the next day, I see Mr. Murray standing by the front office talking to Mr. Johnson. They both look up as I approach.

"Hadley!" Mr. Murray raises his arm to get my attention. He waves me over as Mr. Johnson eyes me, nods to Mr. Murray, and walks back into the office.

Mr. Murray smiles gently as I walk over. I always liked him; he has kind eyes. Eyes really are windows to the soul. If you're a bad person, you just can't hide it. It's right there for the world to see. You just have to know what you're looking for.

"I wanted to talk to you." He wraps his arm loosely around my shoulders, in that barely touching way all the male teachers have so they aren't accused of doing anything improper, as he leads me to his office.

"Um. I was on my way to lunch." I thumb over my shoulder. He closes the glass door behind us.

"Have a seat." He gestures to one of the chairs. "It will only take a couple of minutes, I promise."

Mr. Murray has gray hair, cropped close to his scalp, but a young face. Behind his desk are crudely drawn crayon pictures of "Daddy" pinned to his bulletin board. He's either an older father who got a late start having a family or the students of Melville High School have prematurely aged him.

I sit in the orange felt chair that has seen many asses over the years. Instead of sitting across from me at his desk, he chooses the matching orange chair next to mine, reserved for those parent/student meetings. It's meant to put me at ease, make me more comfortable. Loosen me up to talk.

Mr. Murray plants his elbows on his knees and leans forward. "So, you're a senior now. Big decisions coming up. How's your year going?"

"Good so far," I say, flexing my facial muscles into a smile.

"Good! Classes aren't giving you any trouble?"

"Nope." I shake my head.

"Good, good." He nods, pleased. "Still playing lacrosse I hear. Travel team, right?"

His eyes hold me with their kind, attentive gaze.

"Yep."

"So." He pivots and shuffles some papers around on his desk. "I spoke with Ms. Morales. Your SAT scores are *awesome*. No surprise there." He pivots back to me. "What schools are you looking at?"

Something's fishy. This is a conversation I should have with

Ms. Morales, my guidance counselor, not the dean.

I swallow hard. "Cornell."

"Cornell is wonderful." Mr. Murray nods in agreement. "Is that your dream school?"

"Uh-huh." I erase any evidence of my father's coercion from my face.

"Great. What about it makes it number one?" He holds his pointer finger up.

"Uh. They have a good lacrosse team," I bat off the first point.

"Lacrosse?" he repeats, laughing. "Well, okay. What else?" He holds his smile, letting the sentence hang, probably to encourage me to fill the dead air.

I shrug, feeling a flush race up my neck.

"Did you get your application in by the first?" he asks, watching my reaction.

I stare at my knees. "No. I kind of really screwed that one up." I scrape a piece of lint off my leg. "I did apply, though," I add, feeling the heavy weight of Dad's hand on my shoulder as he stood behind me until he saw me click the submit button. His fury at me for missing the deadline lingers in the house like a bad odor.

"Okay . . . not a *total* disaster!" He laughs, I think to lighten the mood. "So . . . what other schools are you applying to?"

"My father thinks I'll get into Cornell, but we applied to Harvard, Yale, and Brown as backups."

"*We,*" he repeats, his cheerful facade slipping. "Hadley . . ." He knots his fingers together in his lap and looks down for a moment. "You're a bright—*extremely* bright—well-rounded student. I don't want you to have unrealistic expectations, though. Those are all Ivy League schools you listed. They're very competitive. Do you and your father understand that?"

I nod, even though, no, my father *doesn't* understand that. Or at least he refuses to accept it.

"I'm also looking into Hofstra and Stony Brook," I add, even though my father doesn't know.

His smile is encouraging. "Local schools?"

I nod. Yes, local schools. Because even though Cornell and the other Ivy League schools are where my father wants me to go, I can't leave Lila alone to fend for herself.

"Those are also excellent schools. Still competitive, but not *as.*" He pauses. "Remember to keep the schools in balance. The ones that are a stretch . . . the Ivy Leagues you mentioned . . . and a few safe schools, just in case." He continues to stare, the gears spinning behind his pale eyes. "So by 'looking into,' you mean you haven't applied to those two yet?"

"No," I admit.

"Get on that. October through January is our sweet spot, right? Don't put it off much longer."

I clamp my damp palms onto my knees. The room is getting stuffy. My back prickles with nerves. This conversation is sending my sweat glands into overdrive.

Mr. Murray lets out a loud exhale. "Okay. Well, Hadley, I have no doubt you'll get into an excellent school. But . . ." He grimaces, jutting his elbows out to his sides. "Is it fair to say you may be under a lot of pressure at home to get into an Ivy League school?"

He looks at me with that soft "we're just two friends shooting the breeze" thing teachers must learn while getting their master's in education.

His eyes are just so kind. I feel obliged to give him something more.

"Maybe." I smile.

He opens his mouth to add something, but I look at the clock on his wall pointedly. "I'm sorry. I didn't eat breakfast this morning, and I'm starving."

Mr. Murray stands up. "Of course." He scribbles a quick pass.

Handing it to me, he says, "I've been meaning to tell you how sorry I am that you weren't able to be a Peer Helper. I was hoping I could talk your father into it. But he—"

"I know." I let him off the hook. No one should ever feel compelled to finish a sentence about my father. With the pass in hand, I turn to leave.

"One more thing, Hadley," he calls me back. "Even if you're not *in* the Helper program, you can still reach out to any one of them to talk. Or me. Anytime. You know that, right?"

I nod and smile. "Thanks, Mr. Murray. I will . . . if I need to, I mean."

I make my way to the cafeteria, my frayed nerves sparking like live wires. Is Mr. Murray worried about how much pressure I'm under or something else?

Noah and Meaghan are already at our regular table by the window. "There she is." Noah waves me over.

Meaghan pulls out a chair for me between them.

"You do *not* ditch us *today* of all days!" she says, miffed.

"Why? What's today?" I look at them blankly. They both stare at each other in disbelief and shake their heads.

Noah glances up at the heavens and then gestures to me. "This is what you give us to work with?"

Meaghan leans far into my personal space. "How did last night go?"

"Ohhh . . . right!" I reach for her iced tea and take a big sip. My mouth is parched after that awkward conversation with Mr. Murray. I haven't had a chance to fill them in yet about last night, what with Mr. Roussos not letting Noah and me even sit together in World Lit and Charlie sitting in between Meaghan and me in Spanish. "It didn't." I wipe my lips with the back of my hand.

They look at me, confused.

"What . . . ?" Meaghan shakes her head.

"I chickened out." I shrug.

"Oh, sweetie." Noah puts a hand on my shoulder. "Was he too much man for you to handle?" He nods knowingly with a teasing glint in his eyes.

"Ew." I push his hand off my shoulder. "Stop reading those erotic stories online. They're messing with your head."

"So?" Meaghan asks again. "What happened?"

"I don't know." I gaze out at the sea of people eating lunch. How many of them have done it? Are *doing* it? I know I'm in the minority when it comes to dating. But maybe there's something wrong with me and I'll never find the courage to go through with it.

Meaghan chimes in. "Can I offer my two cents?" She twirls her iced-tea cap on the table.

"Even if we said no, would that stop you?" Noah asks, and she reaches across me to shove him.

"Maybe putting it on your to-do list just sucked the fun out of it," she offers with the lift of her shoulder.

I nod. "You're right," I say, hoping she is.

Meaghan claps her hands once to change the subject. "Okay, I didn't want to steamroll you, but I have news. I got into Potsdam!"

I reach over to squeeze her hand. "That's great! Congratulations!" I point to Meaghan, then Noah. "She's going all the way north, and you can't get any farther south than Miami!"

His eyes dart over to Meaghan's as he pulls a deck of cards out of his pocket. "She's nuts. It snows there from October through May. I *better* get into Miami." He puts the deck down and crosses his fingers on both hands. "As God as my witness, this is the last New York winter I'll ever suffer through again."

Meaghan giggles. "That's exactly what my grandfather said right before he retired in Boca."

It goes quiet. Too quiet, the kind of silence that's filled with unspoken words. Finally, Meaghan clears her throat and looks over at Noah. She raises her eyebrows and nods toward me, ever so slightly.

Noah shuffles and deals. "Well, anyway, that just leaves you."

I pick up my cards without looking up at him. "Yep."

Meaghan picks her cards up off the table. "I have a theory. Want to hear it?"

"Not really," I say.

Undeterred, she plows ahead. "I think you forgot the deadline on purpose to sabotage your chances of getting in." She takes my silence as an admission. "I knew it! *Hadley!* You don't *have* to go to Cornell just because your father wants you to."

A different kind of flame scorches through my body.

"Why the fuck is everyone suddenly so obsessed with what college I go to?"

A few heads turn from other tables.

Meaghan and Noah stare at me with openmouthed, gobsmacked expressions.

"Sorry," I backpedal from my outburst. "Mr. Murray was just grilling me about it too."

Meaghan still looks startled, but she nods, letting it go.

A few more awkward seconds of silence pass. Noah exhales and shrugs, looking at his cards.

"Not for nothing, but sex really is an amazing tension reliever." He glances up, his eyes holding on to mine, and laughs softly under his breath.

I smile in relief. Noah's talent for turning something ugly into something funny is what I love most about him.

BRADY: *Today's date is January 10. Time 2:17 p.m. Please state your name and that I have permission to record your statement.*

MM: *Meaghan Maki. And yes, you have my permission . . . again.*

BRADY: *Meaghan, tell me about Charlie and Hadley. Were they close?*

MM: *Yeah. Ridiculously close.*

BRADY: *You don't sound pleased. Did you think they were too serious?*

MM: *No . . . I mean, I don't know. Maybe?*

BRADY: *There are no wrong answers.*

MM: *[exhales] I don't know. I mean, I think they fell crazy in love with each other right away. Like really fast. Scary fast.*

Look, I love Hadley. I wanted her to be happy. Maybe it was how intense they got. That's what worried me.

BRADY: *Worried you? How?*

MM: *Maybe not worried. I don't know anymore. Everything just happened so fast after they started dating. Everything.*

then

The travel lacrosse team practices at Duck Pond Park, a town park with two large playing fields and stadium lights for our night practices. Tonight, there's a weird atmosphere on the team. Every time I turn around, girls are laughing, whispering. At one point Faith holds her fist by her mouth, snorting. When she sees me she pulls her hand away and runs off.

At the end of practice, I go to use the bathroom. Inside, by the sinks, on the cinder block wall in black Sharpie is a crude drawing of someone giving a blow job, with my name written above it. Mystery solved.

That little flame that flared up during lunch bursts into a five-alarm blaze. I tear out of the bathroom, my feet barely touching the ground.

"Who did that?" I point to the bathroom door while everyone packs up their bags for the night. Claudia and her gang giggle. It stokes the anger building inside of me.

Coach Kimmel walks over. "Did what?"

"In the bathroom. Someone wrote my name and—"

Coach Kimmel holds her hand up to silence me. My heart hammers in my ears, throbbing behind my eyes while I wait. She walks to the bathroom and comes back shaking her head.

"I'm disappointed in you girls," she says.

"WHO DID IT?" I holler. Olivia looks at me and then her eyes chart a course over to Claudia. Something inside me detonates.

"You *bitch*!" I scream, and launch myself at Claudia. Fueled by adrenaline, I barely touch the ground before I land on top of her. I get two blows in before Coach Kimmel drags me off her by the back of my shirt with such force that I stumble and fall on my butt.

"HADLEY!" She screams my name in my face. It startles me out of my rage.

Pulling myself up, I look over at Claudia being yanked up off the ground by two of her friends. She takes her hand away from her mouth and there's blood on it. The sight sobers me.

The shaking starts in my legs and travels up my body, until my teeth start to chatter. I sit on the bench before my legs give out.

Coach Kimmel breaks out the ice pack and puts it to Claudia's face. She speaks quietly to her. Claudia glances over at me with hateful eyes. I've taken our feud to the next level.

Coach Kimmel sends everyone home. She saves me for last. Sitting down next to me, she exhales loudly, putting her hands on her knees.

"Hadley," she begins, her lips a thin white line as she shakes her head.

"I don't know what happened," I say, on the verge of crying. "I just lost it."

She stares at me, probing, trying to reach beneath the surface, just like Mr. Murray. Her lips tug down with the weight of her displeasure. "I can't say I didn't see something like this coming. You're under too much pressure. Anyone with eyes sees it. The question is, what are you going to do about it? Because *that*"—she points to where the fight broke out—"is unacceptable."

I nod, and a tear slips out. Then another.

"What's going on, Hadley?" she asks point-blank.

I can't meet her eye.

"You can tell me," she says with a reassuring squeeze of my knee.

I shake my head. "Nothing. I just . . . Claudia and I have bad history together."

Coach waits a moment, maybe for the truth.

"Well." She puts her hands by her sides on the bench, lowering her head. "There's going to be some fallout. I have to bench you tomorrow."

My head snaps over to her. "I can't miss the game." Tomorrow is the Peer Helper retreat, the one I wasn't allowed to go to because Dad insisted I had to play.

"Should have thought of that before you let your anger get the best of you. I'll call the Wileys and try to smooth over at least some of it. If I bench you, maybe they won't press any kind of charges."

"Charges?" I cry.

"Trust me. Benching you for one game will be the lesser of the evils."

"Yeah, but there are only two games left," I groan.

"C'est la vie." She shrugs, then stares off into the field, lit up like daylight by powerful stadium lights. "I should give your father a call too," she adds softly.

"No! Don't do that!"

She raises a silencing hand. "He's going to want to know why I'm not playing you tomorrow. I want to try to defuse this a bit, for your sake. He's already a hothead at these games." She exhales. Her shoulders slump. And then she looks at me again, purposefully, allowing me another opportunity to open up to her.

"You know you can talk to me about anything. Right?"

I pretend to not understand. "Sure. Yeah."

I get up, leaving Coach Kimmel to clean up the mess I made.

Later that night in the shower, I let the steam and scalding water soothe me. Even with Coach Kimmel calling, my father exploded and then grounded me. Which means the house would have to be engulfed in flames this weekend for me to leave. I can't see Charlie until school on Monday.

After draining every ounce of hot water from the tank, I step out of the shower and dry myself off, quickly slipping on sweats, warm socks, and a sweatshirt before the chills kick in again. When I get to my bedroom, I find a Tillys catalog on my bed, open to an outfit circled in grape-scented marker. A yellow sticky note is stuck to the page, written in the same purple marker:

For Xmas, I'd LOVE this outfit!
Hint, hint!
xoxo
your favorite sister

Lila. My sister. My shackle.

I was ten when my father started my lacrosse training sessions, the same age as Lila is now. When I couldn't do one hundred crunches, my father called me a baby. When I told him it was too cold to run, he told me to suck it up. Looking back, he was taking it easy on me then. It got worse as I got older.

Three years ago, when I was fourteen, I decided to flex my backbone. Meaghan put it in my head. "I mean, seriously, it's not like he can force you to run with him if you don't want to."

I was too scared to defy him openly, so I faked really bad period cramps to get out of our morning run. He was in a foul mood all that morning.

Making myself invisible had become a survival skill. I had learned to read the signs and move silently around him. But Lila hadn't learned how to decipher his wild Dr. Jekyll and Mr. Hyde moods yet, how to stay out of his crosshairs. Maybe I had protected her too much. That morning, Lila clamored downstairs for breakfast, *too* happy. Too cheery. Too much like a seven-year-old.

"What are you so happy about?" Dad snapped at her as soon as she came galloping into the kitchen.

She sat down at the table and poured herself a bowl of cereal, still singing under her breath some song she woke up to in her head. She was wearing a Hello Kitty nightgown and matching furry slippers. Her blond, wispy hair swirled dreamily around her head. She picked up the gallon of milk.

I should have seen it coming. I should have helped.

The weight of the gallon was too heavy. She lost control while pouring and dropped it on the table. Milk spilled across the table in every direction and onto the floor.

It was literally spilled milk that did it. He was across the room hauling her out of her seat by her arm in the time it took me to gasp.

"Jesus Christ!" He rattled her, her feet dangling like dead weights in the air. She howled. "You're going to clean up every last drop, if you have to *lick* it up!" He shook her again by her arm.

Her face twisted with something greater than fear.

"Leave her alone!" I ran over and scooped her away from him. Her eyes were wild. Her mouth was open in a silent scream that turned into a piercing wail. She held her shoulder.

"She's fine," Dad said, but there was a worried flash in his eyes.

She wasn't fine. She didn't stop crying. And finally, she gasped, "MY ARM!"

Mom was out shopping, so Dad and I took her to the emergency room. When they asked what happened, my father played the role of concerned parent. "We were having fun. Hadley and I were swinging her. I guess Hadley pulled too hard."

We took her home in a sling, none of us speaking. The next day, an expensive Victorian dollhouse from the toy store arrived, shipped overnight. Mom always gets flowers, or jewelry, or spa days after one of their fights. Lila got an expensive toy. Me, I never get anything. I don't know why he never feels the same kind of remorse for riding me the hardest. Why he hates me more than everyone else combined.

But I promised myself that day I would do anything to make sure he never hurt her again.

I text Charlie.

All bets off tonight. I'm grounded.

I wait for his text. Instead he calls. I'm already standing at the precipice of completely losing it; hearing his voice would push me over the edge. I send it to voicemail and then turn the phone off.

I sneak into my parents' master bathroom, where my mother keeps her sleeping pills in the medicine cabinet, for when she needs more help than Chardonnay to silence the world. Popping the cap off with my thumb, I spill one out into the cup of my palm, chugging it down with faucet water. Before I put the bottle away, I stare inside. It's a full bottle. It would be so easy to make this all go away right now. Quickly, I cap it and put it back in her cabinet. I've hated myself plenty over my lifetime, but this is the first time I've ever *terrified* myself.

I pad silently back to my room, curl up in bed, and let the drowsiness wash it all away.

The next morning, my father drags me out of bed to go watch the lacrosse game. My head is still fuzzy, but the pill did the trick. It tuned out the noise in my head, the whirling thoughts.

I stand on the sidelines watching my team score without me, far enough away from my father's foul mood and the Wileys' dark looks. My father thankfully stays away from them also.

There was a gleam in his eyes when I told him I hit Claudia, a simmering approval of a side of me he related to. What he flipped out about was that I got myself benched. Hitting Claudia brought out something in me that scares me. It brought out the part of me that my father created.

Coach Kimmel walks over during halftime to check in.

"Everything okay?" She lifts her black wraparound sunglasses to get a better look. I nod.

"He didn't give you a hard time?" she asks, jutting her chin in my father's direction.

Digging the toe of my sneakers into the ground, I answer, "Depends what you mean by a hard time."

Her eyes bore through me, measuring, thinking, contemplating. Before she can get any ideas in her head I reach over and grab her arm. "I was wrong to hit Claudia. I know that. I deserve this." I gesture to the field.

She shakes her head and opens her mouth to say more.

"Coach Kimmel!" Olivia hollers, jumping up and down and waving her arms. "They want you!"

She looks over her shoulder and nods then turns back to me.

"Hadley, you have my number. You call me anytime, day or night. You hear me?" She jabs a strong finger into my shoulder to drive her point home.

When she's out of earshot I hear him.

"Hadley!"

I pivot to my left. Charlie's standing by the public bathrooms, waving me over. I glance over to my right; my father's busy chewing Faith's mom's ear off, a huge grin on his face. Faith's mom is as wide-eyed as she is wide-hipped, basking in his attention, *giggling*. My father has that effect on people, especially women. His piercing eyes have a way of making strangers feel nothing else matters but their shared moment. Too bad for Faith's mom, their "shared moment" is complete and utter bullshit. Back home, Dad's going to tell Mom how this woman's "mom jeans" were screaming for mercy.

I run to Charlie, and we hide behind the public bathrooms.

"You can't stay!" I glance around the corner, keeping an eye on my dad.

"I was worried. Why didn't you call me back?" He holds me by my arms.

"I had a bad night." He pushes me back gently by my shoulders to search my face.

"What happened?"

I take him by the hand to the girls' bathroom, both of us looking around the corner to see my father still talking to Faith's mom. Making sure no one is in the stalls, I show him Claudia's handiwork.

"*This* happened." I point to the wall.

He stares at the wall in horror. "What the *fuck*?" His voice bounces off the cinder block walls.

"Claudia did it." He turns to me, his eyes growing cold and

furious. "Ironic, considering I remember her telling you this was *her* area of expertise."

"You're sure?"

I shrug and tilt my head to the side, folding my arms. "Sure enough. If she didn't, then I feel even worse about punching her." I sigh, looking away.

"You . . . *punched* her?" he repeats.

I nod. "Twice. Not my proudest moment. Coach Kimmel benched me today. And I'm still not certain the Wileys won't press charges."

We exit the bathroom, checking on my dad again, who is still gabbing away, not like Faith's mom looks bored or anything. Then we hide on the other side of the building, away from everyone's view.

"You weren't kidding about having a bad night." His fingers weave through my hair. I stare down at my sneakers.

"And then my dad grounded me."

"Until *when*?" If I get grounded, *we* get grounded.

"Until he forgets." I shrug. With so little freedom to begin with, it's hard to really take away more. I still need to go to school and lacrosse practice. Dad's long hours at work make it impossible for him to keep tabs on me, and my mother never enforces anything after she's into her wine.

I lean up against him. I can pretend for a little while with Charlie. He radiates heat and energy and life; I absorb it through my skin, hoping maybe it will jump-start something dying inside of me.

His hand skirts down my side, and I flinch away from it. The pain in my hip is back.

On the other side of the squat cement building, one of the teams scores. Cheers drift over to us. Two seagulls swoop over the trash can by the parking lot and squawk at each other. A girl squeals nearby, and a boy laughs.

Life goes on, with or without me.

BRADY: *The date is January 12. The time 5:28 p.m. Please state your name and occupation.*

DK: *Dolores Kimmel. Lacrosse coach for the Freedoms.*

BRADY: *Do I have your permission to record your statement?*

DK: *Absolutely. You wanted to talk about Hadley?*

BRADY: *Actually, I'd like to focus on her father.*

DK: *[groan] Good idea.*

BRADY: *What can you tell me?*

DK: *Where do I even begin?*

BRADY: *Well, what was your impression of him?*

DK: *Not good. Not good at all.*

I've been coaching girls' lacrosse for over twenty years. I've dealt with my share of overbearing parents. But this guy . . . this guy was a real prize. He thought he was so damn charming. We had words at almost every game. Contradicting me in front of my players, yelling at the ref, yelling at the other coaches, even the other team's players. But what really stuck in my craw was the way he yelled at his own daughter. She was just never good enough.

Look, I know the signs of abuse. I lived it myself. I just about came right out and asked Hadley if he was messing with her at home. Emotional abuse, for sure. That was plain as day. But . . . I had a feeling he might have been physically abusive too.

BRADY: *Why didn't you ever report him?*

DK: *I had no evidence! How do you report someone on a hunch? My gut said so. But Hadley was tight lipped. And I never saw any physical evidence. No bruising, cuts. You know how many times I told my teachers I fell down the stairs when I was a kid?*

I regret it, to be honest. Every time I was ready to make a call, I'd look at her and she seemed so pulled together.

BRADY: *Did Hadley ever tell you anything?*

DK: *No, never. And I tried to get it out of her.*

Here's the rub. She's turning eighteen in a couple of months. I asked her about college. She said her father wanted her to go to Cornell because he went there. I was just glad she had a plan to put distance between him and her. But I asked her, "Where do you want to go?"

This surprised the hell out of me. She said she wanted to stay home and commute to a local college. I figured she'd bolt out of that house like a bat out of hell the first chance she got, you know? What kind of a mind fuck did that guy pull on that girl? 'Scuse my French.

now

Rowan and Melissa follow me back to my room. I didn't invite them, but it doesn't look like I can shake them either.

Rowan leaps on my roommate's bed. As her head sinks down into the pillow, it clicks.

"*You're* my roommate?"

"Lucky you!" Rowan says, crossing her feet at her ankles. Melissa makes herself at home on my bed. Her fingers absently roam along her forearm until she finds what she's looking for and plucks at a lone hair. Rowan yells, "Stop!"

Rowan looks at me, her pursed lips coaxing one deep dimple from below the surface. "Do you know she plucked every single one of her pubes?"

I flinch first at the word, then at the visual.

Melissa blinks back, her face a placid lake. "People pay good money for a clean cooch."

That makes Rowan laugh. Melissa follows with a slower

chuckle. My chest tightens, reminding me there is nothing to be happy about. I clear my throat and shuffle the cards in my hand.

I sit down on the other end of my bed, away from Melissa. "One more round?" I'm not entirely comfortable around these two; cards are a neutral activity to keep us occupied.

Rowan pulls her legs up under her as I deal onto her bed. Watery sunlight streams in through the window, bringing out all of the dark red in her curls. She is thick and hearty, with creamy skin and healthy flushed cheeks. Melissa is the opposite: pale and fragile looking, her skin almost translucent, like she's made of glass.

"Sooo." Rowan peeks up from her cards. "You know you're kind of a celebrity, right?"

I glance up at her, frowning. "Huh?"

She shoots Melissa a glance, like Noah and Meaghan used to. Melissa isn't cut out for covert cues; her eyes are glued to her cards, the thin skin of her forehead puckered in confusion. Rowan sighs in exasperation.

"Have you watched TV at all since you got here?" Rowan asks.

"No." Something unpleasant stirs back to life, the tingling after the Novocain wears off.

"You've been on the news every day. They're calling you Miracle Girl." After she puts down three twos on my mattress, she picks up a card and kicks Melissa to let her know it's her turn.

"WHAT?" I jump up off my bed.

Rowan's face lights up, both dimples at attention. "Good to see you coming back to life. I'm so sick of all the zombies around here." This time she makes an exaggerated wide-eyed head tilt toward Melissa.

Melissa takes a long time poring over her cards, so Rowan continues. "We know everything about you. Did you know you were going to be the saledictorian?"

"Salutatorian?" I correct her, sitting back down. "No. They don't make that decision until March anyway." Talking about life before the crash stirs those last ghastly images back to the surface. I change the subject. "Why are *you* here?"

Melissa finally puts down two sixes. Rowan stares at her in disbelief then shakes her head. "Melissa . . . you can't put down unless you have three of a kind of something."

Melissa blinks. "Oh." She then takes back her cards and starts all over.

Rowan looks at me and shrugs, her face an open book. "I'm what they call a cutter." She lifts both arms up.

"Why?" I ask, shaking my head.

"Shit, you think I know?" She bristles. "It helps me let go of stuff."

"They put you in here for *that*?"

Rowan twists her lips sarcastically. "There's other stuff." She cups a hand to her mouth and whispers loudly. "Spoiler alert: we're *all* in psychiatric crisis."

Her eyes dart down to my wrists again. "Some guy came here yesterday trying to see you." *Charlie?*

But judging from the look on her face, I get the feeling it's someone I'd rather not see.

"I think he's a cop."

then

On Monday, I drive over to Charlie's apartment at 6:50 a.m. Since I still have to get myself to school—it's not like Mom's going to start driving me this early in the morning even if I'm grounded—we decided we could drive together to buy us about a half hour of alone time before school starts.

As soon as the car door slams, we're in each other's arms, trying to climb over the armrest, to mentally push the dashboard back a few more inches so we don't crush each other.

"Let's go park somewhere," I say.

He pulls away with a groan. "And when they call your parents to say you ditched first period?"

I fall back in my seat and throw my head against the headrest.

"You ditch all the time, though," I argue.

He points to the road. "*I* don't get grounded. Drive." Then he promises, "We'll figure something out, don't worry." But he can't hide his own worry etched on his face.

Instead of being relieved at his bottomless pit of patience, his reassurance creates a vortex of panic in my stomach. At what point is he going to want to unload his loser girlfriend, who's not allowed to date, who's barely allowed to breathe on her own without asking for permission first? Pretty soon he's going to get tired of me, tired of waiting, and then there'll be a Claudia or a Kim or a Faith at some party, someone who's more than willing to make up for all the things I'm *not* doing.

Do you want a blow job, Charlie?

Why yes, yes I do. Thank you for asking.

I pull out of my spot and turn left at the light, heading up toward the high school. Good thing the roads are empty because my mind is elsewhere, flipping through the kitchen calendar back home for an answer to our problem. Then I remember the embossed invitation that came in the mail a few weeks ago.

"Charlie!" I say, clutching the steering wheel in excitement. "Saturday night!"

"What about it?" He looks at me, confused.

"My parents have some kind of gala in the city. They won't be home until late."

"Ohhh." He raises his eyebrows knowingly. "What about your sister?"

"Right, Lila." How could I forget Lila? "Let me see. Maybe I can work on getting her a sleepover somewhere."

My mind races through the names of Lila's friends. It would actually be good for her to get out of the house. I just have to make sure no one thinks it was my idea.

———•———

Claudia has kicked the game up a notch. Every bathroom at school has the same BJ picture with my name and now my phone number. It's in the boys' bathrooms too. I checked when my phone wouldn't stop buzzing. I can barely understand the voice mails the boys are leaving; they're either laughing too hard or saying it so quietly their propositions sound like they're speaking in Klingon. The obscene calls don't even really bother me. It's remedial bullying.

On my way to Spanish, Mr. Johnson races down the hall, then stops abruptly when he sees me. He lifts a finger, but his open mouth stalls, trying to find the right words.

"I know." I let him off the hook.

Claudia runs around the corner at just that moment, skidding to a stop when she sees me talking to Mr. Johnson. Her mouth drops open; her bottom lip is cracked because of me. She turns and tears down the stairwell so fast her frizzy hair flies behind her like a cape. If only she ran that fast on the field.

He exhales. "The custodian is going to each bathroom to paint over it. By any chance, do you know who did it?"

"No," I lie. It'll just amp up the feud to yet another level if I tell on Claudia. It ends here.

"I'll call your mother and tell her we're taking it very seriously," he says, trying to do damage control.

I shake my head. "It's okay. I'll tell her what happened."

"You're sure?" He eyes me with relief.

"Absolutely." I flash him a wide-eyed smile to put him at ease then wave good-bye.

Meaghan didn't meet me at my locker before any of my classes today, which is strange, because I know she's here. Her ancient Subaru Outback was in the parking lot this morning. When I get to Spanish, she makes a dramatic statement by sitting three rows away from Charlie, her back stiff as a rod. Charlie points to her with his pen and lifts his shoulders. I start to walk to her, but he waves me over.

"Claudia's been—" he starts to break it to me.

"I know." I pull my phone out of my back pocket. "My butt's been vibrating all day."

His eyes go cold.

"I'm fine," I assure him. "Really, it'll blow over." Then I laugh. "Get it? *Blow*?"

He shakes his head, still not able to find the humor in it.

"Let me talk to Meaghan. I'll be right back."

Crouching down next to her, I fold my hands under my chin and rest them on her desk. She pretends not to notice me. Why she never joined the drama club, I'll never know.

"What's up?"

She glances at me out of the corner of her eye. "*Olivia* told me you beat up Claudia at lacrosse practice."

I groan. "Good news travels fast."

She focuses on the open book in front of her. "I called you."

"Oh." I breathe. Now I know what's going on. High-Maintenance Meaghan. "I got grounded."

"Did you have your phone taken away?" She's still not making eye contact.

"No," I admit. "But I was in a bad place."

Her lips twist to the side. "Bad enough that you didn't even talk to *Charlie*?"

I choose my words carefully. "Charlie came and found me at the lacrosse game. Otherwise I wouldn't have seen him either."

She breathes in deeply through her nose. "You know . . . you're dangerously close to turning into one of *them*." She points across the room to Brian and April, sitting hip to hip on the radiator.

I sigh in frustration. My friendship with Meaghan was the one part of my life that was easy. Why is it so out of balance now, just because of Charlie?

"Look, I'm sorry. I should have called." I press my hands together in a pleading gesture. "I throw myself on the mercy of the court."

She glances at me then quickly looks away. But I know Meaghan; I saw the twinkle in her green eyes. I'm almost there. She scans the ceiling for a verdict.

"Um . . . have you been to the bathroom yet?" she whispers.

I lean closer. "I'm suddenly the most popular girl in school." She smirks. I stand up and my hip aches from the effort. "Come sit with us?"

"Promise not to shut me out anymore?" She collects her books and follows me.

"I promise," I assure her, even though I know it's a promise I can't keep.

Grandma's car is parked in the driveway when I get home.

I drop my backpack in the mudroom and rush to the kitchen.

She's at the table with Mom, drinking Lipton tea with lemon and eating the Lorna Doone cookies she always brings over on her infrequent visits. Grandma likes a cookie with her tea, and she can never find one in our house. I also think it's a not-so-subtle "to hell with you and your food rules" to my dad.

"There she is! My beauty!" She stands up and opens her arms for me. My mother sips her tea, watching us with a tight smile as Grandma envelops me in one of her fierce hugs.

"Let me look at you." She holds me at arm's length, admiring everything from my end-of-the-day fly-aways to the tips of my scuffed sneakers. "Oh, Hadley. How am I old enough to have a granddaughter ready to head off to college?" Her veiny hand flutters to her mouth, and she sighs.

My mother frowns. "How do you think *I* feel having a *daughter* old enough to go off to college?"

Grandma carefully sits back down in her seat. She passes the cookies to me, and I take one, ignoring Mom's critical glare.

Her hand reaches across the table to grab mine and squeezes. "So, Hadley, tell me. What schools are you looking at?" Her eyes—blue like my mother's, but kind—gaze at me with pride. Unconditional love must have skipped a generation.

Mom pushes a napkin across the table to catch my falling crumbs.

"Cornell," Mom answers before I have a chance.

"Oh." Grandma's voice is arctic. "Like Miles?" Layers of accusations lie beneath that question.

Mom smiles tightly and takes another sip of her tea.

"What other colleges?" Grandma turns back to me.

Mom answers for me again. "Miles is fairly certain she'll get in to Cornell."

Grandma's eyes lock on mine. "Is that where *you* want to go, Hadley?"

"Mother! Don't interfere! This is *my* family!" It's an old argument between them. The scab never heals, and the two of them pick at it every time they get together.

Grandma shrugs and sips her tea. "Are you sure about that, Courtney?"

With so few words, Grandma made her point. Mom pushes her chair back with a screech. She winces and glances down to make sure she didn't scratch the wood floor.

"You know what? I'm going to pick up Lila from school. Why don't you two spend some *quality* time together?" She storms off to get her purse, leaving behind a cold breeze in her wake. Moments later, the house rumbles as the garage door opens and shuts.

Grandma looks at me with innocent blue eyes. She shrugs. "I can't help myself."

I pluck another cookie from the package. "That's what I love about you, Grandma."

The rain starts not long after Lila and Mom come home.

"Looks like it's not passing anytime soon," Grandma says, watching pensively through the window as a fierce storm blows through, flooding the road. Garbage cans that have waited patiently all day for their owners to return roll down the block, thudding like bass drums. The last of the fallen leaves glue themselves to whatever surface they come across like orange and red papier-mâché.

Lila wraps her arms around Grandma's waist. "Stay over! You can sleep in my room!"

Grandma smiles down at her and runs her fingers through Lila's hair. Then she glances over at Mom, who has traded in her Lipton for her bottomless wineglass.

"Of course, stay," my mother says in a clipped tone, sipping her wine.

Grandma purses her lips. "I don't want to put you out, Courtney."

"Grandma, you're being silly!" Lila argues. "We have *five* bedrooms! We only use three of them! I even have a trundle bed. We could have a sleepover."

"She'll sleep in the guest room, Lila," Mom says sharply then turns to Grandma. "You wouldn't be comfortable in the trundle. It's for little kids."

Grandma nods and smiles, but her chin dimples the way Lila's does when she's holding back tears. She turns away and busies herself opening cabinets until she finds what she's looking for.

"What time does Miles come back from work?" Grandma asks, her voice guarded, as she gathers plates for dinner.

"Don't bother setting a plate for him. He always comes home so late," Mom says over her shoulder.

I sidle up close to Grandma and mumble, "If at all."

Grandma's shoulders stiffen as she closes her eyes and shakes her head.

"Okay, well. Just us four girls then." She looks over at my mother, who is viciously chopping vegetables. Grandma walks over to her and places a hand on Mom's shoulders. "It'll be nice," Grandma says, trying to soften my mother. "Like old times."

Mom dices the carrots with fierce downward chops. "Sure. *Nice.*" She stops dicing to take a long sip of wine.

I reach for the silverware drawer handle at the same time as Lila. Our hands touch.

"Holding hands makes it a lot harder to set the table," I tease. Lila snatches her hand away.

I laugh but Lila doesn't. She glares at me and walks away.

"What's your problem?" I ask. She doesn't answer.

Dinner is a train wreck. Grandma and Mom barely talk to each other and Lila is in a pissy mood, but only with me it seems. She babbles on and on to Grandma, making sure her back is to me all through dinner.

After we clear the table, with Lila still giving me the silent treatment, we head upstairs to do homework. I'm a few steps from my bedroom when Mom and Grandma start bickering.

"I never feel welcome in your home!" Grandma says, and there's a catch to her voice, as if she might actually be crying.

"I'm sorry I didn't roll out the red carpet for you, Mom!"

"That's not it, and you know it! Miles doesn't like me . . ."

She's not wrong. My dad always makes fun of her. "She won't let me throw away the tea bag, Courtney! She says you can get more than one use out of it!" He laughed at that, at Grandma's expense. In *front* of Grandma, while my mother just sat by and watched. She never once stood up for her mother. Not that she's ever stood up for me either.

"I look around your house and you know what I see? Stuff! Nothing but *stuff*! Is that all that matters to you?"

I shut my door and call Charlie.

"Hey, Muscles." His voice turns my insides gooey.

"What are you doing?" I ask, plucking at my fake tiger-skin throw.

"Wondering what you're wearing," he says, obviously trying to sound seductive. Like he has to try.

I look down at the lounge pants I changed into. "Fleece."

"Sexy," he says, and laughs.

"My grandmother is over."

"Yeah? That's nice."

"She's sleeping over because of the storm. It's been *entertaining*. She—"

Music blasts down the hallway from Lila's room, cutting me off. I put my finger in my ear so I can hear myself, but it's useless.

"Charlie? Let me call you back," I shout, and hang up.

I walk down the hallway and pound on her door. She doesn't answer, so I open it and find her doing her booty dance again.

"Lila! Turn it down!"

She turns to me, first in surprise, then she flies into a fit of rage.

"Get out!" She charges me and pushes me out of her room.

I put my arms out to block her. "What is WITH you tonight?"

Red blotches bloom on her cheeks. "You SUCK! That's what!"

"What did I do?"

"THINK ABOUT IT!" she screams, and slams the door in my face.

As I stare at her door in shock, her lock clicks. It's probably a bad idea to let a little kid have a lock on her door. Except in this house.

"Lila?" I tap a few times. "Come on. Tell me what's wrong. Please?"

She turns the music up, some techno instrumental.

"Lila?" I knock again. Maybe she's mad because I haven't been spending enough time with her. "Want to watch *Cupcake Wars* with me?" She throws something at the door.

Finally, I give up and walk away.

In the middle of the night, I get up to use the bathroom. Lila's night-light casts a dim golden pyramid across the hallway through her door, open a crack.

I tiptoe over to check in on her. She's never been *really* mad at me before. Not like this.

She's passed out sideways across her bed, one knee lifted, her hand splayed over her head off the bed. Lila always sleeps like she doesn't have a care in the world. I want to keep it that way for as long as possible.

On the trundle next to her is Grandma. A box of Lorna Doones sits open on the night table between them.

then

Lila's hot rage turns into the cold shoulder the next day. She has dance class every Tuesday after school. I tell Mom I'll drive Lila so we can have some alone time. She brings her iPod in the car with her and plugs her buds into her ears.

We drive down the tree-lined road in silence. Most of the year, the branches form a shady awning down this road. But on this cold November night, the bare branches strain to reach across the red sky.

"Lila," I say, driving down the road. She bops her head, pretending to be immersed in the music. "LILA!" I reach over and yank one bud out of her head.

"HEY!" she howls in protest.

"LILA!" I shout. "Talk to me! What gives?"

Her lip curls up in a sneer. "If you don't know, then I'm not telling you." She tries to put the bud back in her ear, but I grab her hand while steering with the other. We're already at the dance studio. I pull up to the curb.

"You know what? You're not being very nice." I throw the car into park. "I would never treat you like this."

She stares at me with such outrage, I recoil in my seat. Her chin dimple appears, and her eyes well up.

I reach over to grab her hand. "You're scaring me. Please tell me what's going on."

"Forget it!" She yanks her hand out of my reach and reaches for the door handle to escape.

"Lila! I can't fix it if I don't know what's wrong!" I yell as she opens the door.

She stands out on the curb crying, one hand on the door, her lip quivering just like when she was a baby.

"*You're* supposed to know!" she throws at me.

With that she slams the door in my face, the second time this week, and runs into the dance studio behind the parade of ten-year-olds all in matching yoga pants.

"I don't think Saturday's going to work."

I lean against Charlie in the school parking lot the next morning.

He presses his forehead against mine and sighs. "It's okay."

I shake my head. "I'm sorry. Lila's mad at me. I don't know why. Maybe it's because I'm not spending as much time with her as I used to."

His hands rest on my waist and bring me even closer, filling every nook of space between us until we're almost one.

"It's not a sprint, it's a marathon," he says. With my ear pressed to his chest, I listen to the rumble of his laugh.

"What's that supposed to mean?"

"It's what my mom always says when she has a setback. She means that she's in it for the long haul. We can't give up just because life throws a monkey wrench at us every so often."

I look up at him. "Are you in it for the long haul?"

Charlie has the kindest eyes I've ever seen. They smile down at me. "Was there ever any doubt?"

Funny thing about being grounded: now I really do need to go to the library and I can't. The book I need for my history project is reserved for me at the front desk; I just need to go pick it up.

"Mom, *please*." I follow her around the kitchen island. "My grades are on the line here. It's Thursday. I need it to work on my assignment over the weekend."

She stops and takes a long drink of her wine.

"Fine, fine." She waves her hand in the air to make me go away. "Just don't be long."

I run upstairs to change my clothes. I *do* need to go to the library. But that doesn't mean I can't make a pit stop along the way.

Lila walks out of the bathroom toward her room as I'm ready to head down the stairs.

"Hey—"

She slams the door before I get another word in.

It takes me all of five minutes to pick up the book at the front desk. It seems like a waste to just drive back home. Especially since I've already paid for parking. I cross the street and call Charlie from outside Sal's.

"I have a surprise for you," I say when he answers.

"Really? What?"

"Look outside your window."

I wait, watching expectantly for his face to appear.

"Okay?" he says, confused.

"What do you see?"

"A dumpster full of garbage."

I laugh. "No, Charlie! Not your bedroom window! The other one!"

"Oh." I wait as he crosses the apartment. What remains of the setting sun bounces off his window, then the curtain flutters. "OH!" he says in my ear and hangs up.

The door flies open. "Ta-da!"

He grins. "Wow! How'd you pull this off?" His arm reaches for me, half dragging me upstairs behind him.

"I busted out of jail!" I run after him into the apartment. He slams the door shut behind him and pulls me into his arms.

"I'm glad you did." His lips nuzzle against my neck. "Conjugal visits are important to the well-being of prisoners." I lift my head and press my lips against his.

His hand presses against my lower back, and our kissing turns serious very quickly. We stumble toward his bedroom, walking backward, sideways, bumping into corners, the kitchen counter, our lips never once separating. His blinds are down, the room dark.

His bed presses behind my legs, and I fall back, pulling him with me. His fingers tug at the buttons of my shirt, mine pull his shirt up. We've covered this territory before; it's not new. But this time I don't overthink it. I just let myself go, focusing only on his lips on my neck, on my collarbone. I kiss his neck, smelling him, cataloging his natural scent. We kick our shoes off; his sneaker flies and hits the wall on the other side of the room, startling us, and then we laugh.

Before he gets too far, he stops and watches my face.

"Are you sure?"

I nod and pull his face back to mine.

Absolutely no thought went into tonight. And that's why it happens. It's not wonderful. But it's not horrible either, because it's Charlie.

Afterward, he rolls away but holds on to me, pulling me against him. Curling into his side, I watch his chest rise and fall with each breath, absorbing this newfound level of understanding of him, of me, of us. How our tangled limbs fit together, connected in every way.

He turns to me, caressing my arm. "You okay?"

A pleased grin stretches across my face. "Yeah. You?"

He laughs. "That wasn't complaining you heard coming out of my mouth."

I glance at the school district calendar pinned on the wall across his room, the white paper glowing in the dark room, next to all the drawings he's been working on: sprawling dystopian landscapes, utopian cities, superheroes.

I have a nagging feeling I'm forgetting something. "Charlie? What day is it today?"

"Thursday."

I work through the calendar in my head.

"What's wrong?" He kisses my frown lines away.

"I'm forgetting something." It's right there on the tip of my tongue, but his lips erase everything.

"I should get back now before they release the hounds."

I button my jeans then reach for my shirt next to his desk, lying in a pile of pencil shavings. "You have to sweep this stuff up!" I laugh, shaking my shirt to loosen the debris.

He lounges back in his bed, one hand behind his head, the other reaching out to reel me back. I swat his hand away.

"I wish you could stay."

"Me too," I say. "Maybe if you beg nicely I'll—"

It hits me like a bucket of ice water.

"SHIT!" I shove my arms through my sleeves. "What time is it?"

"A little after seven. What's wrong?" He sits up.

"Ohshitohshitohshit!" I button my shirt while running into the den.

He jumps into his jeans, grabbing his shirt and my shoes while he chases me through the kitchen. "You're freaking me out. What's going on?"

I take my shoes from him and hop into them. "The talent show! It's tonight! That's why Lila's been so pissed at me!" I throw my jacket on. "I'm sorry I'm leaving like this!"

"No, it's okay! Go! Hurry!" He runs barefoot with me down the stairs. "Should I come?" He stands by the door.

"No way. My parents will be there. Shit! Why didn't anyone *say* anything?" I kiss him good-bye and race for my car.

But I know why no one said anything. Because no one else cared. I was the only one who did. Until I didn't.

"You're *supposed to know*!"

I let Lila down.

"Held up at the library again?" my father asks, one eyebrow cocked in disbelief as I settle into my seat next to them in the auditorium.

All of Mom's PTA friends whose kids are performing are clustered around her, like always, along with their husbands. Over Mom's shoulder, Mrs. Wiley purses her lips, staring ahead to avoid making eye contact with me. Since she's sitting close to Mom, I guess the Wileys decided not to press charges.

"Sorry," I say, taking my jacket off, praying my shirt isn't inside out and that I didn't miss any buttons. *They must all know!* My body is humming, my lips are swollen, my neck raw from Charlie's stubble. There should be a blinking neon sign with arrows pointing at my head. *Sex, Sex, Sex!*

Mom glares at me while maintaining her painted-on smile.

"What took you so long?" she says through gritted teeth.

I gulp. "I don't know." I can't even come up with an excuse tonight. "I didn't miss her, did I?"

"No. She's coming up soon, though," Mom says tightly,

flipping through the program.

Thankfully, Mom sits between my father and me. He's already in a foul mood for getting roped into tonight. My lateness just added to it.

Mrs. Peacock, the principal, comes out and announces the next performer. A little boy comes on stage in his karate gi and runs around doing chops and kicks to "Eye of the Tiger." The adults all awww at the adorableness. It's a long song, and he starts to get tired by the end of it, his kicks less enthusiastic, his chops more a wave of his hands. Finally he finishes, and we all applaud.

Mrs. Peacock comes back out again, clapping while holding her cheat sheet.

"Wasn't Robbie fantastic! Next we have Lila McCauley, who will be doing a dance routine to . . ."

Please, Lila! Please tell me you picked another song!

"'Beg for It.'"

The music comes on, heavy bass and synthesizer that sets every nerve ending in my body on high alert. Lila swaggers on stage, bumping and thrusting to the beat.

She doesn't just dance. She lip-synchs along to the racy lyrics. The same ones she promised no one would hear.

"I'mma make you beg, I'mma make you beg for it."

She struts along the stage, staring down every member of the audience like a cat on the prowl. My father leans forward and glares at my mom, then me. I won't look at him for more than a second. I'm glued to Lila's performance.

My heart is roaring in my ears. I can't even hear the lyrics. Until I can.

"Am I waist slim, ass fat, you gotta have it."

She turns her back to the audience and bends over and *ohgod-ohgodohgod* . . . she twerks!

Mrs. Wiley leans over the seat in front of her and grabs Mom's shoulder. "Courtney! You must be *dying!*" she howls. In fact, the whole audience is howling.

Sitting in front of us, Mrs. Giovanni turns around next. She's laughing so hard her eyes are streaming.

"Did you know?" she gasps, wiping the tears from her face while pointing to the stage.

Mom has her fake everything's-fine smile, the one she's mastered over the years. Usually she needs half a bottle of Chardonnay to maintain it. But now her cheeks are flaming, and she's smiling and nodding to her friends.

My father shoots my mother a wide smile that never douses the fire in his eyes. "I'll meet you in the lobby." He steps over our feet and out the auditorium door.

That's when Lila sees him. She pauses, losing her words, her footing, panicking under the bright stage lights. My heart slams against my chest *for* her.

And then I remember Charlie on the lacrosse field.

I get up on my feet. "Go, Lila! *Wooo!*"

The music keeps pumping, and I clap along, hooting loud enough so she can hear me, so she knows I'm here for her. The audience joins in, and I'm so grateful that the only assholes here are my own parents. Lila runs around the stage, showing off all her dance class moves with some awkward white girl hip-hop. When she's done she gets a standing ovation, not just from me, but from everyone. Except my mother.

"Go get her and bring her home." She grabs her purse and rushes out of the auditorium to find my father.

Mrs. Peacock comes back on stage with a bemused look. "Well, wasn't that . . . *interesting*!" She shuffles through her papers. "I'm not sure how *that* one slipped by us in rehearsals!" The audience laughs behind me as I push through the side exit.

Down the hall by the stage entrance, I find Lila holding her coat, frozen in a sea of kids practicing their routines. Her eyes are feverish, her cheeks pink. I remember when I finished my *Allemande* flute solo, I was so overcome with exhausting relief that it was over, I was giddy. Lila is not giddy. Lila looks like she might be sick.

"Wow! You were amazing!" I put on a fake smile.

Her chin puckers, and her bottom lip wobbles. "Is Dad mad?"

I help her on with her coat to rush her along. "It'll be okay." Grabbing her hand, I tug her toward the front entrance. Usually she protests that she's not a baby when I make the mistake of taking her hand in public. But tonight, she squeezes my hand and lets me pull her out into the night.

"We have to hurry, Lila, okay?" I run with her to my car parked a block away from the school, making sure she's buckled in before racing home, taking shortcuts when I can, flying over speed bumps, blowing stop signs. I need to get Lila home before they get there.

"I wasn't going to do it," she says, panicked, near tears. "At the rehearsal I used the karaoke version."

I pull up in the driveway. The house is still dark. "Tell me later, okay, Lila?" I say, as calmly as possible while racing out of the car. "Come on," I take her hand again and rush her inside. "We don't have much time."

We're in the foyer when the house roars with the garage door opening.

"Lila, listen to me." I grab her by the shoulders. "Go to your room and lock the door, okay? Then put your iPod in and go to sleep."

She stands frozen, her enormous blue eyes even wider with unspoken questions. What she knows about our father is scary enough. It's what she doesn't know that is far more terrifying. There's no bringing back her innocence once she discovers how much I've hidden from her.

The mudroom door slams open. "Go!" I push her up the stairs, holding my breath until her door slams behind her.

"LILAAA!"

I turn around to face my father charging around the corner, his face red, his hands clenched into sledgehammers by his sides.

I block the stairs with my body.

"Dad, don't!" I stand in his way.

"Get the hell out of my way, Hadley!" He grabs my shoulder and shoves me, but I take two steps in front of him.

"It was my fault!" I push him back down the stairs, away from Lila. "It was my fault," I repeat again, now that his anger is focused on me. "I worked with her on her routine. I told her it would be okay."

He grabs my arm and drags me down the stairs.

"There's something wrong with you. You know that?" His voice bounces off the soaring foyer ceiling. I pray Lila has her earbuds in already.

I walk backward, leading him away from her. He jabs his finger at his forehead. "Something *seriously* wrong." His words are like hissing steam before a pipe explosion.

I keep walking until I'm in the den, far enough from Lila's room so she won't hear.

"You humiliated us!"

He shoves me, hard. I lose my balance and fall to the floor.

"Miles does the disciplining. I can never watch," my mother once told Mrs. Hawthorne in one of those long, drawn-out PTA huddles outside the school at pickup.

"Discipline? How?" Mrs. Hawthorne asked.

"Oh, you know." Mom's lips curled into a coquettish smile. She raised her tiny, manicured hand and made a gentle, sweeping gesture. "Little swats on their behinds. Just to get their attention."

Mom cowers in the car, because if she doesn't see it, it doesn't exist, while I curl up into a ball, biting my lip so I don't cry out as his foot kicks my hip, my butt, my back.

It's almost over. I can take it.

But Lila could never take it, and I could never let this happen to her.

———

Hours later, I wake with a start to my door opening.

"Hadley?" Lila whimpers. She's standing in my doorway in her nightgown. I wave her over.

"Come on." I pull back my covers. She crawls next to me.

"I'm s-s-s-sorry," she stammers through her tears.

"It's okay." I pull the blanket up to her neck.

Her face convulses. She's been crying for a long time. "That wasn't the act I practiced. I was going to dance to the karaoke song, the one with no words. I gave the new music tonight to Ms. Ellison because I was mad at you. Every time I heard you come home, I turned the music up so you'd hear me. But you never came. Not once. Then when you did . . . it was only to tell me to turn it down."

"I'm sorry, Lila. I forgot."

"You never forget," she says with a hitch in her voice. It breaks my heart.

I curl up on my side that doesn't hurt so we're face to face. "I know. Tonight was a big deal for you. I don't know how it happened. I just . . ." I drift off.

But I *do* know how it happened. Charlie became my everything, my escape. I let all my responsibilities slip away. Even Lila. Especially Lila.

"Are you grounded?" she asks me. I search her face to see if she knows more.

"What'd you hear?" I ask.

"He was coming up the stairs yelling. Then it got quiet."

I tuck the blanket under her chin. "Don't worry about me. Just try and sleep, okay?"

She curls up next to me, and I throw an arm over her, holding on to her until we both fall asleep.

now

"Hadley McCauley," Dr. Bruce says, looking at a file in front of him. *My* file. He stands up from his chair. Warm, friendly brown eyes greet me. "May I call you Hadley, or do you prefer something else?"

"Hadley is fine." I nod.

"I'm Dr. Bruce. It's nice to meet you." He reaches over and shakes my hand. He's the first doctor here to treat me like I came to see him willingly. He gestures to the seat across from him and sits down only after I do.

"How's your arm? Any pain?" He points with his pen to my left arm.

I shrug. "It's okay."

"Hadley . . . I'm going to ask you a lot of questions. Okay?"

I nod again. He's asking as if I have a choice in the matter.

"Good. How do you feel today?"

I shrug. "Okay."

He nods. "Do you know why you're here, Hadley?"

"With you . . . now?" I point to my chair.

He nods.

"I slit my wrists."

He nods. Good, I'm acing this test.

"Do you know why we're keeping you here, Hadley?" he asks, his tone gentle.

"To keep me safe," I murmur obediently, telling him what he wants to hear.

"Right. To keep you safe," he parrots back. "Are you feeling suicidal?"

"No."

"Good." His smile leaches into his voice. "Have you ever attempted suicide before?"

"No."

"Have you ever *thought* about attempting suicide before?"

I picture the full bottle of Mom's sleeping pills in my hand. My knee jiggles. His eyes sweep over my knee and then back up to my face.

"No," I say. His nod of approval is slower this time.

He bats off more questions about sleeping, eating, hearing voices, or seeing things no one else sees. He asks me if I've ever considered self-harm before.

"How do you feel now, Hadley?"

Now I can't hide my irritation. "Not great."

"Not great. Why's that?" His searching gaze is familiar, like Mr. Murray and his kind eyes. And Coach Kimmel. And Señora

Moore. And Dr. Sher. So many sets of kind eyes, and not one of them saw anything.

"Why do you think?" I snap. "I'm here." He stares back at me as if he's waiting for me to finish my thought. So I do. "And my mother's dead!" My voice cracks.

The last time I saw her, she was hanging upside down, her frightened blue eyes staring back at me, as if she were asking me why.

His eyes travel to where my fingers play with the bandage on my right wrist. I tuck my hand under my leg to stop myself. But he sees. He sees everything.

He nods and scribbles. "I know this must be difficult for you, Hadley. I can't really imagine how you feel, can I?" he asks.

"No." I shake my head. His words are kind, too kind.

"This must all come as such a shock to you." I nod. "Do you care to tell me what that's like?"

Even though I know it's shrink shtick, my eyes prickle. My leg jiggles until the moment passes. I shake my head, afraid that if I do start talking, I won't stop.

"Hadley, how are you feeling?"

"You already asked me that."

He nods but doesn't say anything. The silence stretches like elastic around the room. His ticking clock counts the seconds.

"Awful," I say, failing the silence challenge.

"Awful," he repeats. "Is that the way you feel about your situation or yourself?"

"Both."

He hums under his breath a murmur of sympathy. "Both," he repeats. "Can you tell me why?" His voice is a warm blanket. It would be so easy to wrap myself around it and let it comfort me.

The silence is unbearable. Dr. Bruce is baiting me to go on. This time I refuse.

"Hadley." He breaks the silence. "Did you feel awful *before* you got on that plane, or after?"

My head snaps up. "What's that have to do with anything?" Everyone knows why I tried to kill myself. Survivor's guilt. Didn't he get the memo or whatever?

"You seem angry. Is it because you're here? Or because you weren't successful in your attempt?"

My breath hitches. Which attempt is he talking about?

"What?" I ask, stalling.

"Are you angry because you're here? Or because you weren't successful in your suicide attempt?" he clarifies.

He watches my reaction and scribbles, his face still kindly.

"I'm not angry," I say, though I hear the bite in my voice.

Dr. Bruce nods and smiles. I'm not acing the test after all. The smile is as much a part of his office decor as the books on his shelves and the fern on his window ledge.

"Hadley, could you help me understand why you would want to commit suicide after surviving a plane crash?"

My mouth falls open.

"Are you kidding me?" I ask, feeling my face flush.

My outburst is met with silence and that everlasting benign smile.

"My mother is *dead*! She was hanging from her seat belt! I couldn't even get her down!" I yell.

Dr. Bruce doesn't flinch. His lips tug down sympathetically.

"That must have been terrible." Balancing his pen between two fingers, he says, "Hadley, I have to ask, though. You've mentioned your mother twice now. But I'm curious why you haven't mentioned your father."

I have nothing more to say.

then

"How about this?" I hold up a pair of Aztec graphic leggings with a long shirt.

Lila shakes her head dejectedly and rummages through her dresser drawers. Last night took the sparkle out of my firecracker of a little sister. She's been withdrawn all morning, her motions limp and halfhearted. I've pulled every trick out of my bag to shake her out of her funk.

She grabs a pair of jeans and a navy cable sweater and gets dressed.

"No self-respecting diva would be caught dead in Lands' End." I watch in dismay as she puts on the boring outfit. "Lila, that's not *you*," I say, pointing to her outfit, and I think, *That's me.*

She pulls her blond hair out of her sweater and throws it over her shoulders. Then she shrugs, her eyes wide and flat.

"Lila." I take her by the shoulders. "Don't let him do this to you."

She looks up at me, and even though she doesn't say it and maybe doesn't even think it, I hear the hypocrisy. Why not? I let him do this to *me*. Lila is the only one of us whose light hasn't been snuffed out by him.

Her eyes dart away. "I'm sorry I got you in trouble," she mumbles.

"I'm always in trouble." I smile for her. "Some people are impossible to please."

She glances down at her feet, weighing her next words, lifting one shoulder with her heavy admission.

"I'm scared. When you go away . . ."

I squeeze her arms. "I'm working on that." She shoots me a skeptical look. "I applied to some local schools. I'm kind of hoping Cornell turns me down." I laugh to take that worried look off her.

Her mouth purses in an *O*. A flicker of light returns in her eyes.

"Is Charlie going to stay home too?" she whispers.

Every ounce of air siphons out of the room.

I bend down so I'm nose to nose with her. "Lila, what do you know?"

"I'm sorry." She bites her lip. "I heard you on the phone."

I gasp a weak, panicked breath. If it was that easy for Lila . . .

"No one else knows, I swear!"

My legs shake. "Lila, you can't tell anyone, okay?"

She sneers. "Duh!" Lila's back.

I had no idea anyone could hear my conversations with Charlie outside my bedroom. And the things we talk about . . . the blush creeps up my neck at the thought. I cover my face with my hands.

"Jee-zus, Lila! What did you hear?"

She walks to her bed where I've put the leggings and shirt. Inspecting them, she quietly changes out of her Lands' End clothes and slips into an outfit much more suitable for her larger-than-life personality.

"Nothing to get your panties in a wad about."

I snort and choke. "You're ten going on thirty, you know that?"

She tries, and fails, not to smile. "I'm actually glad someone likes you. I was starting to think something was wrong with you."

"And why's that?" I ask, swallowing a laugh.

"God, Hadley," she huffs, pulling her leggings up with a hop. "I've already had two boyfriends." She holds two fingers up to emphasize her point. As she stands there jutting out her hip, trying to look older than her ten years, I have a flash of her in her yellow Gymboree dress holding three fingers up—from her pinky to her middle finger—telling the produce clerk at the supermarket how old she was.

"WHAT?" I gasp.

She shrugs with diva perfection, completely indifferent to my shock. I ease back onto her bed, careful of the new bruises. "Even my little sister is running laps around me."

After she changes her shirt, she crawls onto the bed.

"Is he cute?" She plops down beside me so we're both lying back facing her ceiling, the one with the commissioned Peter Pan–in-flight ceiling mural. Pretty, but so not Lila.

"Very," I say.

"Rocking body?"

"Lila!"

She giggles.

"Well?"

"Yes," I concede.

"Is he nice?"

"The nicest."

"Good."

"I'm so glad I have your approval."

Lila sighs heavily. "I think I have to break up with Colin. He's getting too clingy."

"Really?" I ask. "How?"

She stares at her stubby fingernails, painted a glossy sea glass. "Like during recess, he wants me to play fort on the monkey bars with him all the time, but I want to hang out with my friends on the swings."

I nod. "Yeah. Don't let him come between you and your friends. That's always a big mistake. Meaghan got mad at me about that."

She takes a deep breath and exhales, flapping her lips.

"How do you get to see him?"

"It's been hard," I admit, then I have an idea. "Lila, can I ask you a favor?"

"Sure," she says.

"Mom and Dad are going to the city tomorrow for that gala," I say. "Would you want to have a sleepover at a friend's house?"

She stares at me, confused, but then it dawns on her. Hopefully not completely. I hope her precocious brain isn't *that* fully developed yet.

"Casey asks me all the time to go to her house for a sleepover. I'll ask her today, but I'm pretty sure she'll say yes."

"It has to be your idea when you ask Mom, though, okay?"

"I'm not stupid, Hadley!"

I shove her again and again until she rolls across her bed in a fit of giggles.

"Okay. I have to go to school now. Go have breakfast. The beast has left the building."

I kiss her on the forehead and rush out of the house to pick up Charlie.

He stands on the street corner outside Sal's. When he sees me, his smile brightens the darkened road brighter than a street lamp. In a flash, he's in the car, in my arms.

I pull away from our kiss. "You didn't have to wait out in the cold." Once again he's wearing only his hoodie while I'm wearing mittens, a scarf, and my winter peacoat. My car even had a thin crust of ice on the windshield this morning.

"I don't get cold," he says as if it's not the gazillionth time he's told me.

I pull away from the curb, driving toward school, the music on low in the background.

At the red light, he grins at me. "So, how are we not talking about last night yet?"

The blush creeps up my neck, and I bite my lip.

"I haven't been able to think about anything else." He reaches over and twirls a lock of my hair around his finger.

"Me too." It's not a total lie. Had the talent show never happened, it would have been the only thing on my mind all night.

Turning left when I get the green arrow, I say, "I have some potentially good news. Tomorrow night looks like it's back on."

"Really?" He glances over at me. "How'd you manage that?"

"Turns out my little sister is playing the role of cupid for us." I laugh. "She's going to ask to sleep over at a friend's house."

"What time are your parents leaving?"

I work out the amount of time it will take them to drive into the city. "Probably around six."

He nods. "I'll be there at six-oh-two."

"You can't come to the front door, though," I tell him. "Security cameras." I wince, hearing how entitled that sounds. "I'll text you when they leave, and you can come around the back."

Charlie has some kind of magic power that erases all the ugliness in my life. I can almost forget my father's flat, lifeless eyes last night right before he shoved me. The painful run with him this morning. I even forget about the game tomorrow until Olivia mentions it to me in the hallway.

"Are you driving or taking the bus?"

"Huh?" I stare blankly at her.

"To the *game* tomorrow," she says excitedly. Tomorrow is the last tournament of the season. We're playing in New Jersey. My father never misses the last game. That means I'll be stuck in the car with him for two hours there and two hours home.

And suddenly even Charlie and his magic powers can't erase my dread. If only I could fast-forward past the game. I just have to make it till six o'clock tomorrow.

———

Meaghan and Noah have already claimed our lunch table. As I join them, Noah deals from his shuffled deck.

"So, how was Little Miss Sunshine's performance last night?" Noah smirks.

I sigh. "You heard."

Meaghan cackles so loud, tables of people turn to stare. "Holy crap, Hadley! The whole school district heard!"

"The reviews are in," Noah says with his hands in the air. "Lila is a sensation!"

Meaghan plays along. "Lila's performance is salacious . . . raw . . ."

"Transcendent!" Noah adds.

"The best thing to happen to primary school since Taco Tuesdays!" Meaghan dissolves into a fit of silly giggles over that.

I groan, organizing my cards in my hand. If they only knew, they wouldn't be laughing.

Pretending to be looking at his cards, Noah tilts his head sideways, but I can feel his eyes on me. "My mom was there. She said your dad left in a huff."

I nod. "That he did."

He glances at me. "Everything okay at the homestead?"

I pause for a second. It's one of the few times Noah has let on that maybe he has an idea of what happens at my house.

Since he dealt to me first, I pick up a card. I shrug, expertly dodging the question with just enough truth to make the lie believable. "He's pissed at me."

"Shocking," Noah mutters, his eyes shifting to Meaghan, then me.

"It *was* my fault," I admit, focusing on my cards. "I went from trying to talk her out of the song to completely forgetting all about the talent show."

"But . . . what happened? When you got home?" Noah asks carefully.

I shuffle my cards around. "The usual. He yelled, then grounded me. Same shit, different day."

Meaghan and Noah look at each other. I pretend not to notice.

"In other news," I steer them away from the topic, "I am no longer the only virgin at this table."

I discard my queen and enjoy their stunned moment of silence. Then they both gasp.

Noah puts his cards facedown on the table and applauds slowly. "Well played."

I tell them the tiniest details about last night, just enough to get them off my back. The rest I hoard to myself.

then

During the two-hour car ride on Saturday, I pretend to be grateful for every last scrap of my father's scrimmage advice. I smile and nod as we drive down the Southern State Parkway, over the Verrazano Bridge, onto the Garden State Parkway, pretending he's sharing the secrets to a happy life. This advice-giving version of him, even if it's unasked-for advice, is so much better than the other guy, with the sledgehammer fists and Jackie Chan kicks.

With my mouth guard in and lacrosse stick in hand, I play the best game of my life, scoring five goals and three assists. I also get more fouls than ever before. I'm fueled by my pain, which is a constant reminder of Thursday night, of every time my father took his anger out on me. My muscles scream for mercy as I push my body beyond its limits.

I do everything my father told me to do in the car. I shove myself into the other players. I throw my elbow into more than one back. I even "accidentally" swipe one girl in the head with my crosse. It pays off, even when my penalties force me to sit out. Our team wins. My father throws his fists in the air and howls on the sideline as if the victory is his own.

Dad rushes the field and shakes me by my shoulders, ignoring the look of scorn from both teams. "You were fucking *amazing* out there!" he roars to the raised eyebrows of some of the other parents on the field. Coach Kimmel watches us. She shakes her head and walks away, looking defeated despite our big win.

"We should get home now," I say, wandering off the field. "Beat the traffic."

He looks behind him longingly at the players still on the field, wanting to be part of the celebration.

"What's the hurry?" he asks. "Enjoy this, Hadley. It's yours. You earned it."

I didn't earn it, I stole it. I needed to gain some leverage back with him. I had lost too much of it lately. But if I'm going to convince him to let me stay home and go to college locally, I have to at least try to get on his good side.

It doesn't mean I don't hate myself a little right now.

Mom slinks downstairs in a black gown, her dewy, spray-tanned shoulders exposed. She's worked on her makeup and hair for hours. Diamonds glisten off her earlobes, her neckline, and her wrists. She looks like a middle-aged Barbie doll.

Dad comes downstairs a minute later in his tuxedo, tugging at the collar.

"You guys look great," I say, forcing a smile.

Dad scowls. "Tell me why I agreed to this again?"

Mom walks over to him and straightens his bow tie. "It'll be fun." She smiles up at him.

"For *you*," he says. "I hate this shit."

Holding my smile, I watch them collect their things. As Dad pockets his wallet, he turns to me.

"So your sister decided last minute to sleep over Casey's, huh?" His eyes narrow as he scrutinizes me. "What are you going to do here tonight, all by yourself?" He sounds suspicious, I think. Or I'm just being paranoid.

"Study, watch a movie maybe." I shrug. He stares me down, trying to find the crack in my story.

"We better hurry, Miles," Mom says, her smile tight. What's the point of putting up with all of this if she can't show off?

The garage door rumbles open and shut as they leave. I check the time. Six-oh-seven. There's a rap on the back door soon after they leave. Too soon. It's enough to make my heart slam against my rib cage.

I turn on the back-porch light. Charlie's standing there grinning when I open the sliding door.

"Charlie! They *just* left!" I yell, my knees going weak.

"I know." His hands plunge deeper into the pockets of his hoodie. "I'm parked a few houses down. I watched them go."

"Oh." I exhale in relief. We stand there a few more seconds. "Oh right, come in!" Charlie steps in slowly, walking through the den, looking around the kitchen, until we get to the foyer. His neck cranes, following the winding staircase to the second floor, then up to the chandelier that dangles two stories up. To his left, the living room. To his right, Dad's study. He groans.

"It's as bad as I thought." His shoulders slump.

"Bad?" I ask. "Are you being sarcastic?"

"Sadly, no." He leans against the kitchen archway, his hands still jammed in his hoodie pockets. "Why are you with me again? Remind me."

I walk over to him and wrap my arms around his neck.

"Do you really need me to spell it out?" I lean up against him and lift up on my tiptoes to kiss him, to remind him why he's here.

He pulls his hands out from his pockets and wraps them around me. "If you want to slum it with me, who am I to argue?" He laughs, but I can tell he's only half joking. He tilts his head down to meet my lips.

After a few moments, he pulls away and smiles suggestively, simultaneously unzipping his hoodie. "I'd love a tour of the rest of the house." His eyes glance over to the stairs. "My guess is your bedroom is thataway."

He drapes his sweatshirt on the banister as we walk upstairs hand in hand. One step into my hot-pink bedroom and he bursts out laughing.

"Not what I expected." He walks over to my bed and lifts my faux tiger-fur throw, taking in my room with a bemused look.

"Yeah, this is all my mom. She finally got to have the princess room she always wanted." I take the throw from him and rub it against his cheeks. He wraps an arm behind my back and pulls me in, bringing his lips down while his hands skirt down my side and under my shirt.

"Hold on," I whisper. "Let me just shut off the light." I reach behind me for the light switch.

"Don't." He smiles against my neck. "I want to see your muscles."

I laugh uncomfortably. "I'm embarrassed."

"Why?" His hand skims around my waist.

"Because . . ." I pause. "I just don't want you to see me like that in the light."

"Trust me," he murmurs against my chin. "You're perfect."

It almost makes me want to stop everything, right now.

"Charlie, I'm far from perfect."

I find the wall switch with my fingertips and flick it, throwing us both into darkness.

We curl into each other while Charlie keeps a watchful eye on the chandelier overhead.

"What's that song? 'I'm gonna swing from the chandelier.' You must think that every time you go to bed."

I laugh. "Well, *now* I will."

"It's so big," he says, awestruck. "All of it."

I nod. "It is."

"What's your father do again?" he asks, combing his fingers through my hair.

"He's a hedge fund manager." My fingers trace his bicep.

"Those guys practically print their own money." I detect a note of envy.

"It's just stuff, Charlie," I echo Grandma.

He exhales. "Stuff helps sometimes, though." He drums his fingers along my shoulder. "You could go to any private school with that kind of money. Why are you in public school?"

I shrug and smile wryly. "Because we wouldn't be the richest family at private school." Charlie rolls over to face me. "My father likes having the most, being the best. The most money, the prettiest wife. Even my lacrosse team captainship is all about him. At private school, we'd be just like everybody else."

Charlie shakes his head and groans under his breath. He glances over at my alarm clock. It's almost seven. "What time are they coming home?"

"Not till late. Like one or two."

His arms pull me closer.

"Do you want to watch a movie downstairs?" I ask.

"Okay," he says, but his hands start to roam. "Or we could . . ."

"Watch a movie!" I edge away from his reach, laughing. "Let's pace ourselves! This is still all new to me."

I grope around for my clothes, putting on my bra and underwear. My pants are in my hands when Charlie's keys fall out of his pants pocket and hit the floor with a clang.

"Crap." He turns on the light.

With my back to him, I glance over my shoulder. Standing in his boxers, jeans in his hands, his eyes twinkle when he sees me half-dressed. Then they darken and grow cold. Horror, then anger, cross his face as he stares at my hips, taking in my tie-dyed skin: the faded yellow bruises and the deep purple ones from the other day. I spin to face him, hiding the evidence behind me.

"Hadley, what the fuck?" He crosses the room in two steps and stands in front of me.

"What?" I say, jumping into my jeans. They get as far as my knees when he grabs me by the elbow.

He turns me around and moans when he sees all of the bruises. It takes him a moment to speak. "Where'd these come from?"

I want to cover myself, hide, run. Like a trapped animal, I would rather chew my own limb off than face this moment, face the truth in Charlie's eyes.

"Charlie, stop." Shame churns inside me. I try to pull away, but he holds tight.

His stare pierces through me, deeper than anyone's ever dared to look before. "Don't lie . . . Did your father do that?"

I've trained myself to dodge the truth, but I don't want to lie this time, not to Charlie. I pull my arm out of his grip, finish getting dressed, and sit down on the bed. Charlie joins me, waiting for an answer.

"Yes," I say finally.

He bends over, throwing his hands over his face. "FUUUC-CCKKK!"

I press my hands between my knees, a different kind of terror snaking through my veins.

"I knew it! I fucking knew it!" He finally sits up and looks at me. His eyes search mine. "How long?"

I lift a shoulder, looking away. I don't know how to answer that. The first slap was when I was six. I didn't clean up my Lego blocks off the floor of the den like my father told me to, and then he stepped on one with bare feet. I didn't even know what happened until my cheek was stinging and tears were streaming down my face, more in shock than from pain. He didn't hit me again until I turned twelve, when I left the garage door open overnight and someone stole his golf clubs.

Charlie stares ahead, his face twisting with angry thoughts. "There's a reason why my dad doesn't live with us anymore. My mother thought she could live with being smacked around. It was when he hit *me* that she left him. I haven't seen him since."

I see it in his eyes, the burning question: Why hasn't my mother left my father? But he must figure it out as he looks around the room that is one hundred percent my mother, zero percent me. He shakes his head in dismay.

"*You* can leave, though." He turns to me and grabs my hand. "We're almost eighteen. We could get a place together, you and me."

My chest compresses as if there's a foot pressing down on it, threatening to crush me. In my wildest imagination, I would fantasize about just that. About running away with Charlie, about getting away from this.

I swallow hard, fighting back the tears. "I can't. I can't leave Lila."

Over the years, I've learned how to hide my thoughts, my emotions. But not Charlie. It's all over his face, why I really, truly can't leave. And that's when it becomes too real. There is no way out.

■——•

We walk downstairs together. Charlie's arm is around my shoulders the whole way, like he can't bear to let me go, even for a second.

The garage door roars open.

We both freeze in terror on the staircase.

"You have to leave. Now." I rush down the stairs.

Charlie jumps the last three steps. "Why are they home so early?" He races right behind me through the kitchen to the den.

"I don't know!" I throw open the sliding back door, and a gust of cold air blows in. I push him out into it.

He looks back at me over his shoulder. "I hate leaving you like—"

"GO!" The mudroom door slams open as I slide the back door behind me.

Mom walks in first. Her mascara is running down her face. She doesn't even look at me as she runs up the steps, holding one cheek.

Dad comes in a few seconds later.

"Bitch," he says under his breath, staring up the stairs where Mom just took off. The atmosphere crackles around him as he marches into the foyer.

We both see it at the same time.

"What's this?" He strides directly over to the banister.

I reach for Charlie's hoodie. "It's mine." He grabs it first.

Holding it up with two hands by the shoulders, he looks at the size. It's too big for me, and we both know it. His nose wrinkles as he pulls the jacket to sniff it. Then he digs in the pockets and pulls out a pack of cigarettes.

"So you *smoke* now?" His eyes bulge from their sockets.

My heart pounds a familiar beat of terror throughout my body. "No!"

He crushes the pack in his hands and throws it across the room. Then he holds the jacket up in the air in a tight fist. "I'm going to ask you again. *Whose jacket is this?*" He shakes it like an animal rattling its prey to death. Tears spring to my eyes.

Be strong. Be brave. Look him in the eye.

"It's Charlie's. Charlie Simmons's."

He steps forward, bearing down on me. "The *friend* from the game."

I nod.

"You've been dating him behind my back. After I told you to stay away from him."

"Yes." I try to scrape together an ounce of courage, the fearlessness I have on the lacrosse field, the confidence I have in the classroom. But I'm hopeless around my father. The quiver in my voice betrays me.

"And you brought him *here.*" He points to the ground. "While we were gone. To screw around. In *my home*?" His words come out painstakingly slow; we're in the eye of the storm.

I can't look anymore. It's his eyes, always his eyes, that terrify me. Detached. Hot and cold. I turn away like a submissive dog.

I mumble, "I like him, Dad. I can't help liking someone. I'm seventeen."

He tosses the jacket at me; I catch it limply in my arms. Then he grabs the vase off the foyer table and hurls it across the room, where it smashes against the wall. I flinch, absorbing the impact as if it were my body shattering into pieces on the floor.

"IN *MY* HOME!" He screams in my face and then smacks me hard with the back of his hand. My head reels; my eyes struggle to realign. It shocks me, like it always does. But the sting is fleeting, already a memory. It's never about the pain. Pain is quickly forgotten. It's the violence I always remember. The rage. The hate.

His eyes turn sad almost immediately, like they usually do, at what he is and can't seem to control.

This blow changes me, more than all the others. My heart, already calloused, thickens in an instant. Blind, reckless fury consumes me, burning everything in its path, freeing me from my constant fear.

"You can hit me all you want," I scream, tears streaming down my face. "I don't *feel* it anymore! It doesn't mean *anything*!"

He flinches, hot anger giving way to a flicker of uncertainty.

"Go to your room," he says quietly, his shoulders slack, the tension leaving his body. I inch around him carefully, waiting for the surprise kick from behind that will send me flying. But it doesn't come. I race up the stairs.

Charlie texts me all night and morning.

I left my hoodie there! I realized as soon as I got outside but I couldn't come back in to get it.

I know. I have it.

Did your parents see it?

No.

Good. I kind of left a pack of cigarettes in there.

I found them.

I'm sorry. Don't be mad. I'm still trying.

I know.

Why'd they come home so early?

They got into a fight.

Are you okay?

I'm fine.

Are you sure???

Yeah. Don't worry. I'm okay.

I don't think he believes me. Maybe because I've lied to him so many times already.

I hide in my room all morning, avoiding my father. The garage door rumbles; I watch from my bedroom window as his car takes off down the street before I sneak downstairs to get food. In the kitchen, I find my mother sitting quietly at the table, staring blankly at her coffee cup.

"What time is Lila coming home?" I ask, making a quick sandwich to take back upstairs. She blinks and stares at me.

"What?"

"Lila. What time is she coming home?" She looks lost. "Mom?"

"I don't know," she says, her voice flat. I walk over to her. She doesn't have her makeup on yet. One cheek is red. He must have hit her hard, even harder than me. I checked this morning in the mirror; my face just has a rosy flush on one side. Nothing a little foundation and blush can't even out.

"Do you want me to get her?" I ask.

She takes a deep breath through her nose, trying to find her bearings. "Yes. I think that's a good idea."

I walk back to the island and cut my sandwich in half, watching her. It's hard to feel sorry for her. But right now, I feel like she and I have more in common than we want to admit.

Charlie's mother left his father. Mom could do it too, if she wanted to.

I put my sandwich down and pull up a chair next to her. "You don't have to put up with him."

That wakes her up from her trance.

"What?"

"You could leave him. We wouldn't have to put up with this

anymore." I point to her cheek.

She sits straighter, filling every space between her vertebrae with renewed denial.

"I would never leave him," she says. Her lifeless eyes reignite, and the flow of her anger redirects at me, as if I'm the cause of all her problems. "And *you'd* better start making smarter choices."

"He hits me too, Mom!" I cry.

Her lips pinch, and she shakes her head vehemently. "No. It's different. He *disciplines* you."

My throat tightens.

"*Disciplines?* No, Mom. He ki—"

"Someone has to!" She talks over me, stopping me from making it real. "You've been lying to us, and sneaking around! Everyone knew . . . all of my friends . . . except for me! Do you have any idea how *humiliating* that is?"

I open my mouth, ready to drop my pants and show her how he "disciplines" me when she cuts me off again.

"Charlie Simmons, Hadley. *Really?* What's wrong with you?"

Her words are sharp jabs, as painful as his kicks. Maybe more so, because I know now for sure I really am alone in this.

I stand up and wrap my sandwich in a paper towel to eat on the road. "Call Casey's house. Tell them I'm on my way to get Lila."

I walk out of the house, wishing I never had to come back ever again.

BRADY: *The date is January 13. Time: 11:03 a.m. Please state your . . .*

MM: *Meaghan Maki. Seventeen. Yes, you have my permission to record my statement.*

BRADY: *You're getting to be a pro at this. I'm sorry to drag you down here again.*

MM: *Look, I'm only doing this because you said it's to help Hadley. I still haven't heard from her. Do you know if they even let her get letters there? It's weird that she hasn't written back.*

BRADY: *I'm not sure. So, last time you said you weren't certain that Hadley's relationship with Charlie was a particularly good one.*

MM: *I never said that. I said it was just weird how close they got.*

BRADY: *Let's focus on their relationship.*

MM: *Why?*

BRADY: *We feel Hadley may have been in an abusive relationship.*

MM: *What? No. No way. I'd know. She would have told me . . .*

BRADY: *Ms. Maki?*

MM: *Maybe? . . . God! I don't know anymore!*

She was just . . . different after they started dating.

And Charlie started getting really possessive. I'd see them at her locker. He would be holding her, his arms around her, like, all sweet and stuff, until you got closer and saw his face, and then hers. He looked really intense, and she was uncomfortable.

Hadley started getting weird too. Snapping at us, distracted all the time, forgetting things. She forgot about Lila's talent show. That was something Hadley never would have forgotten. Ever. Until Charlie.

BRADY: *The date is January 13. Time, 11:47 a.m. Please state your name and age for the record.*

NB: *Noah Berger. Still seventeen, but the way this investigation is going, I'll be thirty-three when it's over.*

BRADY: *Do I have your permission to record your statement?*

NB: *Sure.*

BRADY: *Noah, would you say Charlie was possessive of Hadley?*

NB: *Charlie, possessive? No. Wait . . . did Meaghan tell you that? She's nuts. I think she's just saying that because she hasn't dated anyone longer than five minutes. That girl has serious commitment issues.*

BRADY: *Did you ever feel that Hadley was in an unhealthy relationship with Charlie?*

NB: *No, never. If anything, it looked like Hadley was really leaning on Charlie.*

BRADY: *Why would she need to lean on Charlie?*

NB: *Things were crappy at home when her father found out about them dating.*

BRADY: *Crappy how?*

NB: *[exhales] I don't know. She'd always say she was grounded. But I think it was worse than that.*

BRADY: *Could you expand on that?*

NB: *Okay, so like, she was ALWAYS grounded, but after a couple of days she'd still go out with us or go see Charlie. So how is that being grounded, right? I started to think being grounded in her house was code for something else, you know? But what?*

then

Charlie waits for me outside Sal's Monday morning, despite the cold mist in the air that makes the road a slick mess.

I pull up next to the curb and lower the window.

"Penny for your thoughts?" I wince as the words come out of my mouth. His face is stormy and bothered. He gets in the car, forcing a weak smile, then leans over and pecks me on the lips, dry and platonic, like we're an old married couple heading for divorce.

I pull away from the curb, trying to focus on the road, but my thoughts are frantic. He stares ahead, not even trying to make small talk.

"Is everything okay?" I ask, waiting for the green turn arrow.

He looks over at me and shrugs halfheartedly.

My hands start to tremble on the wheel. *He's breaking up with me.* The light turns green, and I hit the gas too hard; the wheels spin out, and the car swerves.

"Whoa!" Charlie reaches for the wheel instinctively.

"I got it!" I snap, straightening the car, easing into my turn more cautiously.

Maybe Charlie breaking up with me isn't the worst thing. It will destroy me, for sure. But it will let me focus on Lila. Since I met Charlie, I've gotten sloppy. My plans have gotten muddled.

But I've been happy. For once.

I drive into the school parking lot. Pulling into the first spot I see, I throw the car into park and turn off the ignition, bracing myself for what comes next.

He shifts in his seat.

"I don't know how to tell you this . . . ," he hedges.

I shake my head, staring at my hands in my lap. It was too good to be true. I always knew it.

"Just . . . say it," I whisper. I can take a hit. But a hit would be easier than this. Physical pain passes quickly. Breaking up with Charlie will take so much longer to heal.

We both take deep breaths.

"Your dad stopped by the diner yesterday."

My head shoots up in shock.

"What?"

"He made a big scene," he says. "Told my mom to make sure I stayed away from you." He looks out his window, as if he can't stand the sight of me anymore.

Now I understand why he wants to break up with me. I feel my cheeks flame with humiliation.

"Oh, Charlie. I don't know what to say. I'm so sorry."

"I didn't want to tell you. I knew it would upset you."

A gulp lodges in my throat. "Okay, well . . . I get why you'd want to break up after that."

"What?"

"You don't deserve any of this, Charlie. You deserve way better."

I reach for the door handle, wanting to escape to the nearest bathroom so I can fall apart in private. He grabs my arm and pulls me back.

"Who said anything about breaking up?" He stares at me quizzically.

"Didn't you?" I ask.

"No!" He laughs, despite everything.

I throw my head back in my seat and breathe. "I'd be relieved if I wasn't still freaking out that my father went to your mom's work." I squeeze my eyes shut. "What are we going to do?"

He pulls me into his arms and rests his chin on the top of my head. "I'm trying to figure that out too."

More cars start to park around us; it's time to face the day. Charlie takes my backpack and meets me in front of the car, wrapping an arm around me.

"How'd he find out? Was it my hoodie?" he asks as we walk toward the building. I nod, and he groans. "Crap! This is my fault!"

I shake my head. "It's not your fault, Charlie. He came home in a mood. He could have found anything to get pissed at me about."

"What happened?" he asks.

"He smacked me and then sent me to my room." I look away when Charlie winces. "I expected it to be worse. Does your mom hate me now?"

"No, of course not. She's not a fan of your dad's, though."

Charlie walks me all the way to my locker, clearly deep in thought.

"Listen, Hadley." He ducks his head down to talk to me privately. "You need to report him," he says, trying to make the words stick.

I shake my head no.

"Why not?" He grabs my arm. "He's—"

"Shhh!" I cut him off with a harsh hiss.

I glance around at everyone darting past us. Any one of them could overhear.

"Hey, kiddies." Meaghan slides up to us, making my point. I shoot him an "I told you so" look.

"What's going on?" Her eyes dart between us. "Did I interrupt something?"

"No," I assure her, slamming my locker. Charlie doesn't play along as well.

"Charlie, you look like you're going to have a stroke or something," Meaghan says, eyeing him. "What's my girl been doing to you to get you so worked up?" She winks at me and loops her arm through mine.

Forcing a smile I don't feel, I say, "I'm keeping him on his toes." I reach over to squeeze his hand. "I'll talk to you later. Okay?"

His eyes widen, and he raises his eyebrows meaningfully. "Yes, you will."

Meaghan and I walk over to the stairwell.

"What was *that* all about?" She thumbs over her shoulder. I notice her new manicure.

"I like the new color." I take her hand, admiring the dark burgundy on her nails. "I could never get away with something that dark."

She flips her hands back and forth to show me. "Yeah, you like it? I wasn't sure at first. It's *really* dark. But it's growing on me."

Sometimes I wish I had the kind of problems I *could* tell my friends. But my time with Meaghan and Noah is too precious. I get to choose who I want to be, how *I* want to be seen, without any dark shadows looming over me. I won't give that up. It's bad enough Charlie knows the truth. If Meaghan and Noah find out too, then my father will be everywhere. I'll have nothing left that's mine.

This isn't over. We need to talk.

I know what you're thinking. Trust me, I've thought about it.
A lot. It's not as easy as you think.

I'll help you.

Promise me you won't do anything. Please.

Let's talk more later.

Promise me, Charlie!

"Put the phone away, Hadley, or I'll take it away," Mr. Roussos says, interrupting his lecture. I slide the phone in my pocket and pick up my pen. Friday's notes are underlined three times:

> *Virgil leads Dante through the gates of hell. Inscription: "Abandon all hope, you who enter here."*

"As I was saying," Mr. Roussos continues. "One of Dante's major themes is God's justice. The sins committed on earth have to correlate to the torments received in hell. Today's readers will probably find many of the punishments to be . . . cruel and unusual. Does anyone recall the *contrapasso* . . . the punishment of souls . . . for homosexuality?" Silence. "An eternity of walking on hot sand."

Noah looks at me from across the room and feigns shock with a hand to his mouth. Mr. Roussos glances down at Noah. "What was that?"

Noah lifts a shoulder. "I'm just saying, if the hot sand is in St. Bart's, I'd manage."

The class laughs; even Mr. Roussos with his strict rules—alphabetical seating, no talking ever without first raising your hand—cracks a smile before continuing.

"So let's review. The first circle is limbo, right? The next three circles are for those who harm only themselves through lust, gluttony, avarice." He counts off on his fingers. "Then we have greed, wrath, heresy. Premeditated sins of malice."

He gives us a moment to jot down notes. "The last two circles, as far away from God as you can get, are reserved for fraud and treachery."

Mr. Roussos paces around the classroom for dramatic effect, then stops and looks around the classroom. I glance up from my notes at the worst time, making direct eye contact with him. He lobs the rest of his lecture right at me.

"Treachery. The ninth circle." Mr. Roussos's eyes bore into mine. "'The lowest and blackest place, farthest from heaven.' Reserved for those who betray their loved ones, friends . . . family."

I break away from his intense stare to draw and label the ninth circle in my notebook, but *Inferno* and Mr. Roussos are way too deep for me today. They're downright depressing.

I find Charlie at his locker before Spanish.

"Good," he says as I walk down the hall to meet him. "We need to talk about this."

I come up right under his chin, looking around to make sure no one's listening.

"Charlie, you can't tell anyone."

He shakes his head, arguing already. "You honestly think I can just sit around knowing he's hurting you? No, Hadley. We have to—"

"Listen to me." I grab his hand and squeeze. "I am going to be eighteen in three months. *I* am not the problem anymore!"

He blinks down at me, confused.

"It's Lila I'm worried about," I continue. "The only way for me to protect her is to stay close. Until *she* can leave too."

"Hadley." He bends his head down closer to mine. "That's a

long time from now."

I nod and gulp. "I know."

"You can't honestly expect to stick it out that long." He looks at me as if I have a couple of screws loose.

"It's not a perfect plan."

"It's the most fucked-up plan I've ever heard!" he explodes. I shush him, glancing around the hallway at a few curious stares, waiting for them to pass before I continue.

"I know. I just don't have another one."

"Yes you do!" He hunches down so we're face to face. "You call CPS."

"You say that as if I haven't already looked into it. My mother is the friggin' president of the PTA twelve years running. And my dad donates so much money every which way he makes Bill Gates look stingy. He does it for the tax write-offs, but still. It makes him *look* good."

Charlie pauses, then opens his mouth to argue back. I cut him off. "Look at me, Charlie. I have a good shot at salutatorian, I'm the captain of the lacrosse team, I even went *over* the required number of community service hours by a mile. Do I look abused to you? No. We're a rich white family. No one is going to believe me."

"Convince them," he insists between gritted teeth. "I saw the evidence." His eyes glance down to my hip. "Do it for Lila."

My eyes well up. Everything I do, I do for Lila.

"Charlie, they don't just sweep in and take kids out of their homes after one phone call. They do an investigation. And if CPS interviews Lila, she'll have nothing to say."

He shakes his head in disbelief. "What? *Why?*"

"Lila doesn't know," I say. "She's *scared* of him. Even just the way he yells at us is terrifying. It's like . . . I can't even describe it. Like he's possessed. She knows he's hit my mother a few times. Those nights were horrible for Lila. But she's never seen him hit *me*. I made sure of that."

He blinks several times. Then he shakes his head as if to clear my words.

"No. Sorry, I don't buy it. There's an out; there has to be. You just don't know what it is yet." He pauses, and his face lights up. "Your grandmother! Tell her what's happening. She could get custody of Lila."

I scan the ceiling, my eyes stinging.

"And be publicly humiliated? He'd never let that happen."

"He wouldn't have a choice!" he shoots back.

The bell rings. I sigh, sadder for Charlie than for myself. This is my reality. I've had plenty of time to adjust. This is all new for him.

"*Vamos a llegar tarde.*" I take his hand and walk him to Spanish. We're going to arrive late to class.

Date is January 15, 9:37 a.m.

Reviewing my notes, this case is not adding up.

Weather wasn't a factor; the skies were clear. Pilot never radioed in that he was having any kind of mechanical trouble. Still waiting for autopsy and toxicology reports, but medical records don't show any kind of condition—heart, seizure, diabetes, anything that would incapacitate him. Nut allergy, that's it. And if it were a medical emergency, there were other passengers on the plane who could have radioed in to air traffic control.

The fuselage caught on fire soon after the crash, burning much of the evidence. The sole survivor, the daughter, is being held in the psychiatric wing of the hospital after a suicide attempt. She's the only person who knows what happened in that cockpit that day. I'm waiting for the hospital to allow me to interview her. They don't think she's ready to talk about it yet.

Wondering if there's more to this case. Possibly criminal.

then

My father hasn't made me go running since before the gala. That first Monday, I thought it was because he was still too mad. On Tuesday, I heard the coffee grinder whirring. I was zipping my jacket when I heard the front door slam. Looking out the window, I saw him stretching in the driveway and then he took off down the darkened street alone, the motion lights tracking his path. I should be relieved, but I'm not. The reprieve is a ticking bomb that's sure to detonate when I least expect it.

On Thanksgiving, we go to Grandma's like we do every year. Dad is in one of his dark, brooding moods. We walk into her house like a storm front, all of us tentative and silent, careful not to set Dad off.

Dad goes out of his way to avoid talking to me. Mom and Lila do their best to fill the awkward moments of silence with safe conversations. Grandma glances between Dad and me with concern all afternoon. I want to take that worried look off her, but I can't seem to find a conversation that's safe to talk about in front of Dad. College, lacrosse, school, Lila's talent show . . . they're all land mines that could blow up in my face with one misplaced step. As soon as Dad finishes his coffee, we're out the door and heading back home, leaving Grandma to clean up by herself.

On the Monday after Thanksgiving, I make Charlie study with me for Wednesday's Spanish test. Even though he's ridiculously smart and barely needs to crack a book, I still have to keep my grades up.

As we review together at his small dining table, I ask him something that's been on my mind.

"Sooo . . . are you looking into any colleges?"

"Sure," he says, like it's a no brainer. He glances up from his notes. "Probably Suffolk Community."

I uncap my highlighter, something mundane to deflect the bigger question I *really* want to highlight. "You could get into a better school, you know. You have the grades."

His pencil digs deeper into the paper as he writes. "I *could*. But Suffolk is cheaper."

"There are scholarships—"

"Let it go, Hadley." His eyes flash as he looks up across the table at me. "I don't have a buttload of cash like you do, okay?"

I flinch. "I didn't . . . that's why I mentioned scholarships . . ."

His cheeks turn red, whether in anger or embarrassment, I can't tell. "I have a plan," he says, focusing on his paper. "I'll go to Suffolk for two years, keep working, save up more money, then finish the last two years at a better school. That way I won't be stuck with huge student loans."

"There's also financial aid—" I stop when his shoulders stiffen. "Okay, sorry. I'm just trying to help."

He glances up at me, his face firm. "I just don't like talking about money. Not with you," he adds, as if to clarify *especially* with me. It stings.

My spine straightens, filling with indignation. "Hey, wait a minute. I've never said anything to make you get all defensive about this."

He shakes his head. "No, you don't have to say anything. But every time you offer to pay for dinner or the movies, you're apologizing for having way more than me."

"What the hell, Charlie? I didn't take you for a Neanderthal! You don't have to pay for your date *every* time we go out!"

He bristles but tries to shrug it off. "It's just me, okay? It bugs me. It's how I feel. I can't help it."

I nod. "Okay. I can't help how you feel. But you can't make me feel bad about my father making a lot of money. It's not even mine, anyway." He rolls his eyes but nods. After a few awkward minutes, he reaches across the table to squeeze my hand.

"I quarter apologize," he teases. I squeeze his hand back, glad our first fight is over.

"Quarter apology accepted."

A few more silent moments pass. He takes a deep breath and then throws his pencil down. "Truth?"

I glance up at him and nod.

He gnaws on his lip. "It's not just the money. I'm afraid once I'm gone, my mother will have no reason to stay sober."

This time I'm the one who reaches across the table to squeeze his hand.

I stare at my calendar pinned to my bulletin board, at the condemning tiny red dot on the day that came and went.

I'm late.

As I take my last placebo pill, I count the empty deflated bubbles in the plastic dome in my hand. I didn't miss one pill. It's impossible. I did everything right. I followed the rules to the letter, even taking the pill the same minute every night.

I do a quick search online.

If you have not missed any pills, it is very unlikely that you are pregnant if you miss one period. It may just be your body acclimating to the Pill.

It's only one period. I'm okay. I'm not pregnant. I'm *not*.

now

Group therapy is like show-and-tell. Tell us who touched you, punched you, hurt you. Then show us the scars, visible or lurking just below the surface. And remember to take turns.

"So then he dragged me to the bathroom by my hood. She didn't wake up when he was kicking my ass. But the sound of my head splashing around in the toilet . . . *that* woke her up." Rowan looks around at the small group sitting in a circle, arms outstretched, unintentionally showing off the crosshatch pattern on her forearms.

Linda turns to me after Rowan is done.

"How about you, Hadley? Anything you'd like to share today?"

I shake my head. "No, thank you."

Franklin rubs his chest with a smug smile. "You're a hoarder."

Tabitha snickers. "It's like a clusterfuck up in there," she says as if I'm not sitting in the same circle as her.

Like an elder statesman, Franklin leans back in his chair and imparts his wise counsel. "You gotta unload some of that shit."

Linda turns to me. "Franklin's right, Hadley. You get what you put into group."

She then hands us each a stubby pencil and a sheet of paper and tells us to write down one negative thought and three positive ones to counteract it. I leave the negative blank, focusing instead on the first positives that pop into my head: Lila, Charlie, Meaghan, Noah, Grandma.

"Everyone done?" Linda pans around the group. "Okay. Let's share them with the group. Maria, why don't you start."

Maria crosses her legs at her ankles and clears her throat. "My negative: that I'll never be okay again." She takes a deep breath to steady herself. Franklin reaches over and rubs her back. "My positives: my best friend, Angela; the beach, especially if I have it all to myself; and running. *God*, I miss running."

"Very good, Maria," Linda says. "Franklin?"

Franklin clutches his list with both hands. His knee shakes back and forth. "My negative: when I found Lenny." He stares at his paper. His throat bobs as he swallows, once, twice. He finds it in him to keep going in a tight voice. "My positives: the Rangers, my grandma's empanadas . . . and my mom," he finishes, blushing.

Linda reaches over and squeezes Franklin's shoulder. "*Great* job, Franklin." She looks around the group, her eyes coaxing us to support Franklin. Franklin had a breakthrough today. Even I know that, and I'm the new kid. Franklin never says his brother's name. He was mad at Lenny for killing himself. "It was the ultimate fuck you!" Franklin said last time, his eyes bloodshot with rage. "How do you fucking kill yourself before you make it right with the people around you? It's like . . . it's like he did it just to fuck me up! He did it to get even with *me*!"

"Donnie? Are you ready, sweetie?" Linda looks over at Donnie, whose shoulder blades still poke out of her shirt like bird wings, even though her calorie intake is being carefully monitored.

Donnie immediately starts sobbing.

"Everyone keeps telling me I'm here to get better . . . but I'm *fine*!" She looks up at the group, tears running down her face. "I'm not *like* any of you! I just want to go back home! Zane's going to find someone else while I'm here . . ."

Thankfully, Donnie runs out the clock, because I misunderstood the assignment. All I did was make a list of people who made me happy *before*. No amount of talking or therapy can absolve me of my guilt, which weighs on me like a collapsed building.

At the end of the session, Linda makes certain we each return our dull, stubby pencils so we can't find a way to pierce an artery with them.

Out in the hallway, I see him at the nurse's station, talking to Janet. The same guy with the kind eyes the day of the crash. Janet has her arms folded, shaking her head.

A hand clamps down on my shoulder.

"Time's running out."

I spin around. "Huh?"

Rowan wrinkles her nose and grins. "Linda's gonna make you talk next time."

The man at the desk sees me standing in the hallway with Rowan and waves.

"Hadley!"

Janet yanks his arm back down. "That's *enough*!"

The walls close in on me, pressing down. I lean my hand against the cinder block wall so I don't tip over. Rowan grabs my arm and drags me into our room.

"Sit down," she orders me, and I fall back on my bed. "Put your head between your knees."

Janet comes in a few seconds later. I hear them talking over me, but they sound far away, like they're underwater.

"She looked like she was gonna pass out," Rowan says. "Or puke. Hadley, here's the trash can if you're gonna puke." She shoves it under my face.

"Hadley? Are you okay?" Janet kneels down next to me.

I nod, even though, no, I'm not okay.

I'm not going to be able to put off talking much longer.

then

Another party is coming up, and Meaghan wants a new outfit for a new love interest, someone to get her mind off Mike. After school on Monday, Noah and I go with her to the mall, which is decked out for Christmas, three weeks away. Santa has his workshop set up in the center of the first floor between Kate Spade and Michael Kors; a long line of kids wait their turn to put in their toy requests. Is wishing your father would disappear something Santa would consider?

We stroll around aimlessly, sharing a batch of Auntie Anne's cinnamon sugar pretzel nuggets.

"I'm just saying, I think I counted a total of two menorahs in the entire mall," Noah argues, glancing around at what could technically be considered nondenominational holiday decorations, though we all know they're really for Christmas. If there's any doubt, Santa's booming *ho-ho-ho* punctuates Noah's point.

"I'll buy you some gelt at the Godiva store." Meaghan pats him on the arm, then turns to me. "So what are you getting Charlie for Christmas?"

"I don't know," I say. "I don't want to buy him something that will make him feel like he didn't spend as much on me." After our argument about money, I don't want to push it.

At that exact moment, we walk by Victoria's Secret.

"Come with me!" She grabs my arm and drags me in. Noah follows.

"What are we doing here?" I look around at the near-naked mannequins with their firm plastic butt cheeks hanging out of satin and lace thongs.

"You are going to get something pretty to wear for your man. *That* will be your present to him!" She navigates me to the back corner with the sexy, *sexy* things.

I put my hand behind a see-through black bustier hanging off a rack, with a bunch of clasps and hooks and straps.

"There is no way in hell . . ." I step back as if it has teeth and is ready to take a bite out of me.

"No, not *that*." She shakes her head at the contraption. "That's way too advanced for you. No I was thinking about something like *this*." She holds up a sheer baby doll nightie in red, with a lace bodice and matching panty, if you can call a fragile, dental-floss G-string a panty.

Heat climbs up my neck just picturing that encounter.

Noah holds it up high and cocks an eyebrow. "Not in red. She's going to look like an heirloom tomato with all that blushing." He flips through the rack looking for another color.

"Guys, seriously. I can't," I protest.

Meaghan is relentless. She whips out her phone and takes a picture.

"Let's see what Charlie thinks." She hits send before I can stop her.

"Meaghan!"

She throws her phone back in her purse. "Hey, you'll both thank me for it, I'm sure. Fa-la-la-la-la."

My phone rings a second later.

"*That* was fast!" Noah laughs.

I don't recognize the phone number; maybe he's calling from work? I answer my phone with a groan. "I swear this wasn't my idea."

"Hadley?"

I pause, forcing my brain to switch gears. "Mom?"

"Hadley . . . there's been a misunderstanding," she says in a strained voice.

Something is very wrong.

"Mom, what's going on?"

She sighs, but it warbles. "I'm sure we can clear this up quickly. But they're being very unreasonable. I think they're just trying to make an example—"

Loud voices swell in the background, followed by someone yelling, "Get *off* me!"

"Where *are* you?"

She tries to inflate her voice with haughty self-confidence but fails.

"I'm at the second precinct."

"The second precinct? Why?"

"There's nothing to worry about. I just need you to come down here and get Lila."

"LILA!" I cry. "Mom, what . . ."

She exhales, exasperated. "Hadley, *please*. Stop asking so many questions. Just come now."

She hangs up. I stare blankly at my friends.

Noah stands frozen like a mannequin, holding a lavender nightie up in the air. Meaghan has her phone in her hand.

"Um." Meaghan holds the phone up. "Charlie likes the nightie."

Noah walks over and wraps me in his arms, which makes me want to cry.

Lila's toes barely graze the floor from the police station chair. She's staring down at her feet, but I can see that she's gnawing on her bottom lip.

"Lila!" I call over to her.

She runs into my arms, burrowing her head into my chest like she's trying to disappear. I hug her and lean to her ear.

"Was she drunk?"

Lila nods against my chest. This is bad. Really bad. Felony bad.

The officer she was sitting with walks over to me.

"Are you the older sister?" she asks, her face stern but somehow also compassionate.

"Yes. I, uh, my mother called me to come down. I'm not sure what I'm supposed to do."

"Can I see your ID?" She juts her hand out.

I open my purse and hand her my license. She looks at it for a second and then hands it back.

"Why is she here?" I ask, afraid to hear her answer.

"DWI. Left the scene of an accident. She hit a parked car on Willow then tried to flee. We pulled her over a block away."

I close my eyes trying to shake the image. What Lila must have seen, felt . . . Why did I leave her alone with Mom, knowing she was drinking more? Why did I think Mom would have the common sense not to drink when she still had to drive Lila?

"Do you have any relatives you can call?"

I blink back. "Did . . . uh . . . was my father notified yet?"

She nods, her face not giving anything away. "He was."

I look down at Lila.

"He's mad," she whispers. I close my eyes.

"Can I bail her out or something?"

The officer shakes her head. "Afraid not. Your father or another adult over eighteen is going to have to take care of that. Until then, she stays here."

"Did he happen to say when he's coming?"

She shakes her head, her lips a straight line.

"Okay, we can call our grandmother." I pull out my phone.

She nods. "Let me know when you get her on the line."

Sitting down in a chair, I stare at my phone in my hand. Lila takes the seat next to me. What am I supposed to tell Grandma? This will break her heart.

I look at Lila. "Are you okay?" Her forehead has those tiny

wrinkles she gets when she's really worried or sick, both of which are rare for Lila. Her chin puckers and her lips twist, trying to hold it together, trying to be cooler and older than all of her ten years. But she can't hold it anymore. She buries her face in my armpit and sobs.

I hold her and dial. She answers on the second ring.

"Hi, Grandma." I press my cheek against Lila's soft hair. "We need you."

Grandma and I meet in my bedroom after we convince Lila to take a hot bath to calm down.

"That *bastard*! He won't pay the money to bail her out. He's letting her stay there tonight to teach her a lesson," Grandma says with a huff as we listen to the tub fill up with Lila in it across the hall.

"He has to eventually," I answer. "Just so it doesn't get all around town. It'll be all over Facebook if he doesn't."

Grandma stares at me for a while, her blue eyes turning glassy and pink around the rims.

"Hadley, I don't know what happened to my daughter. I didn't raise her to be like this!"

She sits down on my bed, picking up the faux-fur throw and staring at it like it's the stupidest thing she's ever seen. "We were happy. We struggled, but we were happy. I don't know how *this* became so important to her." Her hands wave around my room in disgust.

I plop down on the bed next to her. Maybe Charlie was right.

Maybe Grandma *is* the answer. I bite my lip and turn to face her. I want to tell her everything.

"You know what your father told me? He told me he has a lawyer on it. He's going to make it go away." She snaps her fingers, her eyes flashing. "That's what money does, you know? Makes bad things just go away."

With a snap of her fingers, all those dangerous maybes and what ifs starting to take root inside me are gone.

Charlie's hopefulness infected me. I allowed myself to start to believe maybe Grandma *was* the answer to our problems. And now I know it would be no use to tell her. Because Dad has the kind of power that makes people and things go away. Even Grandma.

Useless words lodge in my throat. They'll only upset her because there's nothing either of us can do about it.

"Oh, sweetie." Grandma pats my knee. "Everything will be fine. I'm sorry. I didn't mean to frighten you."

I nod and wipe the tears that escaped.

"I know," I assure her.

That night before bed, I check my texts before setting my phone to quiet. There's one from Noah.

I have a feeling things may not be all sunshine and magic at the homestead tonight. You know you can talk to me about anything, right?

I text him back a quick *X* and *O*, then add a gif of a dog chasing its tail in circles before I shut my phone off.

Mom comes home the next day. Dad is now giving both Mom and me the silent treatment. He runs by himself every morning and comes home late from work every night, if at all.

Mom focuses all her energies into getting ready for Christmas. The tree goes up, and she decks the halls from top to bottom. The ten-foot Scotch pine is decorated in gold ribbons and delicate red ornaments. Year after year, the handmade ornaments we made in school never make it onto her perfect tree.

For a few weeks, the house is quiet. I get to sleep in for the first time in years, spending my free time in the afternoons with Charlie when he's not working. I haven't had a flying lesson with Phil since October. After canceling three times in a row, he left it in my hands: "Call me when you're ready to come back." I haven't scheduled a lesson since. Even with all this free time, I don't bother to reschedule just because I don't feel like going.

My life feels almost blissfully normal.

The Monday before Christmas, the atmosphere shifts again. Dad makes his coffee downstairs, the buzzing of the coffee grinder waking me up. Then the footsteps come up the stairs and down the hallway. The bang on the door should come right about . . .

I shoot out of bed in a panic.

Throwing my door open, I catch him as he raises his knuckles to bang on Lila's door.

"What's going on?" I ask, stepping out into the hallway.

He looks at me dismissively, like I'm nothing, a stranger living in his home.

"I signed Lila up for lacrosse this spring. She needs to start training to get in shape." He knocks and reaches for the knob. I race to his side.

"Lila doesn't like lacrosse or any kind of team sport. She likes dancing and gymnastics," I remind him.

He looks down his nose at me. "She'll learn to like it," he says, like when Lila gags at the sight of spaghetti squash and broccoli.

He opens the door and turns on her light. Lila is sprawled sideways across her bed, rubbing her eyes in confusion.

I finally know how my father is going to get even with me for disobeying him and dating Charlie. By going after Lila.

"Come on, get up," he says, lifting his mug to his mouth with a loud slurp.

"What's happening?" she groans, raising her hands to block the light.

"We're going down to the gym. You and me," he says, yanking her blanket off her.

"Hey!" she yells, still sleepy and not sharp enough to dodge Dad's quick temper.

"I'll help her get dressed." I step in between Dad and Lila.

"Meet you in five. Got it, Lila?" He nods once then walks out.

Lila's eyes are wide open now and panicked. "What's going on?"

I deflect my own panic with a wry smile. If I act like there's nothing to worry about, she'll be okay for now. "Looks like Dad needs a new workout buddy," I say, searching through her drawers for something she can wear down in the gym. I pull out a pair of yoga pants and a cotton shirt.

"Hadley?" Her big blue eyes appeal to me to save her.

"I'll come with you, okay? We'll all work out together. It'll be fun," I lie.

It works. She lets go of at least some of her anxiety. I throw on some clothes quickly in my room, and we walk downstairs to the gym. As soon as Dad sees me with Lila, his face goes even colder.

"I thought I'd work out too," I offer. "I can help."

He puts a hand on Lila's shoulder. It's so big, and she looks so small under the weight of it, like he could pulverize her into a fine powder with one firm squeeze.

"We got this. Go back to bed or whatever."

It's not a question.

"You're sure?" I say, infusing my voice with cheer for Lila. "I haven't lifted in a while. I could really use it."

He doesn't even look at me. "You can use the gym when we're done."

Lila stares back at me over her shoulder in horror as he walks her to the treadmill.

"You got this," I mouth, to give her courage.

She can handle this, I know. But I also know it's just the beginning of the deconstruction period. He will chip away at her the way he did with me until there's nothing left. But Lila is not me. She can't lie, she can't hold things in. She is mouthy and fresh and precocious, and he will make it his goal to break her.

We're running out of time.

■——■

The bumper of a minivan in our driveway is decorated with a bunch of self-congratulatory stickers: "My Child Is an Honor Student at Melville High School," "PTA: Every Child, One Voice," and the pink "Lacrosse Mom" sticker in between. It doesn't take too much super-sleuthing to figure out that Mrs. Wiley is here.

Their conversation in the kitchen trickles over to the mudroom as I kick my shoes off.

"He'll get his, don't you worry. Karma has a way," Mrs. Wiley says then whispers, "I think Hadley's home from school. I heard the door."

On cue, I walk in. "Mom? What's wrong?"

There's a half-empty bottle of wine and a box of tissues on the table between them. Mom doesn't have on a spot of makeup. Not that she cried it all off; there's no sign of any ever making it to her face today, which is not like her. Mom won't go get the newspaper from the driveway without a full face of makeup on, just in case she runs into a neighbor.

She sniffs and looks at me, then at Mrs. Wiley.

"Nothing, honey. I just needed a friend to talk to." Mrs. Wiley reaches across the table and squeezes her hand. "Why don't you go get started on your homework."

Her eyes, so swollen and bloodshot they look beaten, tell me to give her some privacy.

I nod and carry my backpack with me, stopping on the stairs wrapped in boughs of holly to listen.

"I should just fry the asshole's food in peanut oil and be done with him," Mom says through her tears and then laughs darkly.

"Courtney!" Mrs. Wiley admonishes her, but they both laugh.

"It's not like I didn't know," Mom confides.

"I'm so sorry. I didn't know if I should tell you."

"Stop apologizing," Mom says. "You were just being a friend."

There's a long pause.

"Why are men such idiots?" Mrs. Wiley says abruptly. "Look at you. You're gorgeous. What else could he possibly want?"

Mom sniffles. "It's never enough with Miles. He's never satisfied with what he has. He always has to have more."

At that, I walk away. Because my mother is typically myopic: all she can see is how Dad hurt her. She still refuses to see how much damage he's done to all of us.

then

Thursday morning, I squeeze into a pair of jeans. I hold my breath, suck in my stomach, and still can barely get the zipper up. They must've shrunk in the dryer. It takes me almost as long to take them off as it did to wrestle them on. I pull out another pair of jeans from my closet. They barely button.

Standing in front of my mirror, I lift my shirt, looking, *really* looking at my body. I pull my shirt up and touch my belly. It's bigger, rounder than usual. And softer. I reach up and touch my breasts. They're also bigger, and tender.

I rush over to my desk and flip open my laptop.

Almost every website on birth control convinces me I have nothing to worry about. Except for this one condemning article: eight out of one hundred women can still get pregnant, even when taking the Pill correctly. *How is that even remotely 99.9 percent effective?*

My heart races, and my palms sweat as I go over the nightmare conversations I'm going to have to face: *Charlie, I'm pregnant. Mom, I'm pregnant. Dad . . .*

All day my body buzzes with anxiety. Charlie asks what's wrong bunches of times. I tell him it's nothing, but his lips flatline, like my constant lying is literally killing him. I can't bring myself to tell him, or Noah, or even Meaghan because if I say it out loud, the look in their eyes will confirm my wildest fears and make it that much worse. But I can't go on not knowing. I have to find out.

After school, I drive to Walgreens and park, watching people come and go through the glass doors. When Mrs. Hawthorne marches in, her purse slung over her arm, my mouth goes metallic with fear just imagining what would have happened if she'd caught me in aisle six reading the back of a Clearblue box.

"Courtney, I hate to be the one to tell you this, but . . ."

I start the car and peel out of the parking lot, down the road to Planned Parenthood.

The receptionist glances up from her computer screen. "Can I help you?"

"I'm on the Pill, but I think I'm pregnant." Saying it out loud unleashes a torrent of tears.

She ushers me into an exam room, probably so I don't alarm the other patients in the waiting area. Candy, the nurse, comes in.

Candy focuses on calming me down. "Take a deep breath, sweetie. How many periods did you miss?"

I hold up one finger. "Just one, three weeks ago. But my breasts are bigger, and sore . . . and my jeans are tight. I think I gained about five pounds."

"You know those are also side effects of the Pill, right? We went over that with you, didn't we?"

I nod. "Yeah . . . but I read an article online that eight in one hundred women can still get pregnant on the Pill." The words quaver.

"Oh, honey. Stay off the internet when you're this upset." She rests a hand on my shoulder and squeezes. "Okay, so you missed a period. Did you start the new pack after you finished the placebos like you were supposed to?"

I nod.

"Did you miss any pills or take one more than four hours later than your usual time?"

I shake my head.

"Were you sick? On any antibiotics?"

I shake my head again and hiccup.

"Sometimes you just spot a little. Just a smudge of brown in your underwear," Candy says with a reassuring smile. "Did you see any spotting?"

I shake my head, trying to stop sniffling and failing.

"Well, it's *not* unusual to miss a period. But let's take a test just to be certain."

She hands me a cup and points me to the bathroom. When I'm done, I hand the urine cup back. She dips a stick in it.

"Now, we wait," Candy says, her face cheery. The room hums with the fluorescent lighting. "You know you can buy a pregnancy test at the drugstore? They're very accurate," she says sweetly, but I still feel she's implying that I'm overreacting.

"I know," I say, my voice still trembling. "I was afraid someone would see me."

We wait in silence. Then she looks at her watch and checks the test.

"Negative, honey." She reaches over and hugs me. "Try not to get this worked up every month. If you miss two periods in a row, *that's* when you should call us."

She leans back and rubs her own belly. "I put on about five pounds every time this year. It's the holidays. Plus, I don't get enough exercise in the winter."

Of course. Lacrosse is over and I haven't been working out with Dad every morning. Plus, I've been eating pizza with Charlie every time I'm at his place. That's why I put on weight.

I stop off at home quickly just to check in before heading to Charlie's. Outside the bathroom, I hear Lila's muffled cries.

I knock and whisper, "It's me."

She opens the door and lets me in. Her face is wet and blotchy; her blue eyes are tinged pink.

"What's wrong?"

"Everything hurts." She hiccups and rubs her arms and legs.

"From working out?" I ask, terrified that the nightmare has begun. She nods. I sigh in relief.

"Okay." I open the medicine cabinet and pull out the Children's Advil. I pour her a dose. "Take this." I hand it to her. Then I reach over her and push the shower curtain aside, turning the tub on. "Then take a hot bath. It'll help, I promise."

She starts peeling her clothes off, still crying under her breath.

Her head convulses a little, the way it does when she's been on a crying jag.

"I hate him." Her conviction scares me.

I put my hands on her shoulders and squeeze to make sure she understands. "Lila, you really have to go out of your way not to piss him off, okay? Promise me."

Her eyes flare, ready for battle. It's a trait I have always both admired and feared most about my little sister. She's fierce; she's defiant. She is a ten-year-old powerhouse full of self-confidence. And he will do everything he can to squash her.

"I hate him too." I mean it with all my heart.

Curled up on the couch that night, Charlie and I watch TV.

"So, hey . . . my mom wants to go to Midnight Mass on Christmas Eve. She wanted me to ask you if you might want to come with us." Charlie asks casually, as if it just occurred to him, but I get the feeling he's been trying to work his way up to the question for a while. He bites the inside of his cheek, pretending to watch the show. But as the studio audience's laughter rolls by and he doesn't react, I know this is a big deal.

"Yeah, sure," I say, threading my fingers through his hand hanging over my shoulder.

"Your parents won't mind you slipping out on Christmas Eve?"

I focus on the TV. "No." I hesitate. "I mean, it's not like we do anything special." Seeing how important this is to him, I'll just have to find a way to get out of the house, even if it means shinnying down the drainpipe.

I could give him his present then, on Christmas Eve. I went back to the mall without Meaghan and Noah, both of whom were just going to try and talk me into the nightie we abandoned after my mom called from the police station. I ended up buying him a short-sleeve blue cotton shirt, the kind that looks really, *really* good on him. It's wrapped and hidden in my closet.

"I know you don't want anything, but I got you a present for Christmas. It's nothing major, so don't be a jerk about it, okay?"

I expect him to get annoyed that I spent my "buttload" of money on him. Instead, his eyes brighten. "Is it the outfit in the picture Meaghan sent me?"

The blush climbs up my neck like mercury in a thermometer. "No, you perv."

He takes that as an invitation to do some kind of weird wrestling move where he flips me on my back and straddles me, pinning me to the cushions with a delighted grin on his face.

"You like my perviness," he says.

I laugh. "You've perv-fected it."

He leans forward to kiss me and then stops.

His head lifts quickly, like a dog keenly tuned into a sound only he can hear. I recognize the look from the last time, even before footsteps creak up the stairs. His eyes are round with panic; he's going to make me hide in his bedroom again.

"Why don't you—"

I reach up and touch his cheek. "It's okay. I want to meet her."

"Not now," he argues, sitting up, pulling me up with him.

"Yes, now."

The door opens. She walks in with her black waitress skirt and crisp white shirt, her comfortable black sneakers on stockinged feet. Her cheeks sag with exhaustion. But when she sees me, her face brightens.

"Hadley?" she asks, a big smile on her face.

"Hi, Mrs. Simmons." I walk over with my hand out to shake. "It's nice to finally meet you."

"*Phhhh.*" She waves a hand in the air and smirks at Charlie. "So formal. Come here." She spreads her arms wide and gives me a hug.

I smell the booze, but I don't care. So what? We both have mothers who drink. We both have fathers who hit. But unlike my mother, Charlie's mom chose living over a pizza parlor over staying with an abusive husband. If only for that reason alone, I have way more respect for her than he can ever imagine.

"Sit down." She waves over to the couch. "Are you hungry? Want me to make you something?"

Charlie shakes his head. "No, we're good. Unless you—" He glances over at me.

"No, I'm fine, thank you."

She smiles at us, a real smile, a happy-to-see-her-son-happy smile. I kind of love her right now.

"Well, I'll leave you kids alone. I just want to take a hot bath and go to bed."

She glances over at me and smiles again, all the way to her kind eyes. Charlie's eyes.

"It's nice to finally meet you, Hadley."

"You too, Mrs. Simmons."

She stops and gives me a warning look. "*That* we're going to have to work on. Call me Nancy."

I nod warily. I'm not allowed to call adults by their first names.

She walks off, and I hear the wood-on-wood shove of the bathroom door being forcefully pushed into the jamb, followed by the rush of water into the tub.

Charlie exhales next to me.

"See? That wasn't so bad." I reach my arms around him.

His eyes are fixed on the TV. "People talk about her."

"Charlie?" I try to get him to look at me. "All those old witches who talk trash about her are always at my house guzzling gallons of wine. They're a bunch of hypocrites."

Instead of being vindicated, it just makes him angrier. He shakes his head.

"They've always been nasty to her. And she's . . . she doesn't deserve it."

I squeeze him a little tighter. "No. She doesn't."

I can smell that someone's using the fireplace from outside in the driveway.

Once I walk in the house, the fire smells toxic, unnatural. In the kitchen, Dad sits at the table, alone, with a glass of scotch.

He raises the glass to his lips, the ice clinking as his eyes meet mine.

Lowering the glass back to the table, he asks, "How was the *library*?" My stomach clenches.

"Fine. Where are Mom and Lila?"

He smacks his lips together, enjoying his drink. "Bed."

"It's early," I say, my heart rate picking up.

There's a familiar spark in his eyes. He's looking for a fight.

The smell assaults my nose again.

"Something's wrong with the wood," I say to steer his attention away from me. "It smells weird."

He ignores my concern about the wood and picks up his iPhone. "You know, Hadley, if you're going to lie, you should at least be smarter about it."

My heart pounds against my ribs. What does he know?

His finger taps and scrolls around his screen.

"Since Jillian Wiley knew where your boyfriend's mother worked, I asked her where they lived. Over Sal's." He looks up from his screen. "Conveniently located across from the library. Where you've been spending *so* much time studying these days."

He stands up now, pushing the chair back behind him with a loud scrape that slices the thick tension in the air. He walks toward me slowly, and I back up, edging into the den.

He's still holding his phone as he crosses the room. "I used this app to help find your phone." He glances at the screen. "Today I saw you were at 532 Republic Avenue after school. I thought that was weird. It's a medical office building."

I take another step back into the den. The smoke reeks like chemicals, stinging my nose. It hits me: burning plastic.

"So I looked up the directory."

He stops in the den and puts his hands on his hips, waiting for me to confess. I couldn't talk if I wanted to.

"Do you think I'm an idiot, Hadley? This whole time you were thinking you're so smart. *So* fucking smart, you forgot to clear your search browser."

Terror overrides any kind of outrage over his invasion of my privacy. My vision starts to darken at the edges.

He's been using my phone to stalk me. He's been snooping around in my room, searching through my computer.

"Are you pregnant, Hadley?"

"No!" I yell, finally finding my voice.

My heart pounds violently in my chest.

He nods and turns toward the fireplace, picking up the poker and stirring the ashes around. That's when I see it. My pack of birth control pills, smoldering. The fire hasn't melted the plastic packaging completely yet. But there's some fabric in there too, still burning.

With tense shoulders, he pulls the poker out of the fire. It's a subtle cue, a distant rumble before the storm. The way his fist clenches around the rod, the white knuckles pressing against the skin. His rapid breathing. I wait for him to drop the poker and come after me with his fists and kicks. But that's not what happens. There's no time to react. Hot metal slams into my hip.

I clamp my teeth, trapping my scream before it escapes. The heat penetrates the fabric down to my skin. Falling to the ground, I wiggle out of my pants, pulling them down just enough that the material isn't in direct contact with my skin. The burn throbs, mining deeper into my hip, radiating outward. I hold my breath, waiting for the pain to ebb like it usually does. But not tonight. Tonight, everything changed.

"You're never going to see him again! Do you understand?"

I curl into a ball at the first kick.

"DO YOU UNDERSTAND?" He kicks again.

"Yes!" I lie.

I wait for another kick that never comes. I lift my head just as he hurls the poker across the room, cracking the drywall.

"Christ!" He falls on the couch, dropping his head in his hands, howling something so primal it scares me even more than his anger.

With his face still in his hands, he screams, "Go to your room!"

I jump up and run upstairs as fast as I can, trying not to limp.

My room is ransacked, torn upside down. The mattress is half off the box spring. My clothes are scattered all over the floor, still on their hangers, thrown in a fit of rage. The shirt I had wrapped for Charlie is gone, burned to ashes in the fireplace.

then

I text Charlie telling him I can't pick him up because I'm running late, when really, I just can't face him. I know last night is written all over me, the hot poker branding more than just my hip. The burn is minor, a swath of red between two dark bruises like a railroad track. My jeans acted as a buffer, protecting me from it being much worse. I put Neosporin and a bandage over the red skin. Not seeing it helps. But every agonizing step reminds me of last night.

Charlie sneaks up behind me at my locker, his breath tickling the back of my neck. I spin around, startled to find him holding a piece of mistletoe over my head. He leans in and kisses me quickly. I hide my misery away, not wanting to bring him down when he's so happy.

It's the last day of school before break. Way too many girls are dressed like naughty elves, looking like a bunch of *Mean Girls* wannabes. Even Meaghan is wearing her stiletto boots, a short black skirt, and a clingy red sweater, topped with a Santa hat. She and Noah join us at my locker.

"Look." Noah holds her red floppy hat straight up by the pom-pom. "Now she's almost as tall as a regular-size human." She really does look like one of Santa's helpers next to him, even in her heels.

"I'm so ready to bust out of here," Meaghan squeals. "I'm going to sleep till noon every day for the next two weeks." Then she turns to us. "Does anyone have Christmas Eve plans? My parents are going to my aunt's tomorrow night. Let's have a party at my house. Just us, so we can exchange presents."

Noah shrugs. "It's just another night for me, so I'm open."

Charlie glances at me. "Well, we have plans with my mom tomorrow night. Maybe before?" He tries to read my face, but I've wiped it clean of any anxiety, doubt, or fear.

"Maybe," I say. "Let me check."

"Yeah, see if the Drill Sergeant lets you out for the night." Meaghan laughs and makes a cracking whip noise in the air.

Charlie's face falls. Completely, like he absolutely cannot play along with Meaghan's joke.

"What?" Meaghan looks at him aghast. "It's a joke! She knows it's a joke!" She points to me, panicking.

I smile and nudge him. He readjusts his hand from my waist, dropping it just slightly, just enough to hit the sore spot. I groan and bite my lip. Charlie lifts his hand immediately, fingers flared, as if my hip still carries some of the heat from the hot poker and I've scalded him.

"You okay there?" Noah asks, scrutinizing me.

"Yeah." I breathe, pulling it together. "Banged my hip yesterday. No biggie."

The hallway thins out. "I better get to class," I say, slamming
my locker. I won't look at Charlie. I can't tell him about last night.
How much worse it's getting.

I hurry down the hallway without looking back.

"No more secrets."

Charlie finds me before Spanish and pulls me to the side of the
hallway.

I open my mouth, but he cuts me off. "And no more lies." My
lips close as I try to pull my words together. He must take my
silence as resistance, because he offers me something in exchange.

"I never want to be anything but totally honest with you,"
he says, leaning close to me. "I called CPS." He waits for me to
respond.

It doesn't shock me. It doesn't scare me. It doesn't even make
me mad that he did it behind my back. I just look up at him and
nod. I understand why he did it. And because I believe in Charlie,
I want to believe he did the right thing.

"I think that was a good idea." He blinks. It was obviously not
what he was expecting.

The bell rings.

"We're late," I say.

He looks around. "We're not going today." He grabs me by
the elbow and wheels me around to a stairwell that leads down to
the basement. There are shop classes down there, and a couple of

art classes. Otherwise, the basement is a completely underutilized space.

"We're cutting?" I ask in amazement.

"It's the day before a two-week break in our senior year. No one is going to care, if they even notice."

"We're missing the *Feliz Navidad* party," I say, following behind him down the stairwell.

"I can live without the flan."

It sounds like a summer night down here.

"Am I hallucinating, or do I hear crickets?"

Charlie smiles. "You didn't hear about the senior prank?"

"No," I say, letting him guide me down the abandoned hall. Cutting class is much easier than I ever realized.

"Two years ago, a bunch of seniors poured hundreds of crickets into the school as their farewell gesture. The exterminator couldn't get rid of all of them. It's always warm in here, and the school protects them from their natural predators."

He finds an empty classroom, dark and cluttered, with unused Smart Boards and art supplies. Chairs are stacked up on top of desks. By the thick film of dust coating every surface we've disrupted just by entering, I'd say this room hasn't been used in a while.

With the lights off, he pulls two chairs down, face-to-face, and we sit in a dark corner. No one would ever think to look for us here, even if we bunkered down here for days.

"When did you call?" I ask.

He reaches over for my hands and holds them in my lap. "After Thanksgiving."

I bolt forward. "You didn't tell them your name, did you?"

"No, of course not," he says. "I told her it had to be anonymous."

I scratch my nose; the dust is making me itchy. "What did they ask you?"

One side of his lips pinches back. "They asked if I felt you or your sister were in any immediate danger."

"What did you say?" Maybe I need to hear it from him to believe it.

"I said yes!"

When I looked into how CPS works, I read they had twenty-four hours to investigate a call. "Maybe they interviewed our teachers . . . decided it was a prank."

"I'll call again," Charlie says, thinking it's the assurance I need right now. Instead, panic rushes into my lungs like water. The ball is in motion; I should stop it before it's too late.

I ease back against the chair and close my eyes. "Maybe . . ."

I feel him lean closer to me. "What?"

My father's face looms between us, like he always does. *"What happens in this family stays in this family. It's no one else's business."*

It was down in the gym, two years ago. He was lifting weights and lost his grip. It was funny, something straight out of a blooper show. His eyes went wide and his body flailed, right before the bar with all the weights crashed to the floor. A laugh escaped when it shouldn't have.

I clamped my mouth closed, but a smile still hovered on my lips.

"Wipe that dumb smile off your face before I wipe it off for you."

It was too late anyway, even if I did manage to hastily tuck the smile away.

Usually a switch clicked after a couple of blows and he'd snap out of it. Not this time. He wanted to keep going; it took him everything to stop, I could tell. It was going to be hard to hide it tomorrow, the ache of every step.

"If anyone asks, you tell them you got your ass kicked on the field. Got it?"

I inched away from him on my side, across the rough carpeting, between the treadmill and the Bowflex.

"What happens in this family stays in this family. It's no one else's business. I swear to God, Hadley, if you ever tell anyone, I'll kill you with my own bare hands."

He held his hands out to show me, curling them into big square sledgehammers.

Then he stormed over to the heavy punching bag hanging from the ceiling and punched. I watched as his bare knuckles bled, knowing that each time his fist cracked against the hard leather, he was picturing my face.

There's a small terrified part of me that wonders, or maybe knows, if the punching bag weren't there, it would have been me he beat until his hands were covered in both of our blood.

"It's not *that* bad," I continue, my eyes still closed, measuring the pain in my hip against the pain of the beating in the basement. "I mean, other people deal with really sick stuff." I wince. "You know? Broken bones . . ."

If this were only about me, I'd wait out the next few months and then I'd be free. No one would ever know what happened. We'd be the best-kept secret. But it's not just about me.

He looks down at my hip. "What'd he do?"

I tell him how my father's been tracking me, how he knows I've been sneaking out to see Charlie. I even tell him about the pregnancy scare and the trip to Planned Parenthood. I glance up at that, since I know this is our business. His eyes grow fearful first then go soft and tender.

"That's something you should have told me too," he says.

"If I told you, it would be real." I play with his fingers holding my hand in my lap. "Then he tore through my room and found the pills and threw them in the fire. He threw your Christmas present in there too. And then—"

Last night my father did something he'd never done before. He hit me with an *object*. Like that day in the gym, he lost it completely. He had to throw the poker across the room so he wouldn't hit me with it again. Maybe that's why he's not around as much. Maybe he's not just avoiding my mother or having an affair. Maybe he's avoiding *me* because I bring this hate, this rage out in him.

"He hit me with the fireplace poker. While it was still hot."

Charlie and I sit quietly, alone in this neglected basement classroom. Somewhere in the corner, a cricket alerts us to his presence. I envy that cricket, tucked safely away from his natural predators.

——•——

That afternoon I come home to the warm smells of baking. Rows of banana-nut mini loaves cool on the kitchen island. Mom is getting ready for Christmas, even if Christmas wants nothing to do with us.

"That smells great," I say, leaning over the counter.

"They're for the PTA," she says, pleased. "As gifts."

"Save some for us." I'm tempted to grab one and run to my room with it.

"You know we can't. Your father's allergic."

"So make one without nuts." I grab an apple out of the fruit bowl to stop my stomach from churning with hunger.

She takes a sip of wine and rolls her eyes at me. "It's not just the nuts, you know that. It's the sugar, the flour . . . it's fine for other people—"

"It's Christmas!" I whine around a mouthful.

She turns back to the double oven to check on several more loaves.

"We'll have a nice dinner on Christmas Day," she says.

I wait a few moments.

"Meaghan invited me over tomorrow night." I take a casual bite of my apple.

With her back still to me, she stiffens, like a pole just shot right up her ass.

"Is *he* going to be there?"

I stare at her back, despising her.

"*He* has a name," I snap back.

"Well? Is he?" she demands, turning around.

"Maybe," I say, testing her, taunting her. So much anger and resentment are bottled up inside me; it would be so easy to take it out on her.

She takes a deep drink then lowers her glass carefully. She's broken a lot of wineglasses on the granite countertop when she's had a few too many.

"What do you want me to say, Hadley? You want me to *lie* to your father?"

"Do nothing. Look away, like you always do," I snap.

The phone rings before she can respond. Mom answers it. Her face blanches, and she gets that haughty tone in her voice when she wants to let someone know she's better than they are.

"This is she. Who's this? . . . *Who?* . . . What's this in reference to? . . . You can't be serious. This is some kind of sick joke . . . *Tomorrow?* That's *absurd*," she huffs, pacing around the room. "Tomorrow is Christmas Eve!"

She pauses and listens. "Even if it's in the morning, it's still Christmas Eve . . . I . . . fine, of course, fine. I think this is completely unwarranted. I certainly hope you are discreet about this . . . Yes, yes . . . ten o'clock then. Good-bye." She hunches over, her face in her hands. Then she spins around.

"Did *you* have anything to do with that?" She points to the phone, her cheeks red, her chin dimpling.

"With *what?*" I ask, pretending not to know.

"That was Child Protective Services. They're coming here tomorrow for an interview!"

She looks at my face, for clues, for cracks. I've learned how to hide many dark things over the years. I have her and Dad to thank for it.

"This is ridiculous," she says, holding her glass. "Your father is going to have a fit!"

Yes, he is, I think. And I hope CPS is here to see it.

then

Prisms of light burst overhead from my chandelier as my bedroom door swings open. I blink away sleep, trying to remember what day it is, what I forgot. The smell of his coffee in my room tells me we're back to our old routine. I slide my legs out of bed.

"Get up. You need to run an errand today," Dad says, slurping his cup.

"What?" I ask, stifling a yawn.

"You and your sister. You're going over to your grandmother's."

I blink a few more times, arranging my thoughts in some kind of logical order.

"Isn't Grandma coming over tomorrow for Christmas?"

"Nope." He turns away.

"Why?" I ask, but he's already left.

Of course. CPS is coming today, and he doesn't want us around.

I did my research long before Charlie called. I know what's supposed to happen. They were *supposed* to interview Lila and me at school, a neutral place away from our parents, before talking to them. But school is out for the next two weeks.

What I don't know is if they'll try to find a way to talk to us over the break. My stomach knots at the thought.

As Lila and I leave later that morning, I see the house through the CPS caseworker's lens. The boughs of holly that snake down the banister, the ten-foot tree with stacks of festively wrapped presents underneath, Christmas music piping through the sound system in the background, the smell of one more banana-nut loaf baking in the oven, which apparently only people outside our family are allowed to eat.

Closing the door behind me, I can only hope for a miracle at this point.

"Never, ever, ever, *ever* boil your water in the microwave," Grandma says, putting the kettle on the stove for tea. "Always put a kettle on. Always."

"Why?" Lila asks.

"It's just the civilized way to do it," she says as if that's enough.

"But why? The microwave is faster." Lila presses.

"Just do it for me, dear."

She sets the table for us, putting out cream and sugar for Lila. I take mine with lemon for Grandma, because I know it makes her happy.

"Can someone *please* tell me why you're not coming to our house tomorrow?" Lila asks.

Grandma turns away to gather teaspoons from the drawer, but

her shoulders stiffen. "Your *father* has some kind of surprise for you tomorrow," she says, heavy emphasis on *father*.

"Do you know what it is?" Lila asks.

Grandma turns back to us and smiles, but it wavers. "Yes, but you're not getting it out of me." She makes a zipping motion across her lips, lightening the mood for Lila's benefit.

"Can we give you your presents?" I ask.

She smiles, but it's a sad smile. Whatever surprise Dad has in store for us tomorrow cannot possibly be worth the pain of knowing Grandma will be spending Christmas Day alone.

I hate him.

"Sure," she says. I bring her the box with her favorite perfume. It's our running gag; I've kept her in stock every year since I was seven. She laughs as she unwraps it, and immediately takes it out of the box for a quick squirt to her neck. Lila wrinkles her nose and waves her hand in the air.

Then I give Grandma the box with the peach cashmere scarf I saw hanging on a mannequin. It was something Grandma would never buy for herself, but when I felt how soft it was, I knew I had to get it for her.

She unwraps it and stares at the contents for a moment before touching it gently. Twisting the fabric around for the tag, she reads the care instructions, then clucks her tongue in disapproval.

"Cashmere, Hadley? I'm going to have to wash it by hand."

"But it will feel so soft around your neck," I say, wrapping it around her so she can feel it. Her eyes close in contentment.

"It *is* soft." She sighs. "And I do like the color." Her arms reach up for me, and she squeezes. "It was very thoughtful. Thank you. I hope you didn't spend a lot."

"Of course not," I lie, because Grandma would be mad at me if I did.

Lila passes her present across the table. "I bought this at the Holiday Boutique at school," she boasts.

Grandma opens it carefully and pulls it out. It's a ceramic teddy bear holding a plaque that reads "World's Best Grandma." Grandma's eyes get that pink tinge around the edges, and she reaches over and squeezes Lila until she screams, "Grandma! You're killing me!"

Then Grandma hands us the presents she bought for us. They're always a little off. Lila opens hers first, a CD of some band I've never heard of before. I don't have the heart to tell Grandma no one listens to CDs anymore.

"Who are *they*?" Lila asks me.

"They're handsome, don't you think?" Grandma points to the four cute guys on the cover. "I like the hat on this one. Men used to *always* wear hats back in my day." I shoot Lila a "shut up and say thank you" look.

I open my present next. There's a bottle of perfume, the same one I bought her.

"Since you like mine so much, you should have your own." She takes the bottle from me, squirting my neck, then gives me a big kiss on the cheek. Lila just about falls out of her seat laughing.

Lila wipes her eyes. "Now I have to pee!"

Grandma waves Lila off. "Don't announce it, dear." Lila runs down the hallway to the bathroom, laughing the whole way.

The kettle whistles that it's ready. Grandma gets up to turn the stove off. When she turns around with the kettle in hand, she freezes. Whatever expression is on my face clearly scares her.

"Hadley? What's wrong?"

What's the point in telling Grandma about CPS coming to the house to interview my parents? It'll just upset her. We've already done enough to ruin her Christmas. I don't want to eviscerate it completely.

"All good, Grandma. I'm just thinking how I'm going to miss you." I take a bite of a cookie. "Tomorrow."

After Grandma's, I take Lila to the mall with me. It's a madhouse. Only completely disorganized people do their Christmas shopping on Christmas Eve.

Disorganized people and Charlie.

"Hadley!" he calls from across Starbucks. Then he stops to make sure I'm alone.

I smile and wave him over, watching as he dodges the human traffic that keeps coming in between us.

"What the heck is that?" Lila points to my face.

"A smile. Haven't you ever seen me happy before?"

"*Nobody's* ever seen you *that* happy before."

Charlie comes over and glances at both of us, smiling warily.

"His smile is almost as weird as yours!" She throws her hands up in the air.

He grins down at her, and I watch her melt. Charlie just has that effect on the McCauley women, I guess.

"You must be Lila."

"I must be." She giggles. I'm tempted to embarrass her by saying I've never heard *that* giggle before, but I decide to let her off the hook.

"What brings you to the mall on Christmas Eve?" I ask.

He runs his hand through his hair. "Kind of waited till the last minute. As always."

I grin. "Well, for the first time ever, I find myself in the same boat as the rest of you slackers." My hand waves around the throngs of human traffic.

"Want to shop together?" he asks, again carefully, glancing down at Lila.

"I would," I hesitate, "but I have to pick something up for you."

The light in his eyes dims for a moment, remembering what happened to his last gift. "You don't—"

"Shut up, I do." I glance down at Lila, who's watching us like a tennis match. "But you can help me pick out something for Noah and Meaghan. Then we'll split up."

Charlie walks next to us as we follow the flow of people. "Doubt I can help you with Meaghan. Maybe Noah," he says, glancing at Lila. "So . . . did you mail your list to Santa?"

Lila and I both laugh at that.

"Is he for real?" She thumbs over at Charlie.

We walk into Abercrombie, where I pick the first thing that screams Meaghan's name at me. She's a habitual returner anyway; I'll just have to make sure to get a gift receipt. I find a shirt for

Noah, holding it up for Charlie's approval.

"I don't know," Charlie says, tugging at the front of his hoodie. "In case you can't tell, I'm really not up on the latest trends."

"Hoodies are in," Lila says earnestly.

"Yeah?"

"Totally. You're good."

We walk out of the store, back into the fray.

"Okay, this is where we go our separate ways," I say. We both hover, leaning toward each other, then glance over at Lila.

Lila rolls her eyes at us then shoves her hand out. "Give me a couple of bucks," she says. "I'm going to get a cookie." She gives me a knowing look. Charlie fishes in his pocket and hands a few bills to her.

"My treat. Merry Christmas," he says, and she grins at him.

"He's a keeper," she says to me, and runs across the floor to the kiosk.

"And that's Lila," Charlie says, laughing as she runs away.

"That's Lila."

He puts his hands on my waist and turns me toward him.

"So he got you out of the house for it, huh?" I texted him this morning so he'd know what was going on.

"Yeah. We haven't been home yet. My stomach is in knots." Visions of my father waiting to pounce on me the minute I walk through the door have haunted me all day. If it wasn't Christmas Eve, I would drop Lila off at a friend's house.

"How's your hip?" He glances down then back up to my face with a worried look.

"It's . . . fine," I say, even though the gauze chafing against my raw hip with every step is a constant reminder of Thursday night.

He pulls me closer, and then stops and sniffs, his nose wrinkling. "Is that you?"

"What?" I ask, leaning away in alarm. Does my breath smell? Did I forget to put deodorant on?

"Don't take this the wrong way, but you smell like an old lady." He grimaces.

"Oh yeah. Grandma bought me her favorite perfume and nailed me with a squirt." I laugh. "How do you know what old ladies smell like, anyway?"

He grins and reels me back in. "Sunday morning at the diner, they take over the place. I can't even smell the bacon grease over their thick cloud of perfume."

He kisses me softly. "So, do you think you'll be able to come out tonight?"

"I'm going to try," I say. "At least to Meaghan's. I'll text you when I know."

He nods, then rests his forehead against mine.

"It'll get better, I promise." He kisses me again.

Santa's loud *ho-ho-ho* echoes in the mall behind us.

Like Lila, I stopped believing in Santa years ago, but I guess Charlie still believes in Christmas miracles. I wish I could too.

"We're back," Lila announces loudly from the mudroom.

The house is eerily quiet. Mom sits in the den, her glass of wine in one hand, a magazine in the other.

"Hi," I say, glancing around, waiting to hear the rolling thunder of Dad's footsteps approaching. My stomach clenches with nerves.

Mom smiles up at us, lopsided. Drunk. "Hi."

"Grandma says hi and to give you a kiss." Lila hops over and kisses Mom on the cheek.

I don't smell food cooking.

"What's for dinner?" Lila asks.

She shrugs. "Your father's out tonight. And I don't feel like cooking." A huge wave of relief washes over me. I don't have to face him tonight.

"Want to order in pizza?" Lila asks me. If Dad's out, no one is going to police our carb intake.

"Whatever you want," Mom chimes between tightly clenched teeth. She turns the magazine page roughly, tearing the paper.

I order a pizza, then go upstairs and wrap my presents. By the time I'm done, the doorbell rings. Mom is too far into her wine to care about food, so it's just Lila and me, eating our illicit carbs quietly at the kitchen table.

The house feels weird. Nothing looks broken, the furniture doesn't seem like it was tossed around in a fit of rage. Or if it was, my parents righted it before we came home. But something is still off. It feels like there was a brawl, like something bad happened while Lila and I were gone today.

My skin crawls like an army of ants is marching across my body. I shake my hands out by my sides trying to rid them of their nervous prickling.

Anyone could have called CPS. Anyone with eyes. If he asks, I'll tell him it was probably Couch Kimmel. Or Mr. Murray. I would have to be nuts to call CPS on him myself, right?

Hopefully, he'll ask first.

After we eat, I beckon Lila upstairs so we can talk in peace. "Listen, I'm going out tonight."

"To see Charlie?" she asks with a sparkle in her eyes.

I sit on her bed next to her. "Lila, if I don't tell you things, it's not because I don't want to. I just don't want you to know in case Dad ever gets in your face about me or where I am. Does that make sense?"

She bites her lip. "Okay. But if I guess, can you just, like, blink twice so I know if I'm right?"

I laugh. "No! Now, just stay out of Mom and Dad's way. Hopefully he'll be home really late."

She grabs a pillow and squeezes it.

"I can't believe it's almost Christmas!" she squeals. "How early can I wake you?" And this is when I remember that Lila is still, in fact, only ten.

"Not before seven," I warn her. Even *that* is way earlier than I want to be up on a day off. But I remember being her age and wanting to tear through everything under that tree as soon as I could.

On my way out, I walk past my mother, who is now half-asleep on the couch in front of the television, watching a Lifetime movie about a woman scorned. I shake my head. We *are* a Lifetime movie.

■—■

Charlie's car is parked on the street in front of Meaghan's house. On the front lawn, a huge inflatable snow globe with electrically charged swirling snowflakes bobs in the wind, the kind of Christmas decoration that my mom says is garish. I guess everyone in our neighborhood agrees, since I have to drive across town to find one. I can hear Christmas music blasting as I stand on Meaghan's stoop.

"About time, bitch!" Meaghan opens the door and drags me into a hug. She teeters on her heels.

"Been hitting the eggnog already?" I grin, taking off my coat.

"Hitting it hard!" She laughs, taking my coat and throwing it over the banister. "Come on! The boys are in the den—I'll get you something to drink." She darts off to the kitchen, and I head to the den, my bag of gifts in hand.

Meaghan has a fire going. Charlie's in short sleeves probably dying of heat stroke. He and Noah are both holding playing cards.

He looks up at me with a smile, cheeks flushed from the fire. "Apparently for me to be initiated into your club, I have to learn how to play rummy."

"Our hazing is really hard-core." I sit next to him on the couch. Charlie wraps an arm around my shoulder and whispers in my ear. "Any news?"

I shrug as he leans in for a kiss.

"Stop that, now." Noah huffs in mock outrage. "God! There's no more depressing time of year when you're single."

"Uh . . . what now? *Valentine's* Day?" Meaghan reminds him, walking carefully back into the den with two full cups of eggnog in each hand.

Noah's eyelashes flutter humbly as he shrugs it off. "Valentine's Day is so manufactured, it doesn't bother me nearly as much."

I call his bluff with a laugh. "Yeah. And the fact that you get the most roses in the entire school doesn't hurt."

"Don't be a hater," he tosses back with a smug, crooked smile. "The people love me."

"Well, anyway, you're single by choice ever since you and Matt broke up. You're too picky," I say, taking a cup of eggnog from Meaghan.

Noah shuffles the cards in his hands. "I'm not picky. *She's* picky." Meaghan curtsies on cue. "I just have a smaller pool to choose from." Noah puts down three cards, then discards. "And you broke the cardinal rule: never mention his name in front of me again."

Meaghan sits on the carpet in her short skirt, with her legs folded demurely to her side.

I wince. "Sorry."

Noah shrugs a shoulder. "Anyway, I guess I have you two to thank for finally coming to my senses." He glances between Charlie and me. "I want what you guys have."

I lift my cup and toast Noah. "Thank you."

"You're welcome," he says. "Now give me my goddamn presents."

We scatter around and gather our shopping bags and then come back. Charlie sits on the couch, not moving, and I panic. I know Noah and Meaghan got him presents because they told me. But I thought Charlie figured it out when Meaghan invited him to *exchange* presents. I know he doesn't have the extra money to buy us stuff, and no one *expects* anything. I just don't want him to be embarrassed.

"Okay, first rule," Noah says, pulling out his presents. "You two cannot exchange sappy gifts in front of us. I forbid it." He points between Charlie and me.

Charlie holds my hand and squeezes it. "Deal."

"Good," Noah says, then hands us all presents. "Charlie, open yours first," he says, with an excited gleam in his eyes.

"Okay." Charlie glances up at Noah. "It's heavy." He pulls back the gift wrapping. "Oh . . . wow. Thank you." He lifts it to show us *The Art of Pixar*.

Noah smiles, pleased with himself. "I figure you're always doodling."

Noah hands Meaghan an envelope next. She opens it and waves it around with a scowl. "Really? A gift card? You put more thought into *Charlie's* gift."

Noah narrows his eyes at her and shakes his head. "You *know* you were just going to return anything I bought you. I just saved you a step."

She tilts her head and concedes. "Guess you're right."

Noah ceremoniously presents me with a thin gift-wrapped square. "Bust out the Kleenex."

I pull back the wrapping paper. It's a Shutterfly photo album.

"Oh," I say. Then I see. Really see. I flip through the pages, filled chronologically with pictures of Meaghan, Noah, and me over the years. At field day, birthday parties, school plays, dances, decorating the homecoming float, at Relay for Life. Noah was merciless, capturing all our dorky moments, his gangly praying mantis phase in sixth grade, Meaghan's pink-and-mint-green-braces fiasco, my huge forehead cyst that had Claudia calling me Cyclops all of seventh grade. The last page has a picture of all four of us, a selfie Noah made us take in the hallway at school a couple of weeks ago.

"I had to get one of Charlie in there too." He leans over Charlie to point to it. "He's new to the group, but I don't see him going anywhere anytime soon."

My throat tightens. "I love it," I croak, trying not to cry.

Noah leans back in his seat and takes a sip of his eggnog. He peers at me from over the rim, a "pay attention to what I have to say" look. "I want you to know we always have your back."

Our eyes lock, and in that moment, I feel—I know—that Noah knows more about my life than he's ever let on.

"Well, now, everything I got you guys is totally going to suck in comparison," Meaghan complains, standing up.

We open the rest of our presents. Meaghan, as predicted, opens mine and gives me her tight, wide-eyed smile. "Wow!" She tries, and fails, to muster enthusiasm for the shirt she holds up for everyone to see.

I groan. "The gift receipt is in the box."

She sighs in relief. "I love you."

Charlie holds his loot in his lap, the book from Noah and the plaid wool scarf from Meaghan that he'll never wear because he's never cold. When everyone else is done, he stands up and pulls an envelope from his back pocket.

"So, it's kind of a long way off, but I thought it would be fun for all of us to go to the Taconic Music Festival this summer. I got us tickets." He places the envelope on the coffee table.

Noah and Meaghan lunge for the tickets at the same time.

"It's general admission, rain or shine . . . so we'll be in a field, and it could get muddy, but still," he adds, as if to manage their expectations.

I turn to Charlie and squeeze his hand. "Nice."

Probably what makes me the happiest about his gift is that he plans on sticking around for a while.

"Don't goooo!" Meaghan says, completely tanked, looping her arms around my neck and dangling like a monkey off a tree.

Noah peels her away. "I got this," he says, waving me out the door.

"Make sure she doesn't fall asleep on her back," I remind him, walking backward. "Maybe I should stay?"

Noah rolls his eyes. "I am perfectly capable of putting a child-size drunk to bed." He laughs at that. "Yep, I heard it as soon as it came out of my mouth. So wrong. Just go be horny teenagers. It'll warm my heart." He places a hand over his chest then slams the door in our faces.

"So your mom didn't say *anything*?" Charlie asks as we walk down the driveway.

I shake my head. "She was already bombed by the time we got home. Dad was MIA." I shiver, and not from the cold. "Charlie,

I'm terrified he's going to know it was us."

He wraps me in his arms. "Your mom got pulled over for a DWI with Lila in the car. That's *enough* reason for CPS to pay them a visit, you know?"

"Maybe," I say, because I'd really like to believe it.

"Look . . . I've been thinking." Charlie holds me back by my arms. "Maybe you should come stay with my mom and me."

"Lila," I remind him.

"He doesn't *hit* Lila," he says, his voice a sharp snap in the cold air.

"*Yet.*" He opens his mouth, but I place my hand over it. "I don't want to talk about it anymore. It's Christmas Eve. We're together. Let's try to be happy, okay?"

I pull my hand away, and he takes a deep breath, releasing it in a burst of frosty air. "Okay."

"Should I follow you in my car?" I ask.

He thinks about it. "Give me your phone," he says. I hand it to him. "Open your car." I hit the key fob; he opens the door and throws my phone in my glove compartment.

"There. You were at Meaghan's all night, just like you said."

"He's like NORAD tracking Santa." I laugh bitterly, at myself, at my life. We walk to his car, and he opens his passenger door for me.

Listening to Christmas music on the radio, we drive into town. Charlie pulls into the municipal lot behind Sal's and parks, but he doesn't take the keys out of the ignition right away. Instead, he leans over me and opens the glove compartment, pulling out a thin box.

He hands it to me with a smile. "Merry Christmas."

I hold the box. "You didn't have to get me anything else. The concert tickets—"

"Just open it," he says, exasperated.

Inside the box is a silver pendant. "Oh. It's so pretty." I lift it carefully out of the box and hold it in my fingers, looking at the design: two hands holding a heart, with a crown.

He reaches around me, and I hold my hair up while he struggles to clasp it. "It's a claddagh necklace," he explains.

"Okay," I say, touching where it rests between my clavicles.

"Do you know what the symbol means?"

"No, not really."

"A McCauley doesn't know her fine Irish heritage?" he teases.

I grimace. "We're a few generations away from all of that."

His fingers trace along my collarbone to the pendant, where he holds it gently in his hand. "The claddagh is a symbol of love, loyalty, and friendship. I'm quoting here, but it's 'the visual expression of the creator's heartfelt joy when he came home and found his true love still waiting.'"

"That's the sappiest thing I've ever heard," I tease, fingering the pendant resting in his hand. Sappy or not, I love it.

He pulls me closer. "I know. But I wanted you to have a constant reminder. I'm always going to be here for you, Hadley. No matter what. I can't imagine a world where I won't."

We kiss for a long time, long enough that we fog up all the windows, before I pull away.

"I want to go back to the mall now," I say.

"Why?"

"Because I sure as hell can't give you a stupid shirt after this!"

He laughs. "Is it short sleeved?"

"Yes!"

"Then it is extremely thoughtful. I thought I was going to melt into a Charlie puddle at Meaghan's house. Hand it over."

St. Pat's is standing room only.

Charlie spots his mother saving us seats. She leans over and kisses me on the cheek.

"I'm so glad you could come, Hadley," she whispers in my ear. Charlie and his mom flank me on either side. The mass starts as soon as we sit. We timed it perfectly.

Familiar faces fill the pews. I recognize a lot of them, mostly from when I was coming every Sunday in preparation for my first communion then my confirmation. After that we stopped coming to church. I'll be surprised if Lila makes it to her confirmation. My parents are all about the show, but even they couldn't keep up the pretense of being a devout family week after week.

Two pews in front of us, Claudia turns around, acting like she's searching the whole crowd. But I know she's looking at us. She leans in and whispers something to her mother, who shushes her and focuses ahead.

I don't know what it is about church. Maybe because we come so infrequently. Maybe because people come here really, truly believing in something. Maybe because I *want* to believe that if I just pray hard enough, things will get better. My eyes fill with tears. I try to wipe them away without anyone noticing. But Charlie's mom does.

She clasps my hand in hers, wrapping her fingers around mine, like my mother used to when I was a kid crossing the street with her. She squeezes it reassuringly. When she glances over at me, she just nods, as if she's answering all my unspoken questions.

"It'll be okay," she says.

Brady here.

I interviewed one of Mrs. McCauley's friends, Mrs. Jillian Wiley, who did not want to be recorded, but she did sign a statement. She said the husband was having an affair with someone from work. I think she wants to take credit for breaking the news to the wife.

She also said that Mrs. McCauley told her she "should just fry the bastard's food in peanut oil." As noted earlier, the only health issue that could be related is the male victim's nut allergy. Still waiting for toxicology reports to come in. That could answer a lot of questions.

Also . . . two anonymous calls were placed to CPS. The caseworker assigned on the 23rd couldn't interview the girls before school let out for the break, but she managed to get two phone interviews in: the first with the younger daughter's fifth-grade teacher, Mrs. Beatrice Stevenson, who said she saw absolutely no signs of abuse in the child, behavioral or physical. Mrs. Stevenson reported that the mother was a regular fixture at the school, the PTA president, and very involved in her children's lives. The father donated very generously to the school fund-raisers, and was often seen at the children's concerts and performances. The second call was with the older daughter's World Literature teacher, Mr. George Roussos, who said Hadley was a model student. The caseworker was going to visit the girls at school after the break just as a formality. She says the calls had all the red flags of being a prank.

Working with law enforcement at this stage to review home security footage.

then

"Hadley, wake up!"

I open my eyes groggily and glimpse the gray sky outside before I turn toward my open bedroom door. Lila stands there in her red flannel pajamas, the ones with sock monkeys printed all over them.

"It's Christmas!" She holds up her analog clock to show me the evidence: seven o'clock.

My head sinks back into my pillow. "Okay, give me a second."

She tugs my arm. "Pleaaase? You said seven!"

I pull my legs out from under the cozy duvet. "Okay, okay. I'm up."

We walk downstairs quietly. Mom and Dad made a rule a few years ago that we could each open one present without them. That way they could sleep a little while longer.

I pad into the kitchen first. "Want some hot cocoa?" I ask her.

"Sure," she says unconvincingly; her eyes are locked on the

Christmas tree in the den, stacked with presents underneath. I notice the long, slim presents leaning vertically against the wall. Someone got skis, I guess.

I prepare the mugs, boiling the water in a kettle the way Grandma taught us, even if it's not tea. We walk back to the den.

"One each," I say. "Pick whichever one you want."

She moves presents around until she finds the one I wrapped.

"This one," she says holding it up.

"You sure? That one's from me."

She nods. "I know." My heart pinches a little, in a good way.

"Okay, then you have to give me the one from you too," I say, putting my mug down on a coaster.

Grinning, she hands me a light rectangular present. "Open yours first," she says. I notice a new crater in her mouth.

I tuck my finger under the wrapping. "Did the tooth fairy and Santa bump into each other in the night?"

"Will you stop with that?" She rolls her eyes. "Just open it," she adds, echoing the same words Charlie said to me last night. I touch the spot where the claddagh necklace should rest on my chest, but I don't dare wear it in front of my parents. It's back in its box in my closet behind a stack of sweaters.

Under the wrapping paper is a frame with the word "SISTERS" etched into the wood on top, then "BEST FRIENDS" at the bottom. There's a picture of the two of us taken over the summer. The sun was just setting, the light picking up all of the rosy hues in her cheeks, making her blue eyes even bluer, her blond hair blonder, and highlighting the red in my brown hair. We hardly look like sisters at all, but my arms are wrapped around her shoulders from behind, claiming her as mine.

"I love this picture of us." My finger traces over the etched words. "This is really special, Lila. Thank you." I reach over and hug her.

"Gross. Don't get all premenstrual on me," she says. I squeeze her harder and cover her cheeks in kisses to annoy her.

She opens her box next, and once again I was completely predictable in the present department. She pulls out the leggings and sweater outfit from Tillys and squeals. "Thank you! I was afraid you wouldn't figure it out!"

"You left the catalog on my bed with the outfit circled in grape-scented marker. There was no missing it!" I laugh. "Still . . . I got the better present. I'm sorry yours wasn't as special."

She shrugs and avoids eye contact. "I don't care about a present. You're a pretty cool sister, every day of the year."

Footsteps creak along the floorboards upstairs—they're up and coming downstairs.

"I'm glad we had our Christmas together first." I lift my mug. "Cheers."

"Cheers," she says, and takes a sip.

They both come down in their bathrobes, looking unusually disheveled and happy. Even Dad.

Mom picks up the frame Lila got me and coos. Dad looks at it and nods, a half smile on his face. He goes into the kitchen to make his coffee, grinding his beans first. *Whirr, whirr.* We have to wait for him to finish before we can continue with Christmas. Slurping his enormous mug, he picks up a small box from under the tree and tosses it in Mom's lap. She smiles, almost knowingly.

"What did you do . . . oh, Miles!" She grins, taking the emerald ring out and putting it on her finger. She shows it around the room. "It's *beautiful*! Thank you!" She stands up and gives him a big kiss on the lips. Lila gags. He goes back to drinking his coffee.

Lila searches under the tree for her presents to them. I know she did all of her shopping at the Holiday Boutique at school that the PTA runs every year.

Mom opens up her box and finds a hideous paisley nylon scarf that she'll never wear. "Ooh. So pretty! Um . . . Who helped you pick this out, Lila?"

"Mrs. Hawthorne," Lila says. Mom turns away from Lila just as her smile slips into something closer to a grimace. I bite my lip so I don't laugh out loud.

Then Lila hands Dad his gift. He opens it up and pulls out a coffee mug. I almost choke.

"*Number One Dad*," he reads, and gives her a limp smile. I watch Lila's blank expression, realizing for the first time: she's an even better liar than I am.

"'Cause you like coffee." She shrugs and sits back down.

I give them their presents next. Gift cards, because there's nothing they need that they haven't already bought for themselves.

Mom coos again. "Oh, Lord & Taylor! Thank you, Hadley!"

Dad turns his around between his fingers, looking confused. "The Art of Shaving? Okay," he says, and throws it on the coffee table. "Thanks," he adds flatly.

I'm tempted to mimic Lila and say, "Because you like to shave," but those are fighting words. What was I supposed to get him? A pair of cleats and boxing gloves?

He gets up next and pulls the long vertical presents from against the wall. There are two of them. He hands one to me and one to Lila.

"So," he says, grinning. "If you haven't figured out what these are yet, then you're *both* idiots." He laughs. "We're going to Vermont for the week. Leaving today."

So that was the surprise that made Grandma get uninvited to Christmas. He couldn't wait to leave until tomorrow?

He looks at me, one expectant eyebrow raised, and I know what I have to do if I'm going to survive the next week trapped with him on a mountain.

"That's fantastic, Dad. Thanks *so* much!"

It is so far removed from being fantastic that it takes everything not to cry in front of him. Dad skiing is an even bigger asshole than Dad in the gym. He pushes us to go down the steepest slopes. The more scared we are, the more he wants us to confront our fears. Lila peed herself when she was eight, in her snow pants, because he told her she was going down a black diamond trail with him. It got her out of going, but still.

Upstairs packing, I send a quick text to Charlie:

Dad's Christmas present to us is skiing in Vermont. We're leaving today for a week.

Oh.

It takes him a few minutes to respond in more detail.

I'm worried about you being up there with him.

They haven't said anything about the interview.
If you find out anything, can you text me?

Absolutely.

I'm about to text Meaghan and Noah too, letting them know I'll be gone for the week, when Dad opens my door.

"Bragging to your friends?" he asks, slurping on his coffee.

"Yeah."

He nods and sticks his palm out.

"Hand over the phone, Hadley."

"What?" I ask, quickly deleting my thread to Charlie.

"Hand it over." *Slurp.*

"But—"

"Don't make me say it a third time," he says quietly.

I hand it to him.

"Sixteen sixty?" he asks.

Sixteen sixty is an important date in ice cream's history: it was the first year it was made available to the public. It is also my passcode. My parents insisted on knowing it, in case they wanted to check up on me, which is why I delete all my threads. Now I wish I had changed it. It could have bought me a little time so my father wouldn't have immediate access to my texts.

"Good." He puts it in his bathrobe pocket. "You kids spend too much time on these things. This is a family vacation. Just us. No distractions."

His clenched jaw warns me to leave it at that.

Email. I'll email Charlie as soon as he leaves the room, warn him not to text me. But my dad reads my mind.

"And the laptop," he says, jutting his hand out again. "You won't need that while we're away."

"I have a project due in English when I get back."

"You're off for two weeks. You can do it when you get back. It'll give you something *productive* to do."

He walks with me to my desk, where I unplug my laptop. While he's there, he picks up the brochures to Hofstra and Stony Brook. He doesn't say a word. He just rattles them in the air between us.

Maybe there's some Christmas magic I can draw on today. Maybe the universe owes me a holiday miracle. No matter how horrible our house can be, Christmas has always been a day of peace. Like it was written in the Geneva convention.

"Dad?" I get up my nerve. He turns to me. "I've been thinking . . . I'd really like to go to school locally. I . . . uh . . . applied to Hofstra and Stony Brook."

"Why?" he snaps, then he glares at me knowingly. "Is this because of the boyfriend?"

"No!" I rush to defuse the moment. "No . . . I just don't think I'm ready to go away to college yet. It's . . . scary."

He snorts, a derisive laugh at my expense. "Hadley, you have to grow up sometime."

"But do you think . . . maybe even just for the first year?" I negotiate, trying to find an opening.

He squeezes his eyes shut and pinches his nose with his fingers, trying hard to not lose it completely. "No."

"But why?" I push my luck.

"Why? Because I'm not paying for you to take Intro to Basket Weaving at some goof-off college."

"But they're still good schools."

His anger crackles like a live wire. "Cornell . . . Harvard . . . Yale . . . Brown." He ticks off on his fingers. "*Those* were the schools we discussed, Hadley."

"But what if I don't get in?"

His cold stare tells me everything I need to know.

He tosses the brochures in my trash bin then takes my laptop off my desk. "Hurry up and pack. We're leaving in an hour."

With that, he turns his back, dismissing me. Maybe my Christmas miracle was that this conversation didn't turn into something much uglier.

True to his promise, an hour later we're in the car heading to McKinley Airport. Twenty minutes later, Dad takes off, flying us north to Vermont.

Lila looks out the window as we pass over the fawn-colored, barren grounds of Westchester. The snow is still miles away. I stare out my window, hoping Dad left my phone at home and won't be checking my messages. Because if he finds out Charlie was the one who called CPS and I knew about it . . .

An anxious fist clenches in my stomach.

"How are flying lessons going?" Dad yells back at me over the roar of the plane.

My head snaps up. "Okay."

I stare at the back of his thick dark hair as he pilots.

"I spoke to Phil the other day," he begins. I know where this is going.

Dad turns his head so I can see his profile, his crooked nose, broken during a fight in college.

"So?"

"I haven't been able to get there."

"Don't think I don't know why."

The roaring engine fills the dead air. He may think this is all about Charlie, but it's not. I hate flying. A boulder sits in my belly all day when I have a lesson. In the cockpit, my heart throbs in my throat, in my ears, behind my eyes, drowning out Phil's instructions. My hands tremble for hours after we're done.

"You're close to getting your license. I want you to go back, right after break," he throws over his shoulder.

I open my mouth to say something that will placate him, but Lila speaks up first.

"It's not like she *needs* to have a pilot's license," she sasses. I want to kick her.

"Hey!" he shouts back. "Was I talking to you? No. So mind your own business!"

I catch Lila's eye and warn her with a subtle shake of my head. *Quit it.* There's only so much I can do to save her if she isn't willing to try and save herself.

then

"I'm just going to have a drink."

Mom walks toward the lodge, looking like a snow bunny, with her blond hair, pink lipstick, and tight ski clothes. We don't go skiing often, but when we do, she never hits the runs with us.

"Okay. Let's go," Dad says, leading the way to the ski lift.

Dad gets on a chair with Lila, and I wait for the next one. When I get to the top of the mountain, there's no sign of them. I look down the run and spot Lila's hot-pink jacket, speeding down the hill behind Dad. I shoot down the slope, pushing through the pain in my hip to keep an eye on Lila.

The rest of the day is more of the same. Dad makes a point of leaving me behind. He thinks he's punishing me. He's not. But I know Lila is getting the brunt of it, so I try to keep up. I finally meet them much later by the ski lift.

"But I'm *tired*," Lila whines, and slouches.

"I'm not paying all this money for you to sit around drinking hot cocoa. There's still plenty of day left. I don't want to waste it."

As I approach, Lila's eyes plead for help.

"What if we did an easier trail?" I ask.

Dad adjusts his straps and scoffs. "Easier? No way. By the end of this trip we're going down the Black Hole."

My mouth drops open. "Dad, that's way too advanced for Lila. For *any* of us."

"She can do it," Dad says dismissively. "Come on." He leads the way back to the ski lift, and I nudge Lila.

"Just follow him. I'm right here."

"Hadley . . ."

"We'll figure something out. Don't worry."

Today, we let him win. But there's no way in hell he is taking her down the Black Hole.

The house Dad rented has five bedrooms, but Lila and I take a bedroom with two twin beds so we can share. Dad wakes us up early the next day.

"Let's hit the slopes before the crowds get there," he says in our doorway. Lila and I stare at each other, telegraphing messages with our eyes on how to survive the minute, the day, the week.

We get up and get dressed. Lila winces with each step.

"Sore?" She nods. I pour her a dose of Children's Advil. "Don't let him see that you hurt. It just makes him want to toughen you up more."

She downs her shot of Advil as Dad hollers from downstairs, "HURRY UP!"

Christmas is over. The battle resumes.

I struggle to keep up with Dad and Lila all day. And then a miracle happens: a storm blows in with winds so fierce they shut down the ski lifts.

Dad argues with the ski lift operator.

"This is a ski resort. You *ski* in the *snow*!"

"Winds are too strong, man. Gotta shut it down," he tells Dad.

Even Dad can't win a fight with the elements, so we collect Mom from the lodge and the four of us head back to the house. The storm is a double-edged sword. It prevents Dad from forcing Lila to ski the Black Hole, but it also coops us up in the house together.

Lila tries to turn the TV on, but he shuts it off.

"You kids are addicted to electronics," he says, checking his phone for the umpteenth time.

Lila can't help herself. "But *you're* on the phone!"

He shoots her a laser-beam stare that should vaporize her on the spot, but it doesn't. "I have to check in for work. Not play Angry Birds all day or whatever you kids do."

Lila is as easy to read as a picture book. She opens her mouth to make a crack about Angry Birds, but I give her one of my imperceptible shakes of the head to tell her no. She bites her tongue.

On a shelf by the fireplace is a stack of well-worn board games, the kind that families who get along play together. Mom, sipping her wine, decides we are one of those families.

"I have an idea. Let's play Monopoly!"

Mistake.

Dad sets up the board on the coffee table, appointing himself as banker. It doesn't take long for Dad to annihilate Lila, rubbing it in her face till her eyes well up.

"Oh, c'mon. Don't be such a baby," he teases. She gets up and walks away. "Where are you going?" he asks her, annoyed.

"To go do something else." She pouts.

He points his finger back to the couch. "Nuh-uh. Sit your ass back down. Maybe you'll learn something."

Mom chimes in, "Your father doesn't mess around when it comes to winning *or* money." Her lips quirk, barely suppressing a satisfied smile.

Dad looks up from counting his towering piles of pastel-colored cash. "I don't hear you complaining about the money part while you're busy spending all of it."

Lila flops down on the cushion next to me with a mopey face on, a face he has little tolerance for. Dad stares up at her from time to time, getting increasingly pissed off. To distract him, I purchase every property I land on so I'll be the next one to go bankrupt. Unfortunately, so does Mom.

Outside, the wind howls and the snow blows in every direction so you can't tell if it's falling from the sky or shooting up from the ground. It's like being trapped inside a snow globe. Mom loses next, despite my best efforts to be the next one out.

She stands up with her glass for a refill. "Where should we go for dinner?" she asks, walking away.

Dad's head snaps up. I guess I should thank her for being a drunk ditz; it siphons his attention away from us so fast you can practically hear the loud sucking sound following her out of the room.

"Go?" He looks out the window and back at her incredulously. "We're not *going* anywhere. We picked up groceries. Scramble some eggs or something."

She grabs the wine from the dining table. "I thought I got to be on vacation too." Taking the bottle with her, she storms off to the kitchen, opening and slamming cabinets.

Dad stands up and goes after her. "Which part of the vacation wasn't to your liking so far, *Princess*?" he snarls. "The sitting around in the bar all day? Or the sitting around in the bar all day?"

She walks back out into the main room, holding her now-full goblet. She lowers her voice. "Don't talk to me that way in front of the girls."

"They know! The whole fucking town knows, thanks to your little hit-and-run! Goddamn, Courtney, do you know how much money it cost to get us out of that mess?"

Lila and I sit wide-eyed and frozen on the couch, afraid to move in case we draw attention to ourselves.

Dad storms around, waving his arms like a baboon. "Now I've got CPS breathing down my neck because of you!" He walks over to the dining table, which is being used to hold all their vacation booze, and pours a glass of scotch.

Mom follows him, one hand on her hip. "What makes you think it's because of *me*, asshole?"

That's our cue. "Go!" I grab Lila's arm and run upstairs to our bedroom, shutting the door behind us. We sit on our beds, listening to them scream at each other. They brought the storm inside after all.

Lila stares off into space, her eyes huge, her lips slightly parted.

"Did you bring your iPod?" I ask. She nods. Of course. Dad was only concerned about *my* use of electronics. "Why don't you listen to that instead."

She turns to me. "Hadley? What's CPS?"

Do I tell her? Or do I keep her in the dark a little longer? She's so young, like a peach that needs a little more time on the limb to ripen.

"I think they got into some trouble with that accident Mom got into," I offer.

She accepts my version of the truth and puts her earbuds in. Leaning back into her pillow, she closes her eyes, escaping into her music.

I try to tune in to their fight, in case CPS comes up again. It doesn't. Their argument has moved on to his girlfriend at work, how the whole town knows about *that*. . . .

But it's always the same. In the morning, it'll be like nothing ever happened. He'll shower her with kisses and gifts. They'll get really lovey-dovey for a day, sometimes only a few hours. But it will reenergize my mom. Make her feel like this whole shit show is worth it.

Outside, the storm still rages. I hope it ends soon. I need my parents to leave the house for five minutes so I can search through their room for my phone. The battery would have died by now, but Dad has an iPhone too. If he went to the trouble of bringing my phone and he really wanted to snoop, he could always use his charger on my phone.

If Charlie texts me about CPS, I'm as good as dead.

now

There's individual therapy each day with Dr. Bruce. Group therapy with Linda. And then there's art therapy with Miss Lucy in the cafeteria.

Today Miss Lucy hands us lumps of Play-Doh and tells us to "sculpt our feelings." For a place that's supposed to be working at lifting us up, this clay project is the most demoralizing forced group activity yet.

Sculpting with one arm is impossible. Rowan glances across the table from me as I jam my thumb into my clay as if I'm gouging out someone's eye. She reaches across and grabs my mound of clay, then Melissa's, and molds them together, quickly shaping an enormous rainbow-hued, mushroom-tipped penis.

She holds it up over her head proudly.

"Hey, Miss Lucy!" she calls across the room. "I sculpted my feelings! I'm horny!"

The group erupts in laughter, including me. Everyone stares, not at Rowan's sculpture, but at *me*. It's weird. *I'm* not the one who made a Play-Doh dildo!

After class, Miss Lucy calls over to me. "Hadley? Can you stay a minute?"

Rowan elbows me in the ribs. With her best attempt at a Freudian accent, she whispers in my ear, all hot air and spittle, "Zo, tell me, Hadley, how does zis peniz make you feel?" I laugh again and cover my mouth.

Everyone leaves as Miss Lucy collects the clay off the table. She smiles up at me.

"Looks like you and Rowan are getting along nicely."

"Yeah, I guess."

"It's nice to hear you laughing," Miss Lucy says.

"Thanks."

"It's big, don't you think?" she asks me, her eyes glued to mine, while her hands absently knead Rowan's Play-Doh penis. I hold my breath so I don't burst out laughing.

According to Rowan, the kids that get out of here are the ones who play the game. Donnie still refuses to admit she's trying to kill herself by not eating, so she's not going anywhere anytime soon. Franklin will go home any day now because he's finally working through his problems.

It's up to me whether I get discharged sooner rather than later. I'm like Dorothy from *The Wizard of Oz*. I've always had the power to go back to Kansas. I just need to do what I've done all my life: fake it.

I help her scoop up clay off the table. "Huge!" I say, with too much enthusiasm, I can tell, by the way the happy glint in her eyes dims just a bit.

I hand her a mound of clay, and she shoves it in a large plastic bag. "Well, one day at a time," she says, trying to stay positive.

I walk down the hallway, kicking myself. I can't raise my hand three times to get out of this. I can't hide all the broken pieces inside me behind a smile. I can't make myself invisible so they'll leave me alone.

Back in our room, Rowan is standing by my bed holding a stack of envelopes to her nose.

I look quickly at my pillow, the one area of real estate in this room that was private, which Rowan has now invaded. My feet fly across the room, grabbing her wrist with my unbroken arm.

"Those are mine!" I scream.

"Here!" She breaks her hand free and throws the envelopes up in the air. They flutter over us like ticker tape.

I crouch down, picking them up off the floor with one hand.

"Jesus!" Rowan's fists curl up by her sides. "What the hell is your problem?"

I drop the envelopes on my bed and shove her. "*You're* my problem!"

Rowan shoves me back, hard. My legs bump against my wooden box spring. She lifts a warning finger. "Don't *ever* touch me again." Her eyes are wild. I didn't just push her; I pushed her into her dark place.

"Girls?" Janet is by the door, watching us carefully. There's an orderly behind her, just waiting for his order to drag one of us out of here. "What's going on?"

My knees go weak with panic. How much did she see? By the way they're both eyeing Rowan, my guess is they only caught the tail end. I instigated this fight, but now they're about to haul Rowan out of here. Just the other day, Quentin was dragged out of the rec room for going apeshit over the remote control. We haven't seen him since.

Rowan's cheeks go slack and chalky. I caused this. I need to fix it.

"It was me." I turn to Janet. "We were just goofing around. I shoved her, she shoved me. But like a joke. Not, like, you know . . . *Grrrrr.*"

I crook my good elbow out and make a Hulk angry face, which makes Rowan laugh hard. The timing of her laugh is perfect. It defuses the moment. I laugh too, making it look like they caught both of us in a laid-back, "having a grand ol' time in the psych wing" moment.

Janet exhales heavily, a glimmer of uncertainty in her eyes. "Well . . . you both know there's no physical contact here, ladies. Joking or otherwise," Janet says, trying to read us.

I nod. "It won't happen again."

Janet and the orderly leave. I bend over to pick up the last of the envelopes. When I stand up, Rowan holds my pillowcase open so I can put them back and then throws my pillow back at the top of my bed.

Rowan sits down on her bed. "Sorry. I shouldn't have snooped. But shoving me was a dick move."

I fall back onto my mattress, folding my arm behind my head, closing my eyes. "I'm sorry too."

I've sat through enough group therapy to know that Rowan's been on the receiving end of shoves and worse for a while. Cutting is the only thing that makes her feel she is in control of her own life.

"Hey. Hadley?" When I open my eyes, Rowan is leaning forward. "When you first got here . . ." She gnaws a hangnail. "I didn't mean to give you an instructional on how to *do* it, you know? Like, I would be kind of bummed if you got out of here and you know . . ."

I close my eyes again. "I know."

"So, like, don't. Okay?"

She's quiet for a while. When I open my eyes again, she's staring at me with a worried expression.

"I won't," I say, to take the guilt off her.

Her eyes narrow, searching. I don't think she believes me either.

I used to be much better at this.

then

The storm blows out overnight.

"Come on, get up!" Dad throws our bedroom door open, bringing a blast of cold air in with him. Shadows slice against the ceiling as the sun snakes through the cracks of our vertical blinds. "I'm not going to lose another second of this vacation."

We eat boiled eggs and orange slices out of our hands on the car ride to the slopes. Mom sulks in the front seat. After we park, we take our skis off the roof rack and snap them onto our boots, even Mom. Dad turns to me.

"Take your mother down some of the bunny trails today."

"Huh?" I glance over at Mom, who is doing a bang-up job of avoiding eye contact with me.

"Lila and I are going to do a black diamond." He pulls his ski goggles down and adjusts his wrist straps.

With my goggles still on top of my head, the all-consuming whiteness of the snow smothers me, deafens me, shutting down all my senses.

Lila inches closer to my side. "Dad, can't I go with Hadley?"

"Don't be a baby," he says. "Let's go."

"Miles," Mom calls after him. He turns around impatiently. "Please don't take any risks."

He lifts his hand in the air, whether in agreement or dismissively, it's hard to tell. He takes off, and Lila follows, with one last mournful look over her shoulder.

Maybe that's when it really hits me. All these stupid plans to stay closer to home won't help Lila. I can't save her from her own father.

Mom adjusts her wrist straps. "Come on," she says, surly and childish.

My mind is on Lila all morning, as if thinking of her will somehow protect her on the trail. Mom and I amble down the bunny trails, behind wobbly preschoolers just learning how to balance and bend their knees. Mom doesn't do much better. After a few hours, I catch up to her sitting on her butt in the snow, not even trying to get up. I reach my hand out to help her up. When she wraps her fingers around my hand, I get a flash of that movie *Freaky Friday*, where the mom and daughter switch places. I hoist her up.

I'm itching for a fight, but the words I want to say are too dark and too horrible, so I sucker punch her.

"You really suck at this," I say with so much bitterness I'm surprised bile doesn't spew out of my mouth.

She dusts herself off. "I don't like the snow," she mutters.

"So why are we here?" I bait her.

She sighs, her shoulders slipping with the weight of everything that sucks in our world. "To try and keep the peace."

Her answer surprises me, but it doesn't change anything. "You're doing a shitty job of it then," I say, sailing off on my skis to the bottom of the hill. She follows.

"Hadley." She calls out because she can't keep up with me.

I stop and turn around.

"Let's go inside for a bit and warm up," she says. I eye the midday sun. Guess it's not too early for her to start drinking.

As if she reads my mind, she adds, "For hot cocoa and lunch."

"Fine."

We're seated by the oversize river-rock fireplace; the fire pops and crackles behind me, warm and earthy. We sip our hot cocoa first, then look at the menu. Dad's not here, so I steal a roll from the basket. Mom glances over the menu at the basket, at me, then takes a roll. She smiles at me conspiratorially; it just fans the fire in my belly. An illicit buttered roll is not enough to erase the years of damage she's ignored. It's like putting sunscreen on after the melanoma has spread to your brain.

She studies her menu. "What are you thinking of getting?"

"Pasta," I say, refusing to look at her.

She shrugs. "Get whatever you want. I'm going to get the burger."

I roll my eyes. Oh, big deal, Dad's not here so Mom's pigging out.

The waiter comes, and we place our order. Mom chews my ear off about the PTA. While she talks, I stare past her out the window at the white rivers of snow snaking down the mountain. I try to picture which trail Lila is navigating now, or imagine how she's managing with Dad. When our meals arrive, I plow through my own mountain of pasta.

Mom takes big bites of her burger. "Oh, this is so good," she moans, closing her eyes in rapture. It's going to be hard to go back to steamed vegetables when we get home.

She looks at my plate. "How's your lunch?" She takes a sip of water.

"Amazing." I shovel another huge forkful in my mouth.

"I can't eat pasta," she says. "I mean, I *can*, it just brings back bad memories."

I look up from my plate and frown. "How does *pasta* bring back bad memories?"

She takes another sip of her water and then lifts her burger carefully so it doesn't spit out all of the condiments from the sides.

"When Grandpa went through that bad time with his business, we ate a lot of pasta." She takes an enormous bite of her burger, then carefully pushes the lettuce hanging off her lips into her mouth.

I wipe the excess sauce off my mouth with a napkin. "I don't know this story. What are you talking about?"

I knew Grandpa was an electrician, and I knew times were tough. But according to Grandma, they were happy.

She swallows. "I never told you? Oh . . . well, one of the houses

Grandpa worked on caught on fire. You know how people talk. They all thought it had to be because he had done something wrong, even after they investigated it and found it was a curling iron left on in a bedroom. But when you have your own business, you're only as good as your reputation. People stopped hiring him."

She picks up a fry and nibbles on it thoughtfully. "Money was tight. I'd lie in bed and listen to my parents talking in the kitchen. Grandma was afraid they would lose the house. She took up sewing for a dry cleaner. It was a lot of work for very little money, but that's all she knew how to do. She even made me clothes out of leftover upholstery fabric." She wrinkles her nose in distaste. "The house felt dark during those days. I started getting nervous stomachaches all the time, like I worried *with* them, even though I was just a child."

"How old were you?"

"Seven, eight." She gazes off into space. "Things got better, but we never had anything extra." She scrunches up her nose. "Pasta was the cheapest thing we could eat to fill our stomachs. And now, whenever I see pasta, it makes my stomach knot."

Stuffed, I push my plate away and finish my water.

"There are worse things," I say, and she looks up over her burger at me. Her eyes harden. If she thought she was going to butter me up like a dinner roll, she was wrong.

"You know what your problem is? You're spoiled," she shoots back at me. She picks up her water glass, and I can tell by the look of disgust on her face she wishes it had some kind of alcohol in it instead.

"Spoiled? Where'd you get *that* from?" I snap.

She lowers her glass. "You've never wanted for anything. You don't know what it's like to be hungry, or to want things."

I stare back at her, my mouth hanging open in outrage. I've never *wanted* for anything? How about wanting a father who didn't scare the *shit* out of me?

"Your father is a good provider." She nods like that's the end of that conversation and takes another bite, but not with the same rapturous appetite as a minute ago.

I look out the window again and shake my head. "You keep telling yourself that."

She's signing the check when I hear the announcement.

"Courtney McCauley, please go to the medical clinic."

"Mom." I stand up abruptly. "Come on!" I take the lead, rushing out of the restaurant.

"Where's the medical clinic?" I ask the first red jacket ski patrol I can find.

"It's the big yellow building at the base, by the access road underpass," he says.

Please be Dad. Please don't be Lila, I pray as we make our way past the hordes of skiers coming off the mountain for a break in the day or just heading to the slopes. When we find the yellow building, we run through the doors.

"We just heard an announcement for Courtney McCauley," I tell a ski patrol who's just leaving the building.

He holds his hands up in the air to manage my visible terror. "She's okay."

"*She?*" I cry. "It's Lila?"

He nods and looks at my mother. "She broke her arm, but she's fine."

"Where is she?" Mom demands, putting on her holier-than-thou voice. He points to a room behind him. Through the glass pane, I see a doctor talking to my father while Lila lies on a medical cot.

"Lila!" I shove through the door ahead of my mother.

Explosive wailing erupts as soon as we walk in. I know that cry; she was holding it inside for my father and now it bursts out of her in a rush.

"What happened?" my mother asks. The doctor looks up at my mother with a bored expression. He sees this all the time, he thinks. But he doesn't. He has no idea.

Lila's flushed face convulses; she's too worked up to get a word out. Moaning and crying, she reaches her good hand out to me.

Dad laughs. "This is nuts. She was rock solid until *you* walked in." He points to me but says it to the doctor, who shares a laugh with him.

"Why don't you go wait outside," Dad says to me. "I think you're making it worse," he adds. Lila's moan turns frantic.

"Noooo! Had-ley," she cries in between hiccups.

"Do what your father says," Mom says, pushing me gently, which just makes Lila's moans turn into wails then screams.

The doctor has to know these aren't normal cries. He has to know there's more to it.

"Tell the doctor how you broke your arm, Lila!" I yell over my shoulder as Mom's hand on my lower back changes from gently escorting to a not-so-gentle shove.

Dad turns to the doctor. "Can you give her something for the pain? Something to quiet her?" Mom shuts the door in my face.

Outside again, I listen as Lila's cries warble down to a low moan.

Our plane ride home that afternoon is quiet. Lila's still doped up on something, so she's sleeping, her broken arm cradled against her chest in a cast and sling. Mom stares out the window. Dad bristles with anger.

It was his decision to abort the rest of our vacation.

"What's the point?" he said, packing up the rental car. "You all haven't stopped bitching since we got here."

Lila rested on the couch while we packed up around her, her eyes fluttering open and closed. Every time he looked at her, he couldn't hide his resentment. But even he knew better than to blame her. So he lumped all of us together.

I'm just glad we're leaving. The worst already happened: Lila got hurt, because of him. Her arm again. It's a repeat of the morning he dislocated her shoulder three years ago.

The late afternoon sun shimmers on the plane's wings; the blue Long Island Sound is to our left as we fly east across the island. Dad's anger has been vibrating off him in waves all day, increasing as we inch closer to home.

He turns sideways, so I see his profile glaring at Lila sleeping in her seat. His lips tug down in disgust as dark thoughts rush through his head. I know. I've been on the receiving end of that look too many times.

With an annoyed exhale through his nostrils, he reaches over and jerks the throttle back to idle. The plane drops, nosing down toward the Long Island Sound. Dad's no longer trying to get us home safely and quickly. He's trying to scare the shit out of us as payback.

"Dad!" I shout. Lila's eyes flutter open. She looks at me, struggling to focus, to push through her groggy fog. Then she looks out the window, at the pitch of the plane, and screams.

Dad turns and looks at Lila and *smiles*! To him, the screams of terror coming from Mom and Lila as we nosedive is worth putting all our lives in danger.

Until the engine gurgles and sputters. And then there's nothing but terrifying silence.

"Shit!" Dad shouts.

Outside the cockpit window, the propeller twirls like a pinwheel, no longer guided by horsepower but by the air rushing through the blades as we fall. Without the roar of the engine, Mom and Lila's shrieks pierce holes in the dense silence. Mom clutches her harness as the nose of the plane dips, rushing us to our watery grave. Dad reaches over and restarts the engine.

The reassuring rumble of the engine roaring back to life floods the cockpit. Dad levels the plane and continues on his way as if nothing happened. But as the only two people here who have actually flown a plane, we both know how close he came to getting us killed.

"There's an old saying, Hadley," Phil told me early on in my lessons, walking me around the plane and pointing out the important parts. "'The propeller is a big fan made to keep the pilot cool. If it stops, the first thing you'll see is the pilot break out into a sweat.'"

Hands on hips, he laughed. When I didn't get it, he explained. "It's a joke, see, 'cause if that thing goes, it's all over." He pointed to the propeller. "You can kiss your ass good-bye!"

Now that Dad has regained control of the plane, Mom turns to him, her face white, her lips firm. "Quit it, Miles. I mean it."

"Ooh." He laughs. "You mean it. That's funny."

Lila jostled her broken arm in her panic. Her shrieks of fear have turned into whimpers of pain as Dad prepares for landing.

Trees and homes blur by our window as the plane lowers. I focus on the horizon as he levels the plane with the runway. After two decades of flying, he knows all the tricks, even how to make the landing as bumpy as possible on purpose. Lila cries out with each skip and bounce of the tires along the tarmac.

Once we come to a full stop, Mom and I guide Lila out of the plane to make sure she doesn't fall. Dad disembarks with a lazy, satisfied grin on his face. He found a way to get back at us for ruining his vacation. And now, finally, he's happy.

While Lila cries and Mom digs in her purse for the painkillers the resort medic gave us, Phil races out of the terminal to meet us, trying, but not succeeding, to mask the alarm on his face.

"That was quite a landing. Everything okay, Miles?" he asks, walking the rest of the way. He glances at me, at Mom's white face, at Lila crying.

Dad pumps Phil's hand in a hearty handshake. "Everything's fine, Phil."

Phil takes his aviators off, looking to me for the truth, I guess. "For a second, I thought you guys might be in trouble up there."

Before I can say anything, Dad cuts me off. "I was practicing stalls with Hadley." Then he thumbs over at Lila and Mom. "They don't have a stomach for flying."

I don't think Phil's buying Dad's bullshit. But Dad pays for my flying lessons, so Phil nods gamely.

Phil turns to me with a grin and grabs my shoulders, rattling me so my teeth clatter together. "Hadley, when are you coming back? We're so close to getting you your license!"

The smell of jet fuel and fumes and Phil shaking me adds to my already churning stomach. I'm afraid I might throw up right here in front of everyone. Pasta was a mistake after all. I swallow, forcing my lunch back down. Dad steps forward, the ambassador to all things Hadley.

"Oh, she'll be back. Next week. Let me know what days you're free."

Dad then wraps an arm around Mom's shoulder. "Bring the car around. I'll start unloading." He slips the car keys in her palm then leans forward and kisses her on the lips. A flash of his tongue darts in her mouth before I walk over to a nearby trash can and throw up.

then

Back in my room, I unpack my clothes, sorting out the dirty laundry. My father walks by and stands in the doorway. He reaches in his back pocket for something, then throws it on my bed.

My iPhone sinks into the lofty depths of my frilly white duvet. "I'll need my laptop to do that English paper," I remind him casually.

"It's on my dresser. Get it yourself," he says, walking away. I wait until I hear him clomp down every step before I rush to my phone.

The battery is dead, which hopefully means he left it here while we were away. Grabbing my charger from my desk, I plug it in. While I wait for it to chirp back to life, the garage door rumbles open. I watch out my window as Dad's car pulls out of the driveway and down the road. Mom walks by my bedroom door heading to her room with a pained look on her face that's become all too familiar. She shuts her door quietly behind her. I suspect I won't be seeing either of them for the rest of the night.

When my phone has enough juice to turn back on, I read through my texts, almost all of them from Charlie. Thankfully, he doesn't say anything about CPS. The first one is just "Call me." His messages from there on are panicked *where are you*s, one after the other. They come first every few minutes, then hourly, then daily. These past few days must have been horrible for him. I stop reading and call him back.

"Hadley!" He picks up on the first ring and says my name like I'm a hostage just released from her captives, which I kind of am. Just hearing his voice makes me fall apart crying.

"Where are you? I'll come get you."

I sniff. "I'm okay. I'm home."

He sighs in relief.

"Come over, if you can. If you can't . . . find a way."

I nod, and I gulp. "I'm on my way."

I stop by Lila's bedroom. She's passed out on her bed, doped up on pain meds, feet flopping apart at the heel into a ballet first position. The broken arm rests on her tummy, her other arm holds it protectively. Her rosebud lips are parted, breathing softly.

His deconstruction of her has begun. I can see it in the way she sleeps: vertically, instead of horizontally across her bed. The way her arms clutch inward instead of wide open, embracing and challenging the world all at once. Once she didn't have a care in the world. That's lost now.

Long Island caught some of the storm too. The sidewalks outside of shops are shoveled clean, piled into dingy mountains off to the sides, but there's the occasional no-man's-land that is a sheet of ice, flattened to a fine sheen by the steps of hundreds of shoppers. I skid across one in my hurry to get to Charlie's apartment, nearly landing on my butt.

He answers the door seconds after I ring the bell. Before I have time to absorb how much I missed his face, I throw myself in his arms. We trip upstairs, groping and kissing. He frees a hand to open the door. I pull him roughly inside the apartment with me, slipping out of my jacket and letting it fall to the floor. Next I tug at his shirt.

"Hadley, wait."

He kicks his apartment door shut then leans over to lock it. The air is cold between us, even in those few seconds. I reel him back by his shirt, then lift it by the hem, trying to undress him. His hands are on mine, stopping me. I throw my arms around his neck to hold him still; he's squirming away like a puppy I'm hugging too tightly. As he unknots my arms from behind his neck, it reminds me of how he did the same thing to Claudia that night at the party where he kissed me. Rejection burns inside of me, but it just makes me more determined.

"Wait," he whispers against my lips.

"No," I growl, tearing at my clothes instead. My hands are shimmying the bottom of my sweater up when he grabs them again. Then he wraps his arms around me in a hug that's as romantic as a straitjacket.

"Hadley, slow down."

"Why?" My cheeks flame, angry and hurt.

His answer is a kiss to my forehead, like he's checking for a fever. He leads me to the couch and sits down, his arms still around me.

"Talk to me." He takes my hands. "What happened?"

I shake my head and pull my hands away from him to cover my face. "She broke her arm."

"Who? *Lila*?" He peels my hands off my face, and I nod.

The tears pour out of me as I tell him what I know.

"Did you find out anything from CPS while I was away?"

He shakes his head, his lips a grim line. "They wouldn't tell me anything."

I laugh bitterly. No one needs to tell me the result of that investigation. Lila and I are still here. The evidence speaks for itself. I always knew this was the probable outcome. We don't fit the profile of an abused family. The worst-case scenario happened: we poked the bear and now we're stuck with him.

I know why CPS couldn't dig anything up. I covered my tracks so well, it's like they never even existed.

"I don't know what else to do," I admit. All my life, I've studied hard and done well. I played hard on the field, and I've won. I thought I did it because my father made me. Turns out, defeat is not my thing. I don't like losing. Not when the stakes are this high.

We pick up pizza from Sal's and watch TV. Charlie flips through the channels and comes across *Cosmos*. Neil deGrasse Tyson stands on a cosmic calendar, unfolding the course of the universe's 13.8

billion years in one human year. Each month equals 1.14 billion years, each day equals 40 million years, each hour equals 1.3 million years. The American Revolution, World War II, the *Apollo* moon landing, all happened in the last second of December 31st.

Charlie leans forward, elbows on his knees, riveted. He turns to me wide-eyed, shaking his head. "Crazy."

I nod, but the cosmic calendar's perspective snips at the last fragile threads holding me together. If each second equals 438 years, then this, us, *me* . . . mean nothing. We're not even a flick of static on the radar. Every breath I've taken over the course of my entire lifetime combined, doesn't even make a dent in the timeline of humanity's existence. The world is filled with worse things. Famine, genocide, disease. We're a rich family with a fucked-up father. We're nothing.

My body and mind are exhausted. In this moment, never waking up, never having these dark thoughts again, is the only solution that makes sense. It's not the first time it's crossed my mind, but it scares me enough that it forces me up on my feet.

Charlie helps me with my jacket. His fingers linger on my collar, straightening it, tugging at it, then his head lowers to mine, our foreheads touching.

"I'm sorry about CPS," he says finally. "I thought it would help."

"It'll be okay," I lie, because I can't bear that look on his face. He shakes his head, but I nod, trying to convince him. If he loses hope too, I'm lost.

His arms reach around me again, squeezing tighter and tighter.

I almost can't breathe, but that's okay. This would be the best way to go.

Today is Thursday. Lila has been sleeping almost nonstop since we got home, only waking up as the meds wear off, but then Mom shows up with another dose that knocks her right out again.

"I don't think she should be sleeping this much," I say as Mom checks the clock on the stove for the next dose.

"Your father said the doctor told him to stay on top of the pain," she answers.

"But she's been asleep since Tuesday. That can't be good," I say, walking behind her upstairs as Mom opens the door to Lila's room. The blinds are shut. Lila's room, always active and bright, filled with music and dancing and tons and tons of attitude, is dark and depressing. My usually larger-than-life little sister is just a lump under the covers.

"Hey," I say, as her eyes flutter open. Stretching, she tries to fight off the drowsiness. With a wince, she glances down at her arm, so thoroughly zonked she forgot it was broken.

"Time for your medicine," Mom says, handing her a pill and some water. "I'll bring you some food in a bit."

Resenting my mother for the gazillionth time this week alone, I suggest, "Maybe we should let her eat first so she doesn't sleep through another meal."

Mom purses her lips. "Okay. That sounds like a good idea." She puts the pill and water down on Lila's nightstand. "I'll be back in a minute with a bite to eat."

She leaves, and I turn to Lila.

"How are you feeling?"

"Sleepy." Even her words are sluggish, as if coated in molasses. I walk over to her blinds and open them a bit to ease her back into daylight.

"It's perfect sledding weather," I say. "I wish you were feeling better. I can't go out there by myself; I'll look like a dork."

"More than usual," she adds, and her lips struggle to smile. I'm encouraged by her attempt at sarcasm.

She winces again, probably from the pain in her arm.

"You okay?" I ask, smoothing some hair away from her forehead. She glances up at me.

"Is Dad here?" she whispers. My heart skips a beat.

"No."

Her bottom lip wobbles. "He did it."

"Did . . . *what?*" Needles of terror prickle across my skin.

"I didn't fall," she squeezes out.

"What?" My heart roars in my ears. An avalanche approaches that is going to bury me alive, but I can't get out of its way fast enough.

"I told him I didn't want to go down the mountain. I was scared. And I got mad at him for calling me a baby. *Every day.* Whenever I got scared, he'd call me a *baby!*" Her voice hitches. "It came out by accident. I know I shouldn't have said it."

"Said *what?*"

"I called him an asshole."

"Oh God." My hand flies to my mouth.

"I think because I heard Mom say it—"

"Lila. What did he do?"

Downstairs, Mom putters around the kitchen. The blender whirs, probably a smoothie, Mom's idea of TLC.

"He smacked me," she says. I wince as if it happened to me, the crack of his hand across her cheek, how much it must have stung in the cold. And for a brief second I'm relieved. We have our own scale of aggression to measure against in this house. A slap is a two, a three. But she's not done, even though I want her to stop talking so badly my hand itches to cover her mouth.

"Then h-he grabbed my jacket and pulled me up to his face and yelled at me. He was really mad. And then, I don't know, like, he dropped me or pushed me, but I fell and rolled a long time. I heard it crack . . . my arm. And when I finally stopped, I was alone. And I thought . . . I thought he was mad enough to leave me there."

The blender stops whirring downstairs, and we just stare at each other in the silence.

I'm there on the slope with him, as if it were me he threw down a mountain. Because that's what Lila has always been, the part of me that I needed to protect and save. And I failed.

Blinding anger consumes me, extinguishing any last flicker of hope that lingered inside me.

"Hadley?" she looks at me with fearful eyes. Whatever flashed across my face scared her. "Are you okay?"

"No. But I will be."

I pocket her painkiller.

Mom comes up with a bed tray that she places over Lila's lap.

Glancing over, she searches the nightstand.

"She took it already," I say, fluffing Lila's pillow. Then I hand her the smoothie off the tray, and Lila takes it from me. Without asking, Lila knows. I'm in charge now.

then

Later that night, I rap my knuckles on the doorjamb. "Dad?"

He's in his study, looking at his computer screen, his eyeballs darting left and right, reading numbers that make sense only to him. He looks borderline happy; he must have made some more money.

He glances up at me for a second then back at his screen. "Yeah?"

I walk in hesitantly.

"I wanted to talk to you. About Cornell." I stop in front of his desk. He glances up at me and rubs a hand across his stubble. I guess his girlfriend doesn't have a razor for him at her place. Or he hasn't cashed in my thoughtful gift card to the Art of Shaving yet.

He gestures to the chair across from his desk, which I gratefully accept because my knees are just about to give out on me or start knocking together like in the cartoons.

Inhale, exhale. "I'm sorry I missed the early decision deadline. I screwed up. Especially because the more I think about it, the more excited I am to go. If I get in, I mean."

He leans back in his chair like a pleased king looking down at one of his repentant serfs.

"Good."

He turns back to his computer.

"I'm thinking of taking a ride up there, talk to Coach Jeffreys." I lift a shoulder. "I could ask Meaghan to go with me, but I thought I'd check with you first. See if you had any interest in going?"

His face lights up. "Honestly, I'd love an excuse to visit again."

He grabs his iPhone and checks his calendar, doing that long-armed old person squint before grabbing his reading glasses off the desk.

"Let's go tomorrow."

"Tomorrow?"

He levels me with a suspicious glare over his glasses. "Why? Have big plans?"

"No, I just . . ." Think, think.

He taps his phone and grimaces. "Tomorrow doesn't work. They're expecting a storm. Can't fly in that." His fingers flip along the screen, his lips tug down, contemplating. "We'll go on the second. Clear skies."

Air rushes out of me in a whoosh; I'm not sure how long I'd been holding my breath.

"Okay, good." I stand up on shaky legs, turning to leave.

"Hadley." His takes his glasses off and gestures for me to sit back down. "Do you know who called CPS?"

My heart jackhammers in my ears.

"No." I shake my head slowly, calmly, bottling my panic inside where he can't reach it. "I mean, I just figured it was because of Mom's DWI," I say, throwing the bait away from me.

He leans forward, never breaking eye contact. "I have my suspicions about who made that call. But let me make this perfectly clear: I'm not going to let the government come into *my* house and tell me how to raise my children. Over my dead body. Understood?"

He stares at me, and I nod in agreement quickly.

He waits for me to flinch, to show any signs of weakness that reveal my involvement.

Still nodding, I try to swallow but I gag instead, coughing into my fist to cover it up. "I know."

Dad leaves early the next morning, just as the snowflakes start falling from the sky like confectioners' sugar, soft and harmless. By late morning it's practically a blizzard.

My laptop rings. Meaghan's shiny, makeup-free face appears on the screen, her dark hair pulled back in a ponytail.

"Yay! You're back!" She shakes two fists in the air. I don't dare tell her I've been back since Tuesday.

"Yep," I say.

She finds her mug off to the side and lifts it to her mouth, taking a sip. "When I didn't hear from you on Christmas, I sent Charlie a text. He said your dad was taking you all skiing." She shoots me a warning glare. "Kind of weird to hear what's going on with you from your boyfriend."

I'm not up to managing Meaghan today.

"My father confiscated my phone for the entire trip," I say. "Literally took it out of my hands while I was texting you. He said he didn't want us to be distracted while we were on a family vacation, but it was just his way of keeping me from talking to Charlie."

Meaghan cringes. "That's sick."

She looks away and clears her throat, a nervous habit to stall while she gathers her thoughts, like when Señora Moore calls on her and she doesn't know the answer. I pick up a paper clip off my desk and unfurl it, bend by bend, waiting.

"What?"

"Nothing . . . it's just . . . your dad seems to be getting worse. I mean, taking your phone so you can't talk to Charlie is pretty diabolical."

Having my phone confiscated is the least of my problems. Nearly everyone I know has had their phone taken away at some point or another. That would actually make me normal. I'll bet none of them have been dropkicked for getting a B-minus on a calculus test.

Meaghan gasps. "Oh shit. Do you think he read our texts? Or *your* texts to Charlie!"

"I delete them."

She nods and smiles, ready to move on to something happier. "So . . . ," she says, trying to brighten the mood. "Tomorrow night!"

"What about it?" I ask. There's a chirping on her end.

"It's Noah. Let's add him," she says. My screen adjusts to accommodate both of their faces. Noah's dark floppy hair is damp, with snow still clinging to the tips.

"It's nasty out there. The roads are a mess," he says, shaking the wet flakes from his hair.

"My sister has a doctor's appointment this afternoon. I hope the roads are clear by then."

"Lila's sick?" Noah asks.

"Broken arm. Skiing," I add.

They both gasp. "Oh no! Poor Lila," Meaghan says.

The paper clip, twisted and mangled during my conversation with Meaghan, pokes me under my nail. I drop it and pick up a new one to destroy. They don't know the half of it. If CPS can't help us, I have nothing to gain by telling Noah and Meaghan. And at this point, I have even more to lose.

Meaghan says, "Noah, I was just about to tell Hadley about our New Year's Eve plans."

New Year's Eve has always been my least favorite holiday of the year. Not having someone to kiss at midnight is the equivalent of going to the prom with your cousin. And even though for the first time in my life I actually do have someone to kiss, this New Year's Eve will be the worst one of all. I was hoping Charlie and I could just do something quiet together, alone.

"What about it?" I ask cautiously.

"I'm having a party!" she announces. "And *you* have to dress up!" Her finger points to the screen, but Noah and I both answer, "Who? Me?"

"Not you, Noah!" She rolls her eyes. "I'm not worried about you. I'm worried about Miss Thinks a Grandma Cardigan Is Dressed Up over there!"

"I do not!" I say, before reviewing my wardrobe in my mind. "Okay, well, whatever. I don't think I can make it anyway."

There's a stunned silence from both of them.

"What?" Meaghan's voice squeaks with hurt feelings.

"You know I hate big parties!" I backpedal, trying to unwind the damage my words inflicted.

Her eyes glisten. I can't do that to her, even if the last thing I want to do is ring in the New Year and celebrate, not when I know what lies ahead. But I can't hurt Meaghan like this.

"I'm sorry. That was dumb. Of course I'll come."

Meaghan smiles in relief, but Noah scrutinizes me from under his eyelashes.

"Everything okay over there, Muscles?" he asks.

It's the knowing way he says it that just about destroys me, as if he's putting the last few pieces of the puzzle together and finally seeing my life for what it really is.

Noah would give his left arm to make things better for me if he could, I know that down to my marrow. But no one can stop what's already been set in motion.

I nod and blink hard, trying to will away the tears.

"Fantastic! Can't wait to see you guys tomorrow. What can I bring?"

"Yourself! And your man!" Meaghan laughs, back into excited party-planning mode.

———

Later that afternoon, a plow scrapes a path down our block. Mom's already been hitting the Chardonnay, so I take Lila to her doctor's appointment.

The pediatric orthopedist is pleased with how the bone was set in Vermont. He pats Lila on the head and calls her Suzy Chapstick.

"*Who?*" Lila asks, full of snark.

He laughs. "She was a famous skier back in my day. Try to avoid doing the Triple Lindy again till you get to the Olympics, okay?"

"A *what?*" she asks. Dr. Sher, who's probably around my parents' age, shakes his head. "Rodney Dangerfield? *Back to School?* No? God I'm old!" Lila and I smile to be polite.

He's about to leave the room when I pull out the bottle of pain meds.

"Dr. Sher?" He turns back to me. I hand him the bottle. "They gave Lila these for the pain."

He looks at them and at Lila, nods once. "Just to get her over the initial hump."

"So . . . not every four hours then," I say.

"Only if she needs them." He turns to Lila. "Are you on these now?"

"No," she answers.

"She's taking Children's Advil," I add.

"And it's dulling the pain?" he asks.

She nods.

"Okay." He turns to me. "Really, the ibuprofen should be enough. I'm not a fan of these." He holds up the bottle and hands it back to me. "Bare minimum they'll constipate her." He turns back to Lila. "When was the last time you had a bowel movement, Lila?"

"Gross!" is her answer.

"Lila! Just answer him!" I scowl at her.

She pretends to gag and then says, "I don't remember."

He nods knowingly.

"Pick up a stool softener at the drugstore. That should do it."

He turns to leave again, and I press it further. "It's just . . . my parents were under the impression they needed to give these to her every four hours."

"As needed," he stresses. "And since she doesn't need them . . ."

"Right." I nod. "Okay, good. They were making her sleep a lot," I add. That's exactly what Dad wanted, I'm sure. For Lila to sleep so she wouldn't blab.

"I bet." He stares back at me. Behind his kind eyes, the gears are spinning. "So neither of your parents were available to make it to this appointment?"

I clutch the edge of the exam table; the paper crackles under my fingers.

"No." I like Dr. Sher. He's asking the right questions.

"Do they both work?" He opens his file and clicks on his pen.

"Just my dad," I offer. *Keep going . . .*

"And Mom?" He starts to scribble something.

She was drunk! She got arrested for a DWI with Lila in the car,

303

and now I'll never let her drive Lila anywhere ever again! Tell him! Tell him that she didn't break her arm doing a Triple Lindy, that our father threw her down the mountain because she called him an asshole!

"Couldn't make it," I say, and my eyes plead with him to understand, to read between the lines.

He scribbles something, and I hope he's as good a mind reader as he is a pediatric orthopedist. I envision how Dr. Sher will come to our rescue. He'll red-flag Lila's file, stamp it *suspicious* and demand to speak to someone at CPS who can actually do something to help us.

But as he takes my hand in a limp shake and walks across the hall to greet his next patient with the same level of interest and enthusiasm, I know that file is just going right back in the cabinet when we leave.

I open my mouth to call him back. To tell him. But my father's threatening face looms in front of mine again, silencing me.

Back in the car, I navigate the slushy roads from the doctor's office to the expressway. But taking Lila home is like handing her back over to the enemy. A map unfurls in my mind, tracing detours, exits, and escape routes. As we approach the ramps, I veer onto the westbound ramp.

Lila doesn't notice for a while until we pass the Unisphere, the twelve-story metal globe in Flushing Meadow Park.

"Hey . . . Hadley! You're going the wrong way!"

My foot presses down on the gas.

"Hadley! That's the World's Fair! We're in Queens!"

My hands clench the steering wheel until my knuckles go white.

"Hadley!" she screams now, her voice pitching with a hint of panic. It breaks my resolve.

"Okay!" I say, easing back into the right lane and pulling off onto the next ramp.

I find a gas station and pull in, my legs trembling as badly as if we'd just avoided a head-on collision with an eighteen-wheeler.

"Do we need gas?" Lila asks, a hint of nervousness lingering in her voice.

I roll my head back and forth along the headrest.

"I just need to get it together," I say.

With a credit card in my father's name, a phone my father is using to track my every move, and twenty-three dollars, I thought I could just keep driving and get away with it. As Charlie would say, it was a fucked-up plan.

now

"Hadley?" Janet pokes her head into the rec room as I sit alone at the game table playing solitaire. Rowan left yesterday. Our good-bye was unspectacular. A quick hug and a promise to stay in touch. And then her mother and brother swept her away. Rowan already feels like a lifetime ago.

Grandma pokes her head in next to Janet with a plastered-on smile. She's been here to visit a bunch of times but never with that nervous look on her face. Something's up.

I stand up to meet her halfway. Grandma's arms reach around me and squeeze, but nowhere near the fierce hugs she used to give me before the accident. These new tepid ones are reserved for broken, fragile me.

"The man who's been investigating the plane crash is here to see you," Grandma says, releasing me from her embrace. "He has a few questions." She fiddles nervously with the straps of her purse.

"Okay." Grandma and Janet both stare at me. "Oh. You mean now?"

Janet nods. Then Grandma turns to Janet.

"Before we go, can I have a word with Hadley? Privately?"

"Sure," Janet says, then offers a smile.

Grandma looks around the room and gestures to a smaller table by the window, away from the couches. We sit facing each other.

She sets her purse in her lap. "He's been here a few times, but your doctors were waiting for you to be . . . in a better frame of mind," she chooses her words carefully.

"Oh," I say.

"Do you think you're up to it, dear?" She bites her lip, leaving a film of coral lipstick on her teeth. I run my finger along my teeth to tell her to wipe it away. I won't have people staring at my grandmother like she's a nutty old lady who walks around all day with lipstick on her teeth.

"Yuck. Let me get a tissue." She opens her purse. "Oh, here. I brought these for you." She hands me a box of Lorna Doones then continues searching through her purse. Finding a tissue, she dabs it at her front teeth then hides it back in her purse.

"Oh. This is for you too."

She pulls a sheet of notebook paper with the familiar bleeding purple marker from inside her purse and hands it to me.

I hesitate. Grandma watches me, so I unfold it, pressing it to my nose first, smelling the scented marker, the chemical grape smell still fresh.

Dear Hadley,

Are you mad at me? Why haven't you written back? If I did something to make you mad, I'm REALLY sorry.

I don't like being here without you.

Please, please, please, please, please, PLEASE come home soon.

Circle YES or NO.

Love,

Lila

PS: Grandma lets me eat tomatoes as a vegetable!

"Hadley? Did you hear what I said?" Grandma asks.

I nod. "Sure."

"Are you ready then?"

I've known since the day of the crash that this day would come. I thought I was prepared. But Lila's note has me rethinking everything.

I stand up.

"Ready."

then

Charlie watches me from the bottom of the stairs as I make my way down, clutching the banister for balance. I shrug my shoulders and grimace, offering a silent apology for disappearing during the most revered minute of the year for every couple across the planet. Unfortunately for both Charlie and me, at the stroke of midnight on New Year's Eve, I was puking my guts up in the bathroom.

The downstairs is filled with a dozen or so bodies hugging and kissing, the promise of a new year mixed with lots of champagne bringing out the most lovable version of everyone. Wrapping an arm around my shoulder, he leans close to my ear. "You okay?"

"Better," I offer. He kisses my head. I suspect he's not too excited to kiss me on the mouth after I just hurled.

"For someone who never drinks, you were really knocking them back," he says, waiting for some kind of explanation. One I don't give.

Over in the living room, Meaghan holds on to Noah, crying.

"I just love you so much," she sobs, hanging on to his arm. "And I want you to find someone who *appreciates* what a special person you are . . ."

Noah looks at me beseechingly from across the room and mouths, "Help!"

I shrug and smile. We both know Meaghan gets a bad case of the feels when she's been drinking.

"Do you want to go home now?" Charlie asks me.

Surprisingly, that minute of puking did the trick. My stomach isn't churning anymore. My head isn't even too fuzzy. I don't want to go home. But I definitely don't want to be here either.

"Not home," I suggest, and bite my lip. Charlie takes two steps with me back to a quieter corner of the room. He bends down to whisper in my ear. "My mom is at the apartment."

"We can just go park somewhere." I nuzzle up to him, grazing my fingers down the back of his neck, my thumb circling his ear. His eyes flutter closed for a second, and he groans.

"You're bombed," he says.

"I'm not *that* bombed," I counter with a smile.

He shakes his head, almost to humor me. "I'll get your coat. We'll go for a ride or something." With a quick kiss on my forehead, he heads upstairs. While he goes to weed through the pile of coats on Meaghan's bed, I walk over to my friends. Meaghan lets go of Noah and rushes into my arms.

"Oh, Hadley! I just love you so, so much!" she slurs, and wobbles on her ridiculously high heels.

"I love you back, Meaghan." I hug her fiercely. "I really do. Okay? Like, don't ever forget it."

I reach for Noah next. "You too, Stretch. I love you."

"Not you too," he groans. "The two of you are killing me with your drunk talk! She's actually crying over *my* breakup with Matt!"

I lean back and grab his arms. "Noah, listen to me, okay? You have been my voice of reason and closest friend forever. I love you. I want you to know that."

He laughs warily. "You actually seem kind of sober." His sharp eyes scrutinize me.

"I mean it." I squeeze his arms.

"I love you too, Hadley," he says, measuring out his words carefully. His long arms wrap around me and pull me into a thick embrace.

"Happy New Year," Noah says in my ear, and my throat constricts.

Charlie's behind me, holding my coat. I slip my arms in and take a last look at my friends.

"Call us when you get back from Ithaca!" Noah calls after me.

I pretend I didn't hear him and follow Charlie out the door.

On the walkway, Charlie plucks the keys out of my cold hands. "No driving for you tonight."

The cold air clears my head. "I feel fine," I say, and I do, until I trip; Charlie's grip on my elbow tightens before I can stumble to the ground. I glare down at the walkway that reached up to grab my toe out of nowhere.

He hits my key fob, unlocking the door. "Phone?" He sticks his hand out. I dig it out of my purse and hand it to him. He throws it in the glove compartment and locks the door. With his hand on the small of my back, he helps me into his car before shutting the door.

We drive toward town. I try to sneak closer to him, but the console is in the way.

"Let's get some food in you," he offers as we approach the diner.

My hands are in his hair, twirling around his ear. "Let's go to the beach."

"Hadley . . ."

"What?" I giggle.

He glances at me from the corner of his eye, then turns right at the light and drives toward the bay.

The beach gate is down, blocking us from going to the parking lot. Charlie turns the car around, and I point out a road hidden by the darkness. "Turn in here."

"It's private," he notes, reading the sign.

"I know the family who lives here. My dad golfs with their dad. They're in Hawaii."

We pull over to the side of their private road. Charlie turns the engine off. I reach over to kiss him, and he gives me his cheek.

"That was awkward," I complain. He smiles at me and squeezes my hand. Undeterred, I unbuckle and get up on my knees to wrap my arms around his neck.

"Is it because I threw up?" I murmur against his ear.

He grimace-smiles and shrugs. "Kinda? Sorry."

I kiss his ear. "I rinsed with mouthwash," I offer, tugging on his earlobe with my teeth. I crawl over the console onto his lap, my knees on either side of his hips, pinning him.

"Come on," I tease. "It's New Year's Eve. Push the seat back." He kisses my neck, wrapping his arms around my waist. Then he groans and pulls away.

"Hadley . . . I don't have a condom."

I blink. "Oh." It may have slipped my mind, but not Charlie's. I'm not on the Pill anymore, not since my father threw them in the fireplace a little over a week ago. "Why not?"

He shrugs and looks away uncomfortably. "I knew my mother was going to be home. And I *don't* want to have sex in the car."

"Why?" I press my lips against the corner of his. "I don't mind."

"Hadley." My name is so sweet on his lips. He sweeps my hair behind my ear. "Because I'm a fucking romantic when it comes to you. Because you're bombed. And because hooking up in a Honda Civic isn't all it's cracked up to be."

Everything else he said is eclipsed by his last sentence.

"And you know this from experience?" I snap.

His eyes flash. "Yeah, I do. Happy now?"

I groan, my spine collapsing as my bravado slips away. Of course I'm not happy. I deserved that. The steering wheel presses against my back, a nagging reminder of the crushing disappointment of the night. Charlie doesn't make any movements to inch the seat back.

I get a second wind and lean forward. "It's okay. Just this one time." I kiss his jaw, his neck.

He pushes me back a little more firmly this time. "Hadley, you getting knocked up our senior year is *not* okay."

Rejection and despair and anger and fear and desperation all become one murky stew in my stomach. I put my hand against the window to balance myself. The glass is cold and wet. When I lift it, I leave behind an imprint of my hand in the condensation that's all my doing. I'm the only one hot and bothered in here.

The familiar sting behind my eyes begins, and I don't have the energy to fight it. Charlie's arms wrap around me, consoling me, but I'm in the most vulnerable position, straddling him in my skirt while crying into my hands.

"Hadley, everything's fine. You just had too much to drink."

"It's not fine," I blubber.

His laugh rumbles under me. "You're a mess when you drink, you know that? Come on. We have a lot of time ahead of us. A lot of new years together."

It just makes me cry harder.

"Hadley, come on. Please? I'll make it up to you, okay? When you get back. We'll have a New Year's Eve do-over, at my place. Just you and me. It's going to make tonight look like amateur hour."

The tears won't stop pouring out of me, for everything I still have to lose.

then

Daggers of light slash through my blinds against my closed lids. I shield them with my hand and turn to look at my clock on the nightstand. It's after eleven. No one's ever let me sleep this late before. I worry that something happened, maybe everyone succumbed to carbon monoxide poisoning except for me. Before the anxiety takes hold, evidence of life coalesces in my consciousness: music from Lila's room, the clatter of pots in the kitchen downstairs.

Standing up, I walk across my room to my desk to check messages that came in during the night.

The first one is from Noah:

Charlie and I brought your car home. The keys are in the glove compartment. Go get them before someone steals your car. You know, 'cause you live in such a rough neighborhood.

Charlie drove me back to Meaghan's last night, just to get my phone, then home. He wouldn't let me drive myself. He was convinced that my hysterics last night were because I was drunk.

They weren't.

The next one is from Charlie:

I hate that we started the new year off on the wrong foot.

Let me make it up to you. Can we get together?

Mom's working.

I love you.

I make my way downstairs.

"Good *morning*," Mom says. "How was Meaghan's party?"

I shrug and open the fridge for some orange juice. I'm so parched, I'm tempted to drink straight from the jug. I would, if my mother wasn't standing right here watching me. Instead, I sit down with a glass and pour it to the rim, chugging half of it back, the tart sweetness washing away the nasty taste in my mouth. Mom looks at me knowingly.

"I'm going to let you off the hook today," she says with a smug smile. "I know Noah brought your car home last night."

"Oh," I mumble with my eyes downcast.

"Your father doesn't know. It was here when he woke up. So were you. That's all that matters." She sits down with her coffee.

"Thank you."

"So." She smiles brightly. "Tomorrow's a big day, huh?"

"Yeah." I swirl my juice around, controlling the waves that

almost crest over the top. "I guess."

She pours herself another cup of coffee, and I finish what's left of my juice.

"I need to pick out an outfit." She flaps a packet of sweetener back and forth.

"For what?" I lick the rim of my glass. I'm still thirsty. I should probably drink water, but the orange juice hit the spot. I get up and open the refrigerator door.

"For tomorrow," she says simply, as if we're both on the same page.

A chill runs through my body, but it has nothing to do with the open refrigerator. "Where are you going tomorrow?"

She rolls her eyes and feigns playful exasperation. "We're coming with you to Cornell!"

"We?"

"Yes, all of us." She reaches past me for her sugar-free, fat-free, flavored creamer.

My arm freezes inside the fridge, holding the orange-juice jug handle.

"Why?" It comes out whiny. "Lila's arm," I remind her. "She can't bang it around."

She waves my concern away with her hand. "I spoke with Dr. Sher. He says it's fine."

"It's just supposed to be Dad and me," I remind her. "We're just flying up to look around and talk to the lacrosse coach, then coming back home. There's no point in all of us going. I'm only doing it to make him happy anyway."

She stirs her coffee and takes a sip, stubbornly trying to hold on to her fragile good mood. "Your father decided to make a trip out of it."

"That's stupid." I groan. "It's upstate New York in January! It's cold! It's snowy! There's nothing to do!"

She snaps. "Maybe I'd like to get out of the house!" She shakes her head in exasperation. "For God's sake, Hadley. We're coming. End of story."

My mouth gapes open. There are so many things I want to shout back at her. But the familiar fist wedges in my throat, making it impossible.

"I just really wish you would stay home and take care of Lila." I try to appeal one last time to her maternal instinct.

"Yeah, well, you want to know what *I* wish?" she snaps back.

I don't. I turn and storm away.

The four walls of my room feel like a cage. I put on my running clothes and go to the basement of my own free will. My skin itches with nerves, even after an hour on the treadmill running through my pain, my hip that's still a little sore even though the burn has healed. A hot shower usually calms me, but today I exhaust every last drop of hot water from the tank and I'm still as jittery as that one time I had three cups of coffee to cram for a midterm.

It's this house. Every room echoes with his fury, her neglect. I march back downstairs and grab my bag and shoes.

"Where are you going?" Mom asks.

"I need to run some errands," I say. "And get some air."

She nods. "Be home by six. I'm going to the Wileys' for dinner. You need to stay home with Lila."

Slipping my arms through my sleeves, I turn to face her, processing this new information. "Is Dad going with you?"

The way her shoulders stiffen, I know the answer.

"No," she answers simply. A soft sigh escapes my lips. It didn't have to be like this. *We* didn't have to be like this.

My eyes reach for hers like open arms, pleading with her to be more nurturing, more protective, more of a mother. Right now, it could change everything. She turns her back to me and busies herself fluffing an immaculate pillow.

I turn and leave. In my car, I take out my phone.

Reading Charlie's text, I finger the claddagh around my neck hidden under my collar. It steadies me before I write back.

Can't today. Have to get ready for the trip tomorrow.

He texts back right away:

Okay. Well then as soon as you get back. I miss you. And all that that implies. ;)

Charlie once said he doesn't lie. I believed him. I still do. But I never said the same back to him.

It's a date.

now

Grandma and I take seats next to each other in Linda's office. Linda comes in, followed by the man who has been trying to speak with me since the day of the crash.

"Hadley?" He reaches his hand out to shake mine. They're scratchy and calloused. "I don't know if you remember me."

"I do," I say, and leave it at that. The crinkles around his eyes deepen, reassuring me again that he's a good guy.

Linda finds her seat at her desk.

"I'm Gerald Brady," he says, "senior air safety inspector from the National Transportation Safety Board."

"Okay."

"How's your arm?" His eyes travel down my cast, before landing on my wrists. He looks away as if he saw something he shouldn't have.

"It's fine, thank you."

"Are you up to talking today?" Brady asks, the creases around his eyes easing into a kind smile.

I nod.

He holds up a black device in his palm. "Digital recorder." He holds it out for me to see, as if I were a dog that needs to sniff it. "Do you mind if I record our conversation? It helps me later when I have to file the report."

"I don't mind." The sun reflecting off the snow outside blinds me. Holding my hand up in front of my eyes, I ask, "Can we shut the blinds, though?"

Linda gets up from behind her desk and pulls the cords, lowering them. "Better?"

I nod.

Brady says, "Quite a storm we got the other day, huh?"

I nod again to be polite. He exhales and cuts to the chase. "Hadley, what do you remember about the crash?"

Grandma watches me. It's something she's wanted to ask all along, I'm sure.

"Everything."

There's a shocked stillness in the room. Brady's eyes tighten, and he nods.

He sits down on the edge of Linda's desk, which I can tell by her pursed lips she doesn't appreciate. But it puts him in a better position to speak directly to me.

"Was there any kind of engine trouble?" he asks.

"No," I say.

"What then? Why didn't anyone radio in for help?"

"It all happened too fast." I flinch, remembering how the

plane tossed me around.

"*What* did?" he asks.

My heart pounds against my chest as the ground dips under my feet.

"I wanted to land the plane, and I couldn't."

"What do you mean you couldn't?"

"He wouldn't get out of the seat. And my mom—" I stop, her shrieks present, piercing the air around me, her eyes, one moment wild and terrified, the next blank, lifeless blue marbles.

"Hadley?" His eyes, so kind, search mine. "What *happened*?"

Everyone stares back at me, waiting for me to answer.

then

"Where the hell is my coffee grinder?"

I open my eyes with a start. Outside the window, the sun is just starting to rise, just like Christmas morning. I glance over at my clock: 7:02.

Pots clatter and cabinets slam downstairs. My toes curl into the white shag throw rug as I glance over at my calendar, today's date circled in a red bull's-eye. I get dressed and clasp my claddagh necklace on. I hold the charm between my fingers for a moment, closing my eyes in a prayer, before slipping it under my shirt.

Downstairs, my father's hostile mood is palpable. I pad cautiously into the kitchen.

"Morning," I say, rubbing my eyes.

"What's so good about it?" Dad slams another cabinet. I want to point out that I didn't say "good," but I bite my tongue. He's already showered and dressed, wearing dark-blue jeans and his favorite Cornell sweatshirt.

Mom is on her hands and knees scouring through the bottom cabinets.

"Hadley, have you seen the coffee grinder?" she asks in a panic.

I shake my head and reach in the refrigerator for the orange juice.

"Were the cleaning ladies here yesterday?" Dad barks at my mother.

"No, of course not. It was a *holiday*," she reminds him, most likely a dig at Dad's expense for being gone all day.

"Well, where the hell is it?"

I sit down at the kitchen table, making myself invisible as his fury crackles in the air around me.

My mother holds the countertop to pull herself up. "It couldn't have just walked away." He growls something, and she raises her hands to placate him. "We'll just get coffee at the airport, okay?"

Before he can get another word in, Lila walks in, hunched over, holding her stomach.

"Mommyyyy!" she cries. Lila only calls her Mommy when she's sick.

"Oh no. *Now* what?" My mother says, walking toward her.

"I can't stop going to the bathroom!" Lila whimpers. She spins around and runs to the bathroom down the hall. Mom follows, pressing her ear to the door; her nose wrinkles with distaste.

I watch it all unfold with wide eyes while my father rubs the bridge of his nose between two fingers. I've seen him do it a million times, trying to erase his mounting anger and frustration with all of us. It never works. He looks over at me, and I smile nervously. Stupidly.

"Wipe that smug smile off your face or I'll wipe it off for you."

I stare down into my orange-juice glass.

After a few minutes, my mother comes back to the kitchen, shaking her head in confusion. "I don't know what it could be."

I get up and walk to the bathroom door, knocking gently. "Lila?"

"Go away!" she cries.

"Lila, are you okay?"

"What do *you* think?" She groans as her bowels empty into the toilet, fast and furious.

I walk back to the kitchen. "It's bad." I grimace.

My father throws his hands up in the air in surrender and turns to my mother. "Fine! You stay home with Lila. I'll take Hadley up. We'll come back tonight."

Mom gasps as if she's been slapped.

"No! I was looking forward to this!"

He stares back at her. "Do you have any other suggestions?"

She picks up the phone. "Yes, as a matter of fact I do."

As she dials a number, I walk over to her, to try and talk sense to her. "Mom, just stay home with Lila. Please?"

She turns her back to me and plugs a finger in her ear to tune me out.

"Hello, Mom? It's Courtney . . . yes, I know you have caller ID now . . . I need to ask a favor."

I tug on my mother's sleeve. "Mom. Stay home with Lila. She

needs you," I plead. She ignores me and paces, murmuring to Grandma on the phone.

When she hangs up, her grin is back.

"All settled. My mother will come stay with Lila."

My father complains of being too caffeine deprived to drive to the airport, so I drive them in my car. He sits in the passenger seat, flipping through the radio stations until he finds something with "real" music. He yells at every "asshole" driving too fast or too slow, points his finger in front of my nose to tell me to switch lanes. My nerves are beyond shot. The sudden whoop of the police siren behind me startles me; I pull over.

"He's not pulling *you* over," my father says with a snide laugh as the police car speeds past us. Then he looks at my trembling hands. "God, Hadley, you're such a wuss."

I throw the car in park. My legs shake, my teeth clatter, my throat gets tight. Too tight.

"Hadley?" Mom leans forward from the backseat. "What's wrong?"

I hold my head in my hands. "I don't know."

Without a word, Dad opens his door and gets out and walks around the car. He knocks on my window and wags his fingers impatiently at me. We switch seats. After he throws my seat back several inches and adjusts his mirrors, he tears down the road like he's in the final lap of the Daytona 500.

"I know what it is." He shoots me a sidelong glance. "I get them too. Maybe it's hereditary. The one thing you got from me, that had to be it, huh?" He shakes his head, disgusted.

I press my hands between my knees.

"What?" I ask.

"Fight or flight," he says. "Sometimes you fight, sometimes not."

I shake my head slowly, still not following.

"Hits me every so often. Sometimes even flying does it to me. You?" He turns to me.

I shake my head. "A little. But nothing like this."

He nods. "Well, that's good."

We pull into the airport and park.

I shake my tingling hands out by my side and take deep breaths. Mom wheels her overnight bag across the parking lot toward the tarmac.

"Coffee." Dad looks longingly over at the terminal.

"I'll get it!" It comes out as a shout. "And breakfast. I have to use the bathroom anyway," I offer, trying to erase the hysterics from my voice. He takes forty dollars from his wallet and hands it to me.

"Hurry up."

The tarmac is springy under my trembling legs as I run toward the terminal. At the coffee shop counter, I order two coffees for my parents and three blueberry muffins.

"I just need to make sure there are no nuts in the muffins," I say to the cashier who rings me up.

"Nope," a guy not much older than me answers, handing me back my change.

"Positive?" He looks back at me with uncertain eyes. "Because my father is deathly allergic. And he's flying. Can you check with Lou?" I gesture to the manager's broad back a few feet away from us.

He walks over to Lou and taps him on the shoulder. "Lou? This customer wants to make certain there are no nuts in the blueberry muffins." He points to me.

Lou walks over with a grin. "Hey, Chamomile. Where you been?"

"Haven't had a lesson in a while." I force a smile.

He lifts his hand and pretends it's shaking. "No nerves today? No magic herbal tea cure?" He laughs, teasing me for my typical order of chamomile tea, which I need to calm my nerves after every flight lesson with Phil.

I shake my head. I don't trust my voice. "Nuts?" I squeak, holding up the bag.

"No nuts. You allergic?"

"My dad is." I take the receipt and shove it in my purse. "I always have to double check."

I walk off to the ladies' room. When I'm done, I go back outside and find my parents waiting by the plane. I hand the bag over, still holding the coffee tray in my hand.

Dad peeks in the bag and frowns. "Muffins?"

I clear my throat and try again to shake out the pins and needles poking at my hands. "It's not like they had a huge selection." Then I remember. "I made sure there are no nuts."

He nods, and we all climb aboard. I take the seat behind Mom. Within fifteen minutes, we're up in the air. Once we've reached the right altitude, Dad says to Mom, "I'm starving. Hand me one of those muffins."

While Mom and Dad scarf down breakfast, I stare out the window at the white blanket of earth below.

Dad clears his throat. Once, twice. He takes a sip of his coffee to clear it.

Mom glances over at him. "Are you okay?"

He clears his throat again, then tugs at his collar. "It's just nerves," he says, his words lacking confidence. From my seat, I can see sweat pouring down his temples; the backs of his hands glisten with perspiration.

"Hadley!" he yells over his shoulder. "Look in my coat pocket for my pills."

"What pills?" I pull his jacket off the seat next to me, tearing through the pockets.

Mom rests a hand on his arm.

"It's fine," he says to Mom, clearing his throat. "It happens sometimes. I took a pill this morning though . . . I don't know why it's not . . ." He clears his throat again.

"Miles . . . your face!" Mom cries out.

I lean forward to see my father's cheeks erupting in red blotches.

now

Everyone's eyes bear down on me as I tell them about the muffins I bought at the terminal cafeteria. How Dad thought it was nerves at first, and some pill he usually took wasn't working. How we saw the blotches and figured out it was an allergic reaction. How the EpiPen didn't work.

"Mom gave him two shots," I say.

Brady nods, as if he knows. "We saw that in the toxicology report," he says. "Your father was on beta-blockers. Patients on beta-blockers who develop anaphylaxis are often resistant to epinephrine."

Beta-blockers and my father in the same sentence make absolutely no sense. "That's . . . no, that's impossible. Beta-blockers are for people with heart conditions. Right? Dad didn't have a bad heart. He ran every morning." I turn to Grandma, who lifts her hands up and shakes her head, looking as confused as I feel.

"We spoke with his doctor. Your father used them on occasion for anxiety. Not the way they're supposed to be dispensed," Brady says.

"Is that why the pen didn't work?"

"They were already in his system. His doctor never should have prescribed them, not with his allergies. He probably didn't want to take any of the other antianxiety meds because of their side effects. They can dull you, cut your edge."

I bite the inside of my cheek, digesting this new information. My father, who bullied us into facing our fears, to be better than everyone else, suffered from anxiety?

"Hadley." He leans forward. "Did you know about the security cameras at your house?"

"Sure . . . Outside by the front door and the garage."

"And inside."

My mouth opens and closes. "Inside?"

"Hidden throughout the house."

An anxious tremor runs through me. *Oh God.* "Where?"

His eyes search mine. "The foyer. The den. The study."

I take a deep breath. "Anywhere else?" A trickle of sweat snakes down my back.

His eyes narrow. "Not the bedrooms or bathrooms, if that's what you're concerned about."

My heart is pounding against my rib cage so hard, I'm certain he can hear it, can see my body throb with panic.

Brady stares back at me, waiting.

He knows.

then

When I come home through the mudroom door, Mom gives me her exasperated sigh.

"Let me guess. Library?" she snaps, slipping her arms through her coat sleeves.

As she buttons her coat she mutters under her breath, as if I'm not in the room with her. "New Year's Day, and she has to run an errand. She thinks I'm stupid, like I don't know everything is closed."

I watch her gather her things, flipping her carefully tousled blond hair over the collar of her coat, jingling her keys in one hand.

Once she was a mother to me, taking me to the playground where we'd swing next to each other then walk hand in hand around the park's huge pond, pointing out the turtles and goldfish swimming just beneath the lily pads. There were hugs and laughter, but so much time has passed since then, the memories are blurring, faded.

As she goes to walk out the mudroom door, I rush after her.

"Mom? Wait!" I throw my arms around her, squeezing, burying my head into her neck.

She inhales sharply, then pats me on the shoulder . . . one . . . two . . . three times. The exact number it takes to make unpleasantries go away.

"Hadley, I'm late. The Wileys said to be there at six," she says, pulling herself away from me to meet her friends.

And then she's gone. But she's been gone for so long.

I check on Lila, who's upstairs in bed listening to music.

"You okay up here?"

Her eyes are droopy.

"Mom gave me a pill," she says, her voice mushy, her tongue too tired to enunciate. I groan. I should have flushed the whole damn bottle. But for today, it might not be the worst thing.

"All right. Just sleep." I pull her door closed behind me.

I go back outside to my car, grabbing a bag from the trunk.

Yes, Mom, everything is closed today. Everything except the grocery store.

Back in the kitchen, I reach under the cabinet for Dad's coffee grinder and plug it in. Then I grab the metal can from the bag and pop the lid.

The fact that Lila only broke her arm on the mountain is a miracle. It could have been worse, much worse. She has a mouth; he has a temper. I can't live with the possibility of any more "accidents."

Except for this last one.

Staring at the empty grinder bowl, I pour two generous hand-fuls of unsalted mixed nuts inside and flick the on switch.

Whirr, whirr, whirr.

I find the recipe for blueberry muffins in one of Mom's cook-books and pull out all the ingredients, measuring out flour, sugar, salt, baking powder . . .

My skin prickles, hot and clammy, and my stomach turns to liquid like I'm coming down with something. All I want to do is crawl into bed and sleep, forget, even for just a few hours. But that's no longer an option.

To steel myself, I replay all the kicks and slaps. For leaving the garage door open . . . getting a B-minus . . . missing the early deci-sion deadline . . . getting benched . . . doing a shitty job raking the leaves . . . forgetting to give him an important message . . . dinging his car in the parking lot . . . leaving a water mark on the table . . . liking a boy . . . laughing when I should have been invisible . . . being invisible when I should have been shining . . .

But mostly, the one thing that sees me through is knowing that I was the same age as Lila when it all started. Lila is Dad's new pet project.

I fold in the flour mixture with the pulverized nuts, swirling it all together.

Placing three paper muffin cups in the tin, I carefully ladle in the batter and bake at 375 degrees for twenty minutes. A warm sweetness wafts through the air as the muffins bake. I open all the windows downstairs to chase it out.

When I'm done, I scrub the muffin tin, mixing bowls,

measuring cups, and spoons, drying them carefully before putting them all away just as I found them. I wipe down all around the blades of the coffee grinder, inspecting for hidden residue. But I'm not convinced I've gotten every last trace. I can't risk Dad making his morning coffee and having a reaction before we even make it to the airport, so I toss the coffee grinder in the trash.

When the muffins are cool, I take them upstairs with me, hiding them in a plastic bag in my purse.

Around nine o'clock, Lila wakes up to use the bathroom.

"There you are," I say, as she pads by me, still half-asleep. "Hungry?" She nods and grumbles.

I go downstairs to make her a sandwich. And then I make her a chocolate berry smoothie.

Years ago, Claudia gave me chocolate after one of our lacrosse games. After a horrible morning of not being able to get off the toilet, I still didn't figure out what happened until the following Monday, when Olivia told me Claudia was blabbing all around school how she had given me chocolate-flavored laxatives. As the blender crushes the berries, I toss in two "chocolates." I know from my own experience that Lila will be fine by the afternoon, but she'll be stuck in the bathroom all morning. She won't be able to go up to Ithaca, and Mom will have to stay home with her.

I throw the box of laxatives into the kitchen garbage with the coffee grinder and the can of nuts and take the bag outside to the trash can on the curb. By six thirty tomorrow morning, all the evidence will be hauled off in a garbage truck.

❙━━━❙

My mother's perfume and idle chatter in the car absorb all the oxygen in the air. I gasp the entire ride, trying desperately to get air into my lungs.

She wasn't supposed to come.

Up until yesterday, my plan was that Dad would have an allergic reaction while he was flying, forcing me to land the plane, somewhere remote enough that help would arrive too late. But I've never landed a plane by myself. I knew there was a good chance neither of us was coming home. I accepted that the odds weren't in my favor, if it meant Lila would be safe.

But now Mom is coming.

I almost aborted the plan after Mom called Grandma. But then I looked at Lila's broken arm, pictured my father throwing her down the mountain. I remembered the morning he yanked her out of her seat so hard he pulled her arm out of its socket and told the doctor at the hospital it was my fault.

Next time, she might not be as lucky. It might be her neck, or her head cracking against the corner of the wall after he kicks her. Visions of him beating her the way he beats me propel me forward.

Dad has a way of making our injuries seem like accidents. And now so will I.

I have to stick to the plan. But I also have to nail the landing. My last lesson with Phil months ago was a mess; he had to take over the controls after I came in to the runway too low, too fast.

We pull into the airport. Dad peels off a couple of twenties from his wallet, and I run to the terminal to get coffee and breakfast. My heart sinks when the new guy serves me. He won't remember me. I need an alibi. They need to know I bought the muffins here and I made sure there were no nuts. Then I see Lou's familiar back behind the counter, fiddling with the coffeemaker. Lou will remember that I asked.

My lungs are useless lead balloons in my chest as I walk to the bathroom. I check each stall to make sure it's empty.

I open the paper bag of muffins that I just bought, placing them on the metal countertop by the sink. Next, I take the plastic bag of muffins I baked last night out of my purse. My hands shake as if I'm handling live grenades. Lined up next to each other, mine don't look *glaringly* homemade. I put the store-bought ones in the plastic bag and throw them in the garbage and replace mine in the bakery bag.

After another failed attempt to breathe normally, I head toward the door. With the door handle in my hand, my phone buzzes in my back pocket like a security alarm.

I know it's Charlie even before I check.

With cold, trembling hands, I read his message.

I already miss you. Hurry home.

It's as if he's standing right next to me, smiling. His easy, honest smile.

My shaking knees can't hold me anymore. Leaning up against the bathroom tile, I sink down until my butt hits the ground.

Visions of Charlie, then Lila, disarm me. Lila handing me the framed picture at Christmas. *Sisters. Best Friends.* Charlie pulling those summer concert tickets out of his back pocket. Both of them, with their unwavering faith in *me*. Trusting me to be there for them.

I can't go through with this.

This wasn't just about protecting Lila. This was about getting back at my father for years of being his punching bag. I allowed my rage and hate and bitterness to choke out hope. If I go through with this, he wins. I will have turned into him.

My need for vengeance gives way to a feeling of overwhelming relief.

It stops here. Now.

Carefully, I pull myself back up on shaky legs. I take the plastic bag out of the garbage and switch the muffins again.

Today, we fly to Cornell. When we get home, I will call CPS. I will make them reopen the case. I will stand up to my father. I will be brave. I will fight back.

Cold, bracing air rushes into my lungs as I meet my parents outside by the plane. My body, tense and ready to strike for so long, is limp with relief.

Within fifteen minutes, we're up in the air. While Mom and Dad scarf down breakfast, I stare out the window, imagining a future with a glimmer of hope.

"Miles . . . your face!"

Cold dread replaces all the blood in my body.

I threw them away!

The bag. I must have contaminated the bakery bag when I put the homemade muffins in there.

I unbuckle my seat belt and lean forward between their seats. His sleeves are pushed up to his elbows; red blotches bloom along his forearms.

Mom tears through her purse. "There must have been nuts in that muffin!"

"Hurry up!" he yells at Mom. He faces straight ahead, blinking rapidly, but I feel it, the gradual descent. He's preparing the plane for an emergency landing.

Mom empties her purse in her lap. "Where's the EpiPen!" she cries, as her lipstick, wallet, and tampons fly around the cockpit.

It's home, in the junk drawer, where I put it after I snuck it out of her purse in the middle of the night.

Dad coughs and tugs at his sweatshirt collar as if that's what's suffocating him. There's a second yoke, in front of my mother. I can barely land from the left seat where I've been practicing, let alone the right, which requires me to swap flying hands and read instruments from a different angle. And landings are already the hardest part about flying. I need to get into Dad's seat.

"Dad! Listen to me." I lean forward again, ducking my head between their seats. "You're not okay. You need to let me land the plane."

My father turns his head. His clammy, blanched face looks back at me, bewildered, scared. Vulnerable. Familiar, even though I've never seen this side of him. Then I recognize where I've seen that helpless expression before. In the mirror.

I can fix this. I can make this stop, right now.

"Hadley! Is there an EpiPen in the first aid kit?" Mom cries over her shoulder.

Yes! I had forgotten about the first aid kit!

I look out the windshield at the open sky. He's still in control. The plane is level, slowly descending. I reach behind my seat and grab the first aid kit from the storage cargo. Opening it, I grab the two-pack of EpiPens and hand one to Mom.

Her hands shake, and she's crying and whimpering and praying "Dear God, dear God, dear God" all at the same time. With two hands, she thrusts the needle into his thigh through his jeans. He flinches and cries out.

Beneath us, we pass houses. The steeple of a church. A street congested with traffic. We're getting closer to the ground, close enough now that everything below us looks like model toys. A stream. A mall. A highway.

"Dad!" I yell again. "You need to get out of your seat! I can land, but only from your seat!" I reach for him, grabbing at his sweatshirt sleeve in desperation.

As the tiny toy model of the world beneath us passes by, Mom and I both try to force him out of his seat.

Oh God, help me! Help me, please!

I claw at him, desperate to save us from what I've done.

He nods, finally conceding, and struggles to unbuckle his harness. Mom reaches over to help him, tugging at him to hurry. He's too big, she doesn't even shake him.

"Hadley, give me the other pen!" I hand her the second EpiPen, and she gives him another injection. *"Why isn't this working?"*

With one last groan, Dad loses consciousness and collapses on the yoke.

It's too late.

As we plummet down, I buckle myself in and put my head between my knees.

"I'm sorry!" I scream, then . . .

The acrid scent wakes me.

Smoke ripples before my eyes in waves, distorting my vision. My arms dangle down, grazing the ceiling, which is now the ground.

I'm upside down.

My father's body is crumpled on the ceiling/ground beneath me, his neck pitched at an awful, unnatural angle. One shoe is missing from his foot. Blood seeps through his Cornell sweatshirt.

The smell is stronger now, fuel and smoke, a horrible combination. My brain reboots, transmitting signals to move faster. To get out. But the fog doesn't want to lift, and part of me fights to go back to sleep.

I unbuckle my belt with my right arm—my left is aching and useless—falling on top of my father's lifeless body with a loud cry of horror and pain. I crawl forward to reach my mother. She hangs upside down in her seat, her harness still on, her wide blue eyes vacant but somehow still frightened.

I want to unbuckle her and hold her in my arms, tell her how sorry I am.

Instead, I drag myself across the ceiling to the torn hole in the back of the plane and crawl through.

My world is upside down. The bright-blue sky greets me like the bottom of the ocean.

now

Brady sees right through me. All of them know, I can tell, even in the way Grandma holds herself stiffly in the chair next to me, the inches separating us like miles. He's toying with me. He's about to tell me that my father's security cameras caught me in the act of pouring crushed nuts into the muffins that killed my father.

He exhales loudly, his thin, dry lips flapping from the weight of it all.

"The hospital reported unusual bruising on your body that didn't correspond with the plane accident," he begins. "The bruises on your buttocks had the curved imprint of being kicked. There was a tramline bruise on your hip, from being hit with a cylindrical object. The surveillance camera in the den captured a few of these assaults." His eyes cloud over. Then he clears his throat gruffly.

I glance over at Grandma. Her lips are pursed, the rims of her eyes are pink. She closes her lids and sniffs, then reaches for my hand, giving it a firm squeeze.

"The investigation wasn't adding up. No one radioed in. There was no mechanical failure that we knew of. We needed to dig a little deeper to rule out foul play," Brady continues. "One of your mother's friends mentioned that your mother had made a comment about frying his food in peanut oil to get back at him. The autopsy and toxicology reports indicated that he did in fact go into anaphylactic shock."

I let go of Grandma's hand and knot my fingers together in my lap, waiting for the words that will condemn me.

"The manager at the airport coffee shop said you made a point of inquiring about nuts in the muffins?" I'm terrified to look up at him, afraid of what he'll say next.

Brady continues. "We just found out yesterday that the facility where the muffins were baked is a small operation upstate. It seems they didn't thoroughly clean the lines between different batches. This is the third report of a nut allergy linked to their plant."

My mouth drops open in genuine shock.

"The *third*?" I whisper, repeating it to make sure I heard him right.

"Thankfully, there were no fatalities with the other two cases. But those people didn't have beta-blockers in their systems, or three thousand feet between them and the ground. As the only eyewitness to the incident, I needed to hear your account of what transpired that day. I can file my report now that it was a medical emergency."

He pushes a button on the digital recorder. The interview is over.

It wasn't me.

now

Grandma walks with me back to the rec room, where we sit down at the same table as before.

Fiddling with her purse straps in her lap, she shakes her head and lowers her eyes. "How could I not have known?"

All those times I tried to protect Grandma by not telling her. Tried to protect Lila by not telling her. They both ended up getting hurt anyway. We all did.

"I'm sorry," I say.

Next thing I know, I'm in Grandma's arms, my head pressed up against her chest, sobbing into her blouse. She's rocking me back and forth like a baby, hushing me and telling me it wasn't my fault.

After Grandma leaves, I return back to my room. I'm exhausted after my meeting with Brady. My bed squeaks under me as I collapse on the thin mattress, the only familiar sound. The room is too quiet without Rowan. Now that she's gone, I miss her.

I miss everybody.

Sitting up on my bed, I reach for my pillowcase and shake it upside down over my sheets. All the letters I've received over the past few weeks tumble out, from Meaghan, Noah, so many from Charlie, and the grape-scented letters from Lila that Rowan sniffed out of their hiding spot. All of them still sealed, because I didn't want to know how much they missed me, I didn't want to be tempted to "get well soon" or asked when I was coming home. Going back was never an option.

Visions of my mother's lifeless body dangling upside down will haunt me for the rest of my life. Her wide eyes, frightened, seemed to blame me for the accident. Believing I had killed her was what made me take the blade to my wrists. I couldn't live with myself, with that image always there, condemning me.

I pull one of Charlie's letters into my lap, my fingers tracing his pointy handwriting on the envelope. I tear it open and read his letter, allowing myself to miss him, really miss him, for the first time. Then I read Meaghan's. Then Noah's. Then one of Lila's that includes a clipped-out crossword puzzle from the newspaper "in case you're bored."

Like any muscle that hasn't been used in a while, my heart hurts at first. But the pain lessens with each letter, replaced with a longing to return to the people who love me. Still.

My bed is covered in hastily torn-open envelopes and stacks of flattened letters when Janet peeks in on me. She has a pleased smile on her face. She nods and walks away.

I think I understand now what they've been waiting to see from me.

———•

The day after the meeting with Brady, I check in with Dr. Bruce for our daily sessions.

"Hello, Hadley."

Dr. Bruce gestures across from him to my seat.

"How are you today?"

"Fine." I eye a pencil on his desk, wondering if he wouldn't mind if I used that to get under the cast.

"How's your arm doing?" He watches me dig my finger under the cast to scratch.

"Itchy."

He nods and smiles. "I remember. I broke my arm when I was a kid. When the cast came off, I walked around with it like it was still in a sling for weeks." He crooks his arm against his stomach. "Funny, right? Even when something's gone, it can still hurt. Its presence is still felt."

Dr. Bruce's quiet, ruminative gaze lingers a few beats longer than necessary. His words make more sense than he may have realized. Or, knowing Dr. Bruce, his words were chosen with the absolute precision of a trained marksman.

"Anything *you* want to talk about today, Hadley?"

These sessions are always brutal. The first few minutes of getting started are always the worst, followed by the horrible prolonged periods of silence when Dr. Bruce tries to force me to fill the dead air.

"I got a note from Lila. She wants me to come home."

"I'm sure she does," he says. "Do you miss her?"

"Yes." My throat squeezes every time I talk about Lila. "I just don't know how to face her after what I tried to do," I admit.

He taps his pen on his paper. "You'll find people are more forgiving of you than you are of yourself, Hadley."

I dig my finger deeper under my cast and scratch. "Maybe. I hope so."

He nods and scribbles quickly, then glances back up with bright eyes.

"So, after the cast comes off. Then what? Back on the lacrosse field?" He mimes a toss with a lacrosse stick.

"What? No!" My voice flares with anger.

He startles in surprise. "Really? I thought you enjoyed lacrosse?"

"Where'd you get *that* from?"

He flips through the papers in his lap. "You were the team captain."

I stare out the window. Outside is an impossibly white clean slate. The sun shines too brightly on the snow, hurting my eyes. But I don't look away. "I never want to see another crosse as long as I live."

I hear the scratch of his pen across the paper, as if he's writing me a note excusing me from lacrosse indefinitely. "So no more lacrosse. Will you miss it?"

"No." My eyes sting.

His silence forces me to look back at him. His silhouette shimmers like a halo from the sun glare. "Had enough of it, I guess?"

A fist the size of a sledgehammer lodges itself in my throat.

"Why did you play lacrosse, Hadley?"

I try to swallow, but I can't. "For my dad."

"It made him happy to see you play?"

"I don't think anything I did made him happy."

The silence stretches around us, tightening, binding us in this moment.

"Your dad was tough on you, wasn't he, Hadley?"

Anger swells inside me. I glare at him. "You have the records from the ER about the bruises. You've always known."

He doesn't speak. He just watches me with his fucking clinical eyes, like medical instruments trying to probe their way inside me to cut out what's damaged.

"You knew and never said *anything*! You just let me talk like an *asshole* waiting for me to tell you!"

He doesn't break eye contact, but he doesn't speak. Just waits it out. His clock counts the seconds.

I'm drowning in silence. If I don't break the surface, I'll suffocate.

"I hate him, okay?" I admit, wiping my cheeks, then correct myself. *"Hated."*

Dr. Bruce finally speaks. "You were right the first time. The feelings are still present. Right? They don't just go away." He hands me the box of tissues. I nod and swipe at my face.

Dr. Bruce waits while I cry. When I can speak again, I confess. "I wanted him to die."

Dr. Bruce doesn't flinch. "Many victims of abuse want their perpetrators to die."

"But then he did. I wanted it to happen, and it did."

"We all have thoughts that are inappropriate . . . *cruel*, even. It's a common human experience. But those thoughts don't incriminate you." He reaches down and scratches his ankle, which is such an oddly human thing to do at the moment, reminding me that even Dr. Bruce has itches that need to be scratched.

My insides feel ready to explode from the pressure. Franklin was right. I'm a hoarder. The words come out because they have to. Because I'm choking on them.

"I was going to do it. In the plane. And then I didn't. But it happened anyway."

This time, the silence feels like my judge and jury, my moment to hear from Dr. Bruce what a horrible person I am, why I'm not fit to be allowed back into the world.

He inhales through his nose then leans forward. "But you *didn't*. And you had nothing to do with his death." He watches me, as if to see if I accept his absolution.

"Hadley, it is my hope that someday you will realize that you're not guilty. Having thoughts of anger, of vengeance, is not a crime."

I stare down at my fingers.

"Hadley."

I glance up.

"I want you to try something. Close your eyes." I close them. "Now, picture the people you love with all your heart. Reverse roles. Imagine they suffered the same abuse you have. And they are coming to *you* with these same feelings of guilt . . . of shame . . . Would you forgive them? Would you want them to forgive themselves?"

First, I picture Lila. Then Charlie. Then Noah and Meaghan and Grandma. My fists clench imagining any one of them going through what I did.

Lila looks up at me, her blue eyes wide with worry, her chin dimpling. I want to take the worry off her. I want to tell her it's okay. She's going to be okay. *We're* going to be okay.

With my eyes closed, I can't see Dr. Bruce. But I hear him scribbling on his pad like mad.

A few days later in group, surrounded by new faces, I open up about the night of the poker. This time, Linda reaches over and squeezes my shoulder. "Great job, Hadley." The weight on my chest lessens, little by little.

A week later, they discharge me into my grandmother's care. Dr. Bruce, in his silent, analytical way, determined I was no longer a harm to myself and that I had things I wanted to live for. He's right. At our last session, Dr. Bruce told me, "You still have more work to do, Hadley. But our work *here* is done." He recommended a therapist for me close to home.

Grandma and I pass the rec room on the way out. I hardly recognize anyone in there. Everyone I knew left already.

On the long drive home, Grandma shoots me nervous looks from the corner of her eye, maybe to make sure I'm not planning on throwing myself out of the moving car on the highway.

I watch the familiar scenery of my hometown welcome me back. My fingers press against the window as if I can touch the trees lining the road.

"Is Lila home?" I ask, glancing at my blurred reflection in the window, a stranger, a girl I no longer recognize.

Grandma glances over. "No. She's over at Casey's. They'll bring her back tonight."

I smile. Lila. I can't wait to see her.

She clears her throat. "Your young man has called quite a bit. He's been very worried about you."

My head whips back over at Grandma.

"Charlie?" I touch the empty spot at my clavicle. They gave me my necklace back. I put it away in my bag with my clothes and toothbrush.

Her face folds with worry when mine crumbles. "I'm sorry, sweetie . . . I thought that would make you happy."

I nod. It should. But I'm not sure I can face Charlie yet.

Lila and I have had a sleepover every night since I got home. She's been like a koala bear, hanging on to me, never letting me out of her sight. Or maybe it's the other way around.

Now she lies next to me in bed, fingering the scar on my wrist. "Does it hurt?"

"No," I say, watching her gently trace the puckered lines on my wrists. The pain isn't in my wrist, or my broken arm still in a cast. It's everywhere.

The quiet is a constant ringing in my ears, the emptiness of every room condemns me. But the house noises are worse. The garage door rumbling makes my fingers prickle and my breath quicken. The mudroom door shutting sends an electric bolt down my spine. The hulking shadow of my father looms around every corner, ready to pounce. Every time I walk into the kitchen, I expect to see my mother at the kitchen counter, a hand ready on her glass to silence her world.

And then there's Grandma. Watching her stare out the window, her eyes old and tired, reminds me of what the crash stole from her.

I'm grateful I didn't know about the vertical cuts. Rowan was right; somewhere deep inside of me, I didn't really want to die. But living is hard. And then I remember sitting in front of Lila's baby carrier when she first came home from the hospital, willing her little lungs to keep breathing. I just have to do the same for myself now.

After a week of trying to get me to commit to a day to see them, Noah texts me an ultimatum.

Either lower the drawbridge or we're storming the castle.

Half an hour later, Noah and Meaghan wave at me nervously from my porch.

Meaghan rushes over the threshold first, nearly knocking me down with her hug. She immediately starts bawling. When I look over her shoulder at Noah for some assistance, he walks over and peels her off.

"Okay, my turn," he tells her. Noah's hug is gentler, as if he's afraid I might break. And then the one person in my life who can make a joke out of just about any miserable situation whispers in my ear, "I'm so sorry."

We sit in the den with the TV on, but no one watches. They both bite their lips, eyes darting everywhere and anywhere but my wrists.

Meaghan rambles on, briefing me on what I missed since I was gone. She and Mike are dating again. "We had a long talk. We really like each other, but we're going to take it slow. It's only been about three weeks, but—"

"It's a world record for her." Noah thumbs over to Meaghan.

Meaghan grins in agreement. "Okay, what else? Faith had a party last Friday. The neighbors complained about the noise, and the cops came and broke it up, thank God! I couldn't shake Claudia! She was chewing my ear off all night about how *bad* she felt because she had been so mean to you. She was *so* annoying, I was ready to kill myself just to—"

Noah's mouth falls open.

"I did not just say that," Meaghan gasps.

I snort. "Yeah, you did."

She babbles, trying to explain. "You know how when you try really hard not to say something, but you say it anyway because you're trying *not* to? I was so nervous I'd say the wrong thing and—"

Noah squeezes his eyes shut and slaps his forehead. *"Stop talking!"*

I can't stop laughing. It's the ice breaker we needed. We finally talk to each other again the way we used to.

Eventually, Noah brings up the million-dollar question.

"Why are you avoiding Charlie?"

My fingers flutter to the hollow pit at my clavicle.

"I'm not ready."

Meaghan looks at Noah, then me.

"Ready for *what*?"

They look genuinely confused. They have no idea how hard it is to see everyone I had decided I was willing to leave, especially Charlie. How do I face him and see the pain in his eyes, knowing that no matter how much he loved me, how much I loved him, it wasn't enough?

"The guy is really hurting, Hadley. He misses you," Noah says.

I glance away. "I miss him too." My voice catches.

That's not a lie. I miss him so much it aches.

That last day Brady came to the hospital, I was ready to tell him everything. I *needed* to confess. I couldn't go on living without some kind of atonement.

Until I saw Lila's letter in Grandma's purse. I avoided opening all of her letters because I didn't want to know she missed me. I didn't deserve Lila's love. Or anyone's. But this one changed everything: Lila didn't just miss me, she *needed* me. I was willing to let the guilt burn inside me if that's what it took to come home to her.

And then Brady and Dr. Bruce absolved me of my sins.

Even though I found my way back, the knowledge of what I almost became, what I was willing to do, what I saw through almost to the end, frightens me.

•—•

I know it's him ringing the doorbell even before Grandma calls me down.

She disappears discreetly as I walk down the stairs.

His eyes are dark and haunted. Shifting nervously, he shoves his hands deep into his hoodie pockets as I approach. The closer I get, the more the stress of this past month is apparent, in the dark circles under his eyes, the hollows of his cheeks.

We stare at each other, neither one sure how to move forward. My fingers flutter to the empty space of my clavicle, like they always do, and always will, when I think of Charlie. His eyes follow my fingers, filling with horror as he sees the evidence on my wrist of what until now had just been unfathomable news about his girlfriend.

I glance up at him hesitantly. "Hasn't anyone been feeding you while I was gone?" My lips edge up in an attempt to crack a joke.

He takes his arms out of his pockets and reaches for me, testing to see if I'll allow it. When I don't resist, he wraps them around me and pulls me tight, erasing every ounce of space between us.

I rest my cheek against his chest, closing my eyes. His smell, even the cigarette smoke embedded in the soft cotton of his hoodie, is warm, comforting. Forgiving.

He turns his lips to my ear. "I love you."

Careful of my cast, I wrap my arms tighter around him, soaking in his familiar warmth.

He's here now, and all I can ask for is now. And now is okay. Now is more than I thought I deserved up until a week ago. Our now may be nothing compared to the billions of years and stars that make up our universe, but maybe now is all we can ask for. Now is everything.

Later that afternoon, he clasps the necklace around my neck. We sit in front of the TV, where I ease back into the crook of his arm. Lila's dancing upstairs in her room rattles the ceiling over our heads. I touch the claddagh at my neck, focusing on the pulsing beat of my little sister's feet and the warmth radiating off Charlie. My heart is full. Of love and grief, of pain and happiness. Of life. I take a breath, then another, and another.

A Note from Amy Giles

If Hadley seems familiar to you, please keep reading.

Every year more than three million reports of child abuse are made in the United States.[1]

Abuse doesn't discriminate by race, gender, religion, or socio-economic status. Abuse exists in rich families, poor families, devout families, and educated families. In 2013, just under 80 percent of reported child fatalities from abuse and neglect were caused by one or more of the child victim's parents.[2]

But what about the cases of abuse that aren't reported?

Victims of emotional, physical, and sexual abuse are often made to feel so tiny and insignificant they think no one will care, no one will believe them, or worse, their problems don't matter. I want you to know, you matter. And people care.

It's common for people who are being abused to feel confused, upset, angry, guilty, embarrassed, and even blame themselves. It can be hard to report someone who hurts you. Abusers often try to make you think you did something to deserve it, to deflect attention away from their own actions. Sometimes the abuser

---

1   www.childhelp.org/child-abuse/

2   www.nationalchildrensalliance.org/media-room/media-kit/national-statis-tics-child-abuse

threatens to harm you or someone you love (sometimes even a pet) if you tell anyone what they've done. This is how they convince you that there's nothing you can do to stop what's happening. They're wrong.

If you or someone you know is being abused, there's help. Reporting abuse makes it possible for a family to receive the counseling they need. And it can also save a life. The sooner authorities know about an abusive situation, the sooner they can help.

Help can be as close as a dean, teacher, or school nurse, even a friend's parent. Hadley could have turned to Mr. Murray, Señora Moore, Dr. Sher, or Coach Kimmel. Any one of them would have made the call that Hadley feared to make for herself. Suspicion of abuse is all that's needed to report. Some professionals are required by law to report suspected abuse. Mandated reporters include school personnel, doctors and their staff, emergency medical technicians, foster care workers, police officers, social workers, school athletic coaches, and many other individuals whose professional work puts them in contact with children.

If you take away anything from Hadley's story, it's the importance of talking to someone. To quote one survivor of abuse: "If you don't talk about it, how in the name of hell are you supposed to deal with it? You can't deal with what's not there."[3]

If you are being abused or neglected, or suspect someone you know is, please make the call. Here are emergency numbers and websites:

---

3   http://www.bostonmagazine.com/2006/05/poor-little-rich-kids/

Call 911 if you believe you or someone you know is in immediate danger from child abuse or neglect.

Childhelp National Child Abuse Hotline 24/7: 1-800-4-A-CHILD (1-800-422-4453). Serves the United States and Canada. Assistance is available in 170 languages.

Cybertipline http://www.missingkids.com

National Child Pornography Tipline: 1-800-843-5678. To report the sexual exploitation of children through the production and distribution of pornography.

National Suicide Hotline 1-800-273-TALK

The National Center for Missing and Exploited Children: 24/7 hotline 1-800-THE-LOST (1-800-843-5678). To report child-sexual exploitation, harassment or solicitation, a missing child, or a sighting of a missing child.

Rape, Assault and Incest National Network: 24/7/hotline 1-800-656-HOPE.

National sexual assault online hotline. Free, safe, confidential—does not capture IP address: www.rainn.org

For a complete list of individual state child abuse hotlines, please visit capsli.org/reporting-abuse/individual-state-hotlines or amygiles.net.

ACKNOWLEDGMENTS

Pulling words together into a story is easy compared to arranging words into thoughtful thank-yous to all the incredible people in my life. Words are inadequate compared to the depth of love, respect, and gratitude I have for all of you.

This book would not be in your hands right now if not for my amazing agent, Alexandra Machinist. Your call that night is up there in my top five best moments of my life. Thank you to my superstar editors, Rosemary Brosnan and Jessica MacLeish, for their equal parts enthusiasm and editorial wizardry, and for loving Hadley as much as I do.

Thanks to everyone at HarperTeen who worked on this book, from production to marketing and everyone in between.

Thank you to my earliest readers and best cheerleaders a writer can have, my critique partners, Amanda Jasper and Nicole Sewell. I owe so much to my 2017 debut group for their friendship and support. A special shout-out to Melissa, Stephanie, Robin, and Jeff, for the laughs and impromptu therapy sessions.

To quote Clarence in *It's a Wonderful Life*: "No (wo)man is a failure who has friends." Thank you to my crew: Jenssie, Debbie M, Leslie, Karen, Debbie S, Anna, KT, Lisa, Zina, Dawn,

Debbie P, Lauren, my neighborhood "Ladies Who Wine," and my extended family. I love you all. A special thank-you to Benjamin Baldwin for helping me shape Hadley's therapy sessions. Many additional experts were consulted while writing this story, from pilots to medical professionals. A tremendous heartfelt thank-you for your time. If any errors remain, they're all on me.

To my home team: Mom, thank you for inspiring my love of reading and writing, and for taking me to the library when I was little to see how to go about publishing my short story about the man in the blue hat and his curious monkey (I was writing fan fiction and didn't even know it). Thank you to my brother, Evans, for putting up with all my little sisterly stuff. To my husband, Pat, for the many "bacon" salads during edits and for believing this day would come long before I ever believed it myself. And to my girls, Maggie and Julia. It feels as if there was never a time before you.